Praise for

NEVER HIDE FROM THE DEVIL

McQueen approaches this story with extraordinary sensitivity and lyricism. . . . The story's true strength lies in its heartfelt narration. . . . Readers will feel for them as though they were their own neighbors, in peril of their lives.

—★*Kirkus Reviews* (starred review)

Never Hide from the Devil is not merely a historical reconstruction; it is a jagged piece of shrapnel from 1915 Van, pulsing with the frantic, localized energy of a city under siege.

—*The Armenian Weekly*

Set at the onset of the Armenian Genocide in 1915, this novel plunges the reader with authenticity into a little-known act of defiance during the twentieth century's first genocide.

—Marsha Skrypuch,
author of *Making Bombs for Hitler*
and the Kidnapped from Ukraine trilogy

Through the eyes of a young boy, McQueen crafts a devastating and unforgettable portrait of the 1915 Defense of Van—a story of resilience against impossible odds that delivers the history of the Armenian Genocide to a new generation.

—Eric Z. Weintraub, author of *South of Sepharad*

The horrors perpetrators commit are only half the story of genocide. The other half is the resistance of its victims. N.T. McQueen delivers a powerful novel of courage and defiance in the face of annihilation.

—Dr. Khatchig Mouradian, Columbia University,
author of *The Resistance Network*

N.T. McQueen humanizes a most inhumane history—the little-known but extremely courageous Defense of Van leading up to the horrors of the Armenian Genocide. The resiliency and resistance of the Armenian people shine brightly, all while seamlessly woven into one teenager's coming-of-age experience in a time of heartbreak, hope, family ties, friendship, and the unknown of what lies ahead.

—Laura Michael Gaboudian,
educator and author of *Under the Light of the Moon*

From the perspective of a teenage boy, McQueen masterfully weaves a poignant narrative set against the heavy emotional backdrop of the 1915 Armenian Genocide, where boys are compelled to become men overnight. McQueen's skill in crafting coming-of-age stories provides a rare glimpse of and an ideal lens through which to develop characters as they navigate the untold experiences of the Armenian Freedom Fighters.

—Victoria Atamian Waterman,
author of *What She Left Behind*

In 1915, Armenians in the eastern Ottoman city of Van defended their town, threatened by their own government intent on destroying its people. Almost miraculously, they held off the army until the Russians rescued them—temporarily. N.T. McQueen tells the harrowing story of simple defenders against a predatory, genocidal empire. Vividly written, this moving story reminds us that resistance against tyranny and oppression is possible. Costs may be high, but courage can prevail. A real tour de force!

—Ronald Grigor Suny,
William H. Sewell, Jr. Distinguished
University Professor Emeritus of History,
The University of Michigan

Bold, gripping, and unforgettable, *Never Hide from the Devil* shines a light on the Armenian genocide, an often overlooked chapter in history. Told through the eyes of a young hero determined to protect his people, N.T.'s impactful novel is both heart-pounding and relatable, and stays with the reader long after the final page.

—Melissa W. Hunter,
author of *What She Lost*

N.T. McQueen's scintillating *Never Hide from the Devil* captures the little-known Armenian experience in its depiction of the siege of Van, from the bravery to the sorrow to the ecstasy of love and hope. Read it.

—Mark Mustian,
author of *The Gendarme* and *Boy with Wings*

When a historical truth is undeniable, all that remains is the shadow of innocence. In the 1915 Ottoman Empire, Suren is forced to trade boyhood for a world where genocide is being committed against his people. In a riveting exploration of courage, conviction, and loss, this novel charts humanity's most desperate journey through one of the darkest times in history. McQueen's prose is compelling in its measured, unsparing gaze of devastating truths—where boys become soldiers and how silence becomes a graveyard.

—Tamar Marie Boyadjian,
award-winning author, editor & translator

Inspired by true stories of Armenian resistance, this novel strikes the perfect balance between honesty and kid friendliness. Look out for it, buy it, request it, borrow it, share it!

—Leila Boukarim, author of
Lost Words: An Armenian Story of Survival and Hope

NEVER HIDE FROM THE DEVIL

NEVER HIDE FROM THE DEVIL

a novel

N. T. McQUEEN

CHESTER CO.,
PENN.

PUBLISHED BY CENNAN BOOKS
an imprint of Cynren Press
Chester County, Pennsylvania
http://www.cynren.com/

No generative AI has been used in writing this book.

First published 2026

ISBN-13: 978-1-947976-71-9 (pbk)
ISBN-13: 978-1-947976-72-6 (ebk)

Printed in the United States of America by TPS

Library of Congress Control Number: 2025909009

Content Warning: This book contains themes of War violence and combat scenes; Death of young characters; Genocide and ethnic persecution; Religious conflict and discrimination; Traumatic injury (amputation); Family separation and displacement; Refugee experiences and suffering; Child soldiers/combatants; Psychological trauma and PTSD symptoms; Loss of home and cultural destruction.

For information about special discounts for bulk purchases, please contact Cynren Press Sales at sales.media@cynren.com.

For all Armenians
Past, present, and future

Contents

NEVER

HIDE

FROM

THE

DEVIL

April 17, 1915

Whispers and Rumors

1

A Fight on Holy Ground

The group of boys waits behind St. Boghos, hoping Father Zakarian doesn't come out. I always find it odd they choose to fight behind a holy building. The Bible teaches us to love our enemies, not to punch them in the face. I can see the Topchu Mosque a few streets down rising into the sky and wonder if the Quran teaches to love our enemies as well.

Two boys pace in the center: Razmik, who looks like a man ready to join the army, with a scar under his right eye to prove it, and a new boy who attends the orphanage school run by the Americans. The two dance around the circle in a cloud of dust as the others urge them to fight. The shadow of the steeple cuts through the heart of the circle. A slight crispness in the spring air makes me glad I brought my coat.

Razmik's dark eyes bore into the new boy. He keeps his fists raised and loaded like a wolf waiting to attack while the new boy shuffles. His eyes dart from face to face, and with each pass of the circle, he steps on his own crumpled taraz in the dirt.

"What's his name?" I ask Nshan.

I can hear Nshan wheezing through his nose. "Mardik? Mkhitar? I'm not sure."

"It doesn't matter what his name is. Razmik is an animal," Hamza comments, his fists lifted and punching through the air.

"Why are they fighting anyway?" I ask.

"You know Razmik. He's always looking to hit someone," Nshan replies, removing his glasses and wiping them with his shirt. His clothes hang so loosely on him that it looks like his mother gave him a blanket to wear to school. If Nshan didn't go to Yeramian School, his blood would have been on Razmik's fists by now.

The voices grow louder as the two keep circling without a swing. One of the boys with wide-set eyes, from Hisoushian School, yells "Fight!" in Armenian. Soon, the word catches fire. Each boy punches the air as he chants. Even Hamza, who only knows a few phrases in our language, joins in.

"Mihran! That's his name," Nshan shouts, pointing his finger in the air like a politician.

Razmik and Mihran circle faster, kicking up dust from the street. The cloud builds and a sick, tense feeling surges in my gut—a feeling I hate, but I wait and watch like the others. With a growl, Razmik lunges toward his opponent and swings. A roar fills the air.

Mihran ducks as Razmik's fist swings across the top of his head. The momentum sends him staggering, and he turns, glaring at Mihran. His eyes dart at the chanting faces, and I can see his chest rise and fall with heavy breaths.

Hamza hits my chest, startling me, then points: "The orphan floats like a butterfly, yeah?"

I nod without looking at him. The dust hovers around the two fighters, and the tension in my stomach pushes my insides into my throat. Even when my brothers fought, my body acted as if I were fighting instead of them. Saliva fills my mouth, and I spit it at my feet.

Dancing again, I can see that look in Razmik's eyes. Like a dog sick with madness and only one mission. The same look my dog Chalo had before a gendarme shot him after he was bitten by a local street dog. Razmik lunges at Mihran, wrapping his arms around his waist and driving him into the dirt. I can't see much in the dusty fog except the shadow of bodies rolling around. Even Nshan the Politician starts chanting along with the others.

Then I hear the unmistakable crack of knuckle on bone.

"Is it Razmik or Mihran?" Nshan asks.

I try to say something, but I fight back the urge to throw up.

As the dust clears, Razmik's hunched body and bloodied fist land into Mihran's face. With his hands up, he tries to signal his surrender, but the wild eyes of Razmik see nothing. He lifts his red fist more slowly, as if he's lifting a hammer to drive home a nail. But before he can drop it, a blur flies from my right, and Hamza's lanky figure dives into Razmik's thick body, knocking them both to the ground.

The frenzy grows louder, and other boys rush in to break up the scuffle. Mihran rolls to his side, and the blood from his nose mixes with the dust.

"Get off of me! Let me go!" Razmik screams with so much fury that his voice cracks. As the boys who jumped in begin to spread out, I see Hamza crawl atop Razmik, pinning him to the ground.

"You won, Raz. You joined his nose and his mouth. Everyone knows it. Just relax," Hamza says in Turkish.

"Don't touch me, Turk. This has nothing to do with you," Razmik growls.

The other boys help Hamza hold Razmik down until his legs stop kicking and the wildness leaves his eyes. His long breaths heave in and out, and, watching him breathe, the metallic taste on my tongue begins to fade.

I look back to Mihran. During the commotion, he sits upright with his elbows on his knees and his head hanging. Coated in dust, he touches the dark bruises forming under his eyes and wipes the blood from the gash in his lip. Other boys chatter about the fight and how the Turk wrestled Razmik into submission, but not because they admire Hamza.

From my left, Nshan strolls in front of me, making sure he crosses my path. He holds his hands behind his back, pacing as if lost in thought, before he says, "My Baba always says, 'Dogs that fight each other will join against the wolf.'"

"What does that mean?" I ask.

Nshan pauses, pushes his glasses onto the bridge of his nose, then shrugs. "I don't know. It just seemed like the right thing to say."

I hear some grunts, and Hamza is on his feet now, dusting off his trousers and vest while Razmik scrambles to his feet, spits, and stomps off. Some boys follow him while the others begin to leave for home. Mihran still sits with his head down, facing the dirt.

Hamza walks over, swiping dust from his shirt and trousers. Mihran refuses to look up, and I see a tear trickle down his cheek, leaving a trail through the muddy, caked blood. Nshan and I approach the two.

Nshan clears his throat before speaking. "Razmik always settles arguments with his fists. Something his father sadly teaches him."

Blood drips from Mihran's nose, and he wipes it with the back of his hand. He raises his eyes to the three of us. He squints through his swollen right eye at our faces, then sees Hamza.

"I didn't need your help. I had him," Mihran mumbles.

Hamza looks at Nshan and me before answering. "You don't know Razmik like we do."

Mihran looks at us, and I see something in his face that I haven't seen before, even in Razmik. Something I can't quite understand.

"Why do you allow him here? Shouldn't he be with his kind beyond the cemetery?" Mihran asks in our language, keeping his eyes on us and nodding his head toward Hamza.

We share the same look with the same empty mouths. The rumors I heard at home from Baba and Uncle Tarzi flood back to me. Whether they are true or not, Hamza is different. I glance at my friend, and he stares back, dusting off his arms and legs. For the moment, I am glad he doesn't understand my language well.

Nshan answers, holding out his palms in an almost pleading way, "Look, he even helped you when Razmik lost his mind. Turk or not, he is a good friend."

Struggling to his feet, Mihran stands and glares at us through his swollen eye. He rubs the blood from under his nose. His eyes move away from Hamza and focus on us.

"Tell the Turk to stay away from me," he grumbles. He turns away, pushing through two boys still talking about the fight.

Nshan and I watch him leave as Hamza stands next to me.

He asks me, "What did he say, Suren?"

I pause, unsure if I should tell him the truth or create a lie.

"It's not important," I reply, though his words still linger with me like a bitter taste from a bad fruit.

Nshan shakes his head, making *tisk-tisk* noises with his lips before remarking with a sigh, "Armenians."

"Hey! What are you boys doing?" a deep voice shouts toward us. Our heads snap at the sound and see fat Father Zakarian standing on the steps at the back of the church. His white, wiry beard is bright in the sunlight. His eyes lock on mine, and he points a finger at me.

"I see you, Suren. Don't make me tell your father what you've been up to."

Like a flock of startled birds, we scatter.

2

Uncle's Rumors

The three of us walk through the streets and drop Nshan off at his home near the Shoushanian School. Little girls walk home together, but the girls our age loiter around, whispering as we pass. Waiting for a glance at Hamza, I'm sure. Turk or not, all the girls giggle when he passes. Every day, they whisper or laugh until he smiles or waves. Then they shriek and run off when he does.

We don't talk about the fight on our walk home in the Old City. I keep going over Mihran's words. Not so much what he said but the way he said it. The bitterness of his voice and the darkness in his eyes, even after Hamza had stopped Razmik, still leave me scratching my scalp.

The crowded streets and markets bustle around us, and the vendors—Turks, Armenians, Greeks, Kurds—all shout and call out to the crowds. "Buy this, buy that. Best deal in the city!" Stalls are full of vegetables and fruits. Some are crowded with bottles of wine and *oghi*, while another stall sells fine clothing, blankets, and pillows. Even the wealthy outside of the Old City come in to shop or sell. "Great deal for you," they say. But neither of us has any money. Otherwise, we would live in Aykesdan, where people have land and orchards in which to roam, not cramped, dirty, and poor spaces, like here.

We arrive at my home in the afternoon and remove our shoes outside. I notice two other pairs of shoes next to Mama's and Baba's and hear a familiar voice on the other side of the door. Inside, Uncle Tarzi sits at the table with Baba, waving his hands and shouting in Armenian. I hesitate, thinking it may be better if Hamza doesn't come in when he's worked up, but since his Armenian is so poor, he won't understand Uncle Tarzi's rants. Aunt Yeva and Mama linger around the stove, mixing meat and chopping onions for some kufta.

We walk over to Mama, and she kisses my head before handing Hamza a piece of lavash like she always does after school. He smiles and says "thank you" in Armenian incorrectly, the same way he has since we were young boys. Baba's voice grows louder.

"There is no proof, Tarzi. We can't panic over rumors." He polishes the face of his wristwatch with a soft towel—the same watch Pap gave him before he left to fight in the Hamidian massacre and never returned.

"Bah! He's a butcher. They don't call him the 'Horseshoer of Bashkale' because he races horses."

"Again, more rumors."

"Rumors? These taxes are not rumors—funds for the Ottomans to fight in this Great War consuming the earth. You remember the Avakians? The tanner who moved to Aykesdan? Just last week, two gendarmes arrived and demanded a tax for the war. They took everything but the pork. Everything, Vartan! What will the *pasha* take from you when they come to the Old City? They already took our sons."

Baba and Uncle Tarzi fall silent once they see Hamza as we walk toward the back room. Uncle Tarzi's dark eyes stay fixed on my friend, shadowed by his bushy eyebrows. A hint of suspicion lingers in his pupils. A deep, black beard covers his lips when he speaks, and I remember believing when I was a young boy that he had no mouth.

Baba keeps his eyes on his watch, rubbing its face in a smooth circle. His gaze seems far away, like the times when he sits in the garden, looking at the pomegranate tree, but despite how many times I ask what he is thinking, he changes the subject. Baba's beard seems grayer since the start of the Great War when my brothers were enlisted. From the stove, Mama glances over at the dinner table.

In the back room, I sit by the door frame while Hamza paces around the room, fiddling with his prayer beads around his wrist. His eyes meet mine, and I nod, trying to let him know my family sees him as another son, but I don't think he believes me.

Uncle Tarzi leans forward and speaks in a hushed voice. "Vartan, we knew this was coming. It was just a matter of time before they finally decided to exterminate all of us. We should leave now. Go to France or America before Jevdet Bey brings his army."

Baba places the wristwatch on the table, moving so slowly that it seems he might be afraid he'll crack it. He lets out a long sigh through his nose and places his hand in Uncle Tarzi's pleading palms.

"Trust in God, *yeghpayr.*"

Uncle Tarzi stares at Baba for a moment, then catches me listening. Leaning closer, I hear him whisper, "I trust God, Vartan *jan*. I do. It's the Turks I don't trust."

Baba stares back as Uncle Tarzi stands up from the table. He gathers his hat and bag before heading toward the door.

"Come, Yeva," he orders.

Aunt Yeva turns toward her husband, fists propped on her wide hips. Aunt Yeva's eyes always bulge when she gets angry.

"Come? I'm your wife, not a dog."

He pauses, jutting his chin out and standing straight like a cadet in the Ottoman army. For once, he has nothing to say.

Aunt Yeva hugs Mama and removes her apron, placing it in a heap on the table. She hugs Baba, waves to me at the doorway, and leaves through the door first.

"You come," she barks, waving her hand at him.

He rolls his eyes and ducks through the doorway. Before shutting the door, he pauses and looks at Baba.

"Remember Adana." Their bickering trails off outside as the door closes behind them.

Baba and Mama look at each other. Sometimes I wonder if they can read each other's minds. Maybe when you spend enough time with someone, you don't need to speak to hear each other.

I look at Hamza across the room. "Did you understand any of what they said?"

Hamza thinks for a moment, bobbing his head from side to side with his bottom lip upturned. "I understood 'Adana.'" I can see his fingers fidget with the beads of his *tasbih*, and I wonder if he is praying to Allah or worrying.

His dark eyes look back at me. Some sweat has mingled with the dust still on his temples. To me, it seems he doesn't believe everything the Turkish papers said about that ugly history. I hope he doesn't.

"Suren, come in here," Baba commands, not in anger but in the quiet, stern voice he uses when something troubles him.

With cap in hand, I walk to the table where he sits. He looks past me and beckons with his hand. "You too, Hamza."

The two of us stand across the table, looking at the scratched wood on the tabletop. Hamza's longer hair hangs just above his eyes.

"*Pari eerigoon*, Baron Simonian."

Baba always smiles when Turks try to speak Armenian. He leans forward and examines Hamza's bowed face. "Hamza *jan*, what is on your face?"

My friend lifts his hand and smudges the dark dirt down the side of his head.

"No matter," he says. "I want to ask you both. Have you heard any rumors lately?"

We pause a moment, as if trying to decide which rumors we should mention.

"Some boys talked about news they heard in the villages. I don't know if it is true," I reply.

"Hamza?"

Hamza's black hair sways back as he answers. "Nothing, Baron Simonian."

"From the Shamiram quarter or your imam?" he asks in Turkish.

"Not a word, Baron Simonian."

Baba waves his hand at my friend. "For the last time, don't call me that. Just call me Vartan."

"Yes, Baron Vartan," he replies, his eyes still on the floor.

My eyes connect with Baba's, and despite how hard I try, I can't help but smile. Neither can my father. From the corner of my eye, I can see Mama's shoulders bouncing.

Baba's smile fades, and he leans forward with his elbows on the table, setting the watch down without a sound. In my mind, I believe I can hear the tick of the clock in the silence. Mama stands with her back to us, moving her hands without much purpose.

"Why, Baba?" I ask. Hamza's fingers start to play with his *tasbih* again.

A long sigh escapes my father, one of those sighs that carries much weight but never releases it.

"Nothing. Just curious. Hamza *jan*, it's time you started home."

"Yes, Baron Va—I mean, Vartan," he replies, tripping on the words. Even to me, it sounds odd to hear him call my father by his name.

"Suren, you can walk him to the cemetery."

I nod and follow Hamza to the door as he thanks Mama and Baba. As I close the door behind me, I hear my parents begin to whisper.

3

A Walk to the Cemetery

Though I have walked to Hamza's neighborhood, I have never crossed the invisible border between his world and mine. We live in the same city, in the same country, drink the same water, and eat mostly the same foods—except his food must be halal—but I have never seen what his home looks like. Not even the outside. As we walk past the two-story stone buildings, I can't help but wonder if I will ever understand why.

We pass an uneven table loaded with pomegranates, apples, and walnuts on the side of the street. A bearded man waves a shriveled hand in front of an Armenian woman and the young daughter in her arms. A boy, close to my age, stands behind the man in the background, watching. I can tell he's a Kurd by his large turban.

"I have a right to buy this fruit," I hear the woman argue.

"You are Armenian. What right do you have here?" he shouts.

The woman curses the man in our language—words I only hear Uncle Tarzi use, when he drinks too much or loses a game. The man responds in Kurdish, loud and full of bitterness. The argument continues as we pass, and I keep looking back.

"That was quite a fight today," Hamza remarks.

I turn back to him and see his eyes cast down, as if he's watching his steps.

"I know," I reply in a quieter voice than I intend.

A strange silence follows us on the walk. I look back, but the Kurdish man has disappeared along with the woman, and I hear the conversation between Baba and Uncle Tarzi replay in my head.

"Do you think what the people are saying are just rumors?" I ask Hamza.

He sighs, kicking pebbles with the toe of his shoe with each step. "Maybe."

"Maybe?"

Hamza looks at me. "You know there's a history between my people and your people."

"Why? We are both Vanetsis, born on Van soil just like our fathers and grandfathers."

Hamza shrugs. "I don't know. My father says it's because your people are Christian. But I don't know if that is true."

"Why?"

He tightens his lips, showing the faint, patchy mustache he has begun to grow. I rub my fingers across my own upper lip and feel only smooth skin.

"He says other things as well."

I hesitate a moment, but ask anyway, "What things?"

As soon as the words leave my lips, I already know I don't need to meet his father to know what Turks say about us. I hear the gendarmes say them in the streets, in the market, and in my dreams.

Hamza points ahead. "We're almost there."

Up ahead, I see the stone entry to the cemetery where generations of Turks have been buried. The chiseled headstones stand tall like a small army in the distance. The sun starts to descend over the Old City toward Lake Van, casting shadows from those headstones. I recall the ghost stories my brothers would tell me at night that made me cry. Even after Baba scolded them for scaring me, they still tried sometimes, before they were forced to enlist and the Great War began.

We reach the cemetery and stop at the entrance. A soft breeze blows across our skin as we stand outside the graves. I've walked Hamza to this very spot many times, and each time, there is a strange moment neither of us can put into words. Almost as if the cemetery, which divides my world from his, will grow longer and farther until we may never see each other again. It seems foolish to me. But today, with the rumors and bitter words floating through the city, perhaps these words have added a small distance, centimeters at a time, between our worlds.

Hamza leans forward and kisses my cheek, and I his, before he raises his hand and says, "From the Aegean to the Euphrates."

"Blood brothers," I reply with a smile.

The familiar phrase we created when we were boys is still alive each time we say goodbye. But as I watch Hamza's lanky stride take him through the headstones, passing among the remains of his countrymen, I wonder if their hatred of my name existed in their time and if they curse me in ghostly whispers for being his friend.

Regardless, I wait until I no longer see his figure among the headstones and tombs. A few pairs of feral cats' eyes spy from around or atop the headstones, watching me. I read the Turkish names and realize that even in death, Armenians and Turks are separated. I hope it is better in the next life.

4

A Secret Meeting

When I arrive home, two shapes linger in the darkness outside our door. My heart pounds as I creep toward them. Not until I am a few meters away do I realize that the figures are not spying gendarmes but something worse.

My elder sisters.

"What are you doing?" I ask.

They both shush me as if they'd rehearsed earlier.

"What?"

They beckon me over. As I join them beside the door, I hear muffled voices inside.

"Mama and Baba are arguing," Ani whispers.

"About what?"

"Be quiet and stop asking questions. Then you'll find out."

I glare at Taline. Even in the dark, I can see the outline of her scowl from under her head covering.

"Just because you are twelve months older doesn't mean you can tell me what to do," I snap back.

"Shut up and listen!" she hisses.

Leaning forward, I hear our parents and the nerves that sizzle in their voices.

". . . going . . . to do, Vartan? They've already taken our eldest boys. What if they come after Suren? Or our daughters, God forbid!"

"Calm down, my *sireli*. Please."

"How? How can I calm down? The refugees from up north come into the city each day. The stories they tell I can't even repeat."

A slight pause in the conversation makes me realize I have been holding my breath since I put my ear to the door.

A sound returns, but not from behind the door. Footsteps! Before I can turn, Uncle Tarzi, ignoring the three of us huddled around the closed door, pushes us aside and knocks on the door in a frenzy.

"Vartan! Vartan!"

The chair screeches inside, and soon the door flies open. To me, Baba seems older than when I'd left him that afternoon.

"What is it?"

Uncle Tarzi catches his breath and braces himself against the door frame with his hands.

"Ishkhan is dead."

Baba's face sags. Mama gasps behind him, her hand flying to her lips as she staggers across the room and sinks into a chair. Ani and Taline rush past Baba and help her, putting their arms around her shoulders. Taline strokes Mama's arm and whispers something into her ear.

"How?" Baba asks.

Uncle Tarzi's voice strains. "It's Jevdet Bey, that murderous bastard. I know it. Of course a wolf would target the shepherd before attacking the sheep. The *fedayi* have called a meeting. Come now!"

Baba grabs his coat and cap and looks into my face. Even at fourteen, I am getting closer to meeting his eyes.

"Stay here with your mother and sisters. I'll be back soon."

"But I . . . can—"

"Do as I say, Suren. Please. Look after your mother and sisters."

His grip tightens on my shoulder, and I nod as the two men jog into the night among the lamps being lit.

I hear Ani and Taline continue soothing Mama, whose sobs intensify. I place my hand on the door handle to pull it closed but pause. In the street, I see other men leaving their homes and heading toward the secret meeting—the one I should be attending. With Levon and Narek off fighting for the Ottomans, I am the only man left in the home besides Baba.

I look back at Mama and my sisters, but they don't even see me. It won't hurt just to check out what this meeting is all about, right?

"I'll be back soon," I say and close the door before they can answer.

I sprint into the street and follow the feverish figures into the night.

My stomach churns. Each step sends a jolt of electricity through my shoes and into my veins. Thoughts of Baba beating my backside if he catches me swirl around my mind, but this is different. I am almost a man. There's only one year of school left before I need to work. Also, I want to know who Ishkhan is and why Uncle Tarzi thinks the Turks did it.

I follow the men into the city until I see a tall spire with a cross on top. I am back at St. Boghos. Now I have to worry if Father Zakarian sees me and tells Baba about the fight earlier. I say a short prayer asking God to hide me as I disobey my father. Can God answer prayers like that?

The men file through the front door into the candlelit sanctuary as I hide behind the stone wall surrounding the grounds. Among the shadowy figures, I can't see Baba or Uncle Tarzi anywhere, but I see others I know from the market, from church. Short, tall, round. It feels like every man in the city has been summoned.

"Suren!"

A harsh whisper startles me, and an odd noise tumbles from my mouth.

"It's just us," a familiar voice says.

In the light of the church, I see Nshan's glasses and Razmik's square jaw hiding behind the wall with me.

My breath catches up to me, and I hope I didn't wet my pants. "You scared me!"

"I can see that. You moaned like a ghost," Razmik remarks with a chuckle.

"It's not funny," I say with a scowl. "What are you doing here?"

Nshan states, "Disobeying our parents."

"Not me," Razmik replies. "He's drunk."

We all exchange a glance before I answer with a smile. They join me on both sides as we peek over the top of the stone wall. From what I can tell, the last few men enter the church, and Father Zakarian glances around before pulling the large doors shut.

"I should be in there," Razmik claims. Even in the faint light from the lamps, I can see his right knuckles discolored and swollen.

"We all should. But it must have to do with the refugees from the villages and the news about Ishkhan's murder," Nshan informs, removing his smudged glasses and using his shirt to clean them.

"I heard that too. Who is Ishkhan?" I ask.

"Yeah, who is that?" Razmik chimes in.

Nshan's eyes open wide as he replaces his half-cleaned glasses. "Are you joking? You don't know who Ishkhan is?"

Razmik takes a step closer, towering over Nshan. "Why don't you tell us?"

"All right, all right," he replies and takes a deep breath.

"His real name isn't Ishkhan, but he is the leader of the *fedayi*. The man all the militia fighters from the Armenian Revolutionary Federation follow. He armed many of the villages outside Van when the Turks and Kurds attacked."

"I thought Armenians weren't allowed to have weapons?" I ask.

Nshan shrugs. "I guess Ishkhan was not a good listener."

I glance around to see if anyone had spotted us crouching behind the wall. "This is bad."

Nshan nods. "Very bad. My Baba mentioned there are three leaders, but I don't know their names."

"We have to listen to that meeting," Razmik asserts. "I am going in there right now."

"How?" Nshan asks.

"Through the front door."

Razmik stands, moves, and we clamber after him, grabbing at his bulky arms, but I feel like nothing more than an annoying fly.

"Wait! Wait!" I say and stop in front of Razmik with my hands on his chest. His pupils are large and black in the darkness as he stares into my face. His nostrils flare above his tense lips.

"There's another way we can get in," I tell them.

"Then let's go," he replies.

The three of us huddle behind the long stone wall toward the other side of St. Boghos. Through the stained glass, the light from the candles makes the sanctuary look empty. We jump over the short wall and cut across toward the back door where Father Zakarian shouted at us earlier in the day. Once we scurry up the steps and onto the landing, we catch our breath for a moment and survey the area, then I turn to Razmik and Nshan. Even with the cold night air, my body is burning.

"This leads to the altar," I tell them.

"And?" Razmik asks.

"I don't know who will be on the other side."

Nshan walks past me and wraps his skinny fingers around the metal handle. His lips curl into a mischievous grin.

"Let's find out."

5

Terrible News

A shaft of light hits us as we file into the back of the church. The altar where Father Zakarian gives his sermons is filled with silhouettes facing a church full of the city's men—young and old. The lamps and candles shine off the white ceiling and walls. In the upper balcony where Mama, my sisters, and all the other women sit during service, all I see are men. A stocky man I have never seen before speaks to the faces in the pews.

A curtain hangs near the side where the three of us entered, and we hurry behind it. No one seems to notice us. I can feel Razmik's breath on my neck and Nshan's bony elbow in my ribs, but since the area behind the curtain is so small, I grimace and listen.

". . . have spread across the outer villages like wildfire over the past months. I have seen it. We fought against the Turks and the bloodthirsty Kurds. In Bashkale, Tashlou, Hazara, Ardamed. Unspeakable acts against women and girls. The young men shot like dogs in front of their families. Some of the children were kidnapped, and some have said they are being raised as Muslims now in the West. Because of Ishkhan, we were supplied with enough weapons to fight back. But we did not do enough to protect our . . . protect our families from . . ."

The man's voice breaks, and he stops. Another person steps to his side and places a hand on his shoulder, gently ushering him to the side of the stage. Though I can't see this other man's full face, I do see a cloth wrapped around his head. It's mostly white, and the rest is stained red.

I look through a small break in the curtain toward the audience. Right away, I see Baba and Uncle Tarzi sitting off to the side of the wooden pews. Baba holds his watch in his hands and rubs its face in slow circles, while Uncle Tarzi's arms are crossed on his chest, and his eyes give away the scowl behind his beard; he leans over and whispers something to Baba.

After the speaker stands off to the side, this new man walks forward, and I can see his profile. The bushy hairs on his mustache and chin stick out in all directions. His hair is combed in a swooping wave across his scalp as he approaches the pulpit.

"Hey! Do you know who that is?" Nshan whispers.

I stare at the man's profile, and as he begins to speak, I recognize the voice I'd heard every day at the Yeramian School for years.

"Our comrade from Varak has told us of the atrocities in the villages of Vaspurakan. Massacres and violations beyond what we have endured in this country. Even worse than when Hamid ruled over us. We can claim it started with the war tax, then stealing our young men to fight for a country that hates them. But it goes further back in our history. The hate they carry for us has grown, decade by decade, until it has become an unspeakable evil. Sadly, I fear that what plagues the villages is coming to Van. Refugees have begun to wander from all sides to the Old City and will spread to Aykesdan in the east. Ishkhan foresaw this. Before he left for Jevdet Bey's 'peace talk,' he sent me a note expressing his fears, urging me not to listen to the lies of the Butcher of Van. Thank God, I listened."

Professor Manukian pauses a moment. I see a smirk on Uncle Tarzi's face, and I imagine he enjoys proving how right he is to Baba.

"Unlike their promises, it appears the Committee of Union and Progress has only a thirst for Armenian blood. Talat Pasha is the new Sultan Abdul Hamid. The new enemy of the Armenian people. All their promises of change have fallen short. The only promise they have kept is to deny us freedom and land. Deportations have begun in the surrounding areas, sending young and old Armenians into the desert and to their deaths. But we are not cattle led to the butcher. It is time we make a choice to fight or to flee. To protect the land of our ancestors that God had given to us long before the Ottomans."

The men in the pews rustle and murmur among each other. Razmik straightens a bit and whispers, "If Professor Manukian lectured like that in school, I could have stayed awake in class."

"He's not a miracle worker," Nshan comments, and a quick nudge from Raz nearly sends Nshan's small frame tumbling onto the altar.

"Quiet! I want to hear," I tell them.

Some of the men in the pews shift and squirm in their seats. From the back, a man stands and clears his throat.

"This is most alarming, Aram. But what can the few of us do against an army? We are merchants, tanners, salesmen. Not trained fighters."

Grunts of agreement fill the sanctuary. I try to keep my eyes on Baba.

Professor Manukian raises a hand, and the men settle.

"I understand, my friend. Doubt and fear seem appropriate for this hour. But we are not just common peasants. We are Armenians. Sultan Hamid could not extinguish us. At Adana, many of us fell, but so did many of them. We come from the line of Tigranes the Great, King of Kings."

Short cheers arise among the men, and the comrade who had spoken earlier claps his hands so loudly the sound pierces the air.

"Yes, we have different views as a people. We don't always agree. We fight. Some of us are Tashnags. Some are Hunchags. Some of you may be Nationalists, while others may still have hope in the Young Turks. Despite our political stances, when we are faced with a common enemy, we come together. I am asking you now, as proud Armenians who have suffered an existence less than what we deserve, to join in the fight. Our group has stockpiled weapons across the city right under the gendarmes' noses for this inevitable moment. Will you raise your weapons with me?"

The men fall silent in their seats, glancing across the pews at each other like when a teacher asks a question in class but everyone is too afraid to be wrong. Murmurs float around the room. Professor Manukian waits at the glossy, wooden pulpit. The three of us huddle together, waiting and watching, and I can't tell if Nshan or Razmik has stopped breathing as I have.

To the side, I see Baba, watch in hand, lean forward and place his hands on the back of the pew in front of him. He rises to his feet so slowly I fear he might fall over, but Uncle Tarzi simply sits and watches him along with the hundreds of other eyes.

The white in Baba's beard catches in the candlelight. In his hand, I can see the glare of the watch as he rubs the face a moment in the silence.

"What do you say, Vartan?" the professor asks. His words echo now more than any other words he'd spoken that night.

Baba lifts his eyes and scans the sea of faces. Then he looks down at Uncle Tarzi. In a soft voice just loud enough to carry through the air of the sanctuary, he says one, short phrase.

"Remember Adana."

The men across the room nod their heads solemnly—whether to agree or because their heads feel too heavy with the memory, I can't tell.

Even the professor nods as he repeats, "Remember Adana."

Uncle Tarzi springs to his feet and shouts, "Adana!"

His cry bounces off the walls and around the sanctuary, and soon all the men pump their fists in the air and shout, "Adana! Adana! Adana!" Over and over, they repeat the word like the beating of a drum. Each shout surges through my body, and I begin to wander out toward the pulpit with my fist pumping in the air.

"Suren, what are you doing?" Nshan asks, and he grabs my shirt, pulling me backward.

"Adana!" I shout. I push at the fingers gripping my shirt as I walk forward. I'm Armenian and must protect the land.

With a sudden jerk, I lose my balance and tumble forward past the curtains. Razmik's heavy body lands on my legs, and Nshan lays across my back in a heap. The men continue chanting as I look out at their faces, ignoring us boys piled at the foot of the cross. However, one face does not ignore us.

The same face I will have to meet when I go home.

6

The Gendarme

Baba, silence, and I walk home in the dark streets after the meeting. Uncle Tarzi stayed behind to give his strategy for how the Armenians could fight the Turks, but I think the *fedayi* know better.

I glance at Baba often as we walk, and each time, I am sure his disappointed eyes will pierce my soul. But instead, he looks at the street with his hands tucked into the pockets of his long coat. I think of Razmik and Nshan and wonder how each of them walked home. Did they receive a lecture about being good Armenian boys and listening to their fathers? I'm sure Nshan will never hear the end of the lesson. But in Razmik's case, the lecture probably came in the form of a fist. I could see his father's bloodshot eyes as he stomped toward us at the altar, his callous, thick fingers gripping Raz's arm so tightly that he winced. Even after seeing him pummel Mihran earlier that day, I wished I could have stopped Raz's father from digging his nails into his skin.

Baba says nothing. Not a sigh or a clearing of his throat. We pass each lamp, and it looks as if the bags under his eyes carry a heavy weight. I smell the grease of some goat meat over a fire as we pass one of the homes, and my stomach grumbles. When did I last eat?

The sweet smell turns sour as we walk down the street past the police station. My heart pounds with each silent step. The mystery of a possible beating or fatherly lecture gnaws at my bones. Maybe it will never come, but the fear still grips me, and, unable to contain it, I speak up in a cracking voice: "I'm sorry, Baba."

He doesn't reply but only lets go a long sigh through his nostrils. Without a break in his stride, he places a hand on my shoulder. His thumb digs into my collarbone, not in a painful way, but with a grip just tight enough to make it uncomfortable. Is he angry? Disappointed?

"I would have done the same," he says.

A pressure eases in my chest. "You would have?"

"You are getting older, Suren *jan*. By spring, you won't be a student anymore. It's only natural you want to know what men speak about. I'm afraid this world may force you to grow up sooner than you should."

"Is all of what Professor Manukian said true? About the Turks wanting to kill us?" I ask, Hamza's face flashing before me.

"There's no use hiding it now. They have always resented us and our faith since I was a boy."

An old Armenian woman wearing a head covering stands outside her front door, sweeping dirt from the stones. She sweeps as if nothing is coming, as if everything is as it always was. Is she unaware of what tomorrow could bring? Or the day after? The week? Should I tell her she may not have a step to sweep in a matter of days?

"Are you going to fight, Baba?"

His lips tighten behind his beard as he opens his mouth to speak.

"Hey, Armenian!" a man shouts from one of the buildings. We freeze. Baba looks to his left at two men in uniform standing in the doorway of the Turkish gendarmerie. In the light behind them, smoke curls in the air as the butt of a cigarette glows. The taller gendarme tosses the stub onto the street, then stomps it out with the toe of his boot.

The woman sweeping keeps her head down and slips back into her home. The slam of her door echoes in the street. In his dark uniform, the tall gendarme walks toward us while the other leans against the doorway, smoking and watching. His shadow stretches across the dirt street and nearly touches our feet. The crunch of his boots grows louder and louder, and Baba shifts his body in front of mine. The gendarme approaches from his side. The smell of incense from the church still clings to Baba's clothes. Can the officer smell it too?

The gendarme stops in front of us, and now the stench of tobacco mingles with the holy smell.

"You are out late," he states, almost as if he asks at the same time. His long, pointed mustache curls up at the ends and seems to spread from ear to ear. In the dark, his eyes are as black as his uniform. The brass buttons catch flecks of light leading to the sword at his waist.

Baba bows his head. "Forgive me, officer. Is there a curfew I am unaware of?"

The gendarme twists one end of his mustache to a point. "You don't ask the questions. I do."

"Yes, sir."

The gendarme comes closer. “Here’s a question: I see many of you people out tonight. Why is that?”

“April nights in Van are perfect for a walk, sir.”

The gendarme examines Baba’s face, twisting and turning his mustache until the point looks as if it could pierce skin.

“It’s common knowledge that you can’t trust an Armenian. So, as you can imagine, I think you are lying to me. Are you a liar, Armenian?” The gendarme’s voice is calm, full of patience. Cold.

“No, sir. It is against our faith to lie. In fact, many of us were at St. Boghos for Mass.”

The gendarme outwardly maintains his calm, but his nostrils flare.

“Your faith,” he repeats.

With a sick groan, Baba bends in half and clutches his stomach as the gendarme’s fist collides with his gut. He swung so fast I feel like I’m seeing it happen after the fact. My hand grips Baba’s shirt as he gasps.

“Your faith,” the gendarme growls once again, swinging another blow into Baba’s stomach with a sickening thud. My body tenses watching my father struggle to breathe. In my throat, I feel the need to shout, but the words lodge there; they clamor to get out, but nothing comes. Have I stopped breathing too?

Baba drops to one knee, and spit dribbles into his beard. His gasping breaths fill the street. I look around for help, for a familiar face to intervene. But the only faces I see are silent shadows in the windows. My mouth fills with saliva, and I think my body can no longer stomach another thrown fist.

The gendarme crouches down onto his haunches without taking his eyes off Baba, blowing smoke into our faces. Lamplight catches his face. Until now, I’d not noticed that his cap had fallen to the ground. His black hair hangs in front of his young eyes, not much older than my brothers’—at least from what I remember before they enlisted to fight.

"You do know that the Sheikh has issued a jihad. But your kind is quite empty up here, so maybe you don't," he says in a gentle voice, tapping his temple. "That means you and all the other *gavur* in our country should leave this land to whom it rightfully belongs."

Baba's breath returns, and he looks at the man crouching before him.

"This land was always Armenian."

The man pauses, reaching toward my feet where his fez has fallen. He brushes the black fabric before placing it on his head.

"Of course, there is the other option," he says with a smirk before lifting himself to his full height. He flicks the remains of his cigarette into Baba's face, but Baba doesn't even flinch.

The gendarme's shadow falls over us as he pulls another cigarette from his jacket and places it between his lips. His dark eyes look at me for the first time as he searches for a match.

"Think of your son, old man. Or Vali Bey will."

The light flares as he takes a strong drag and tosses the burned match at my feet. Then he turns and walks back to the gendarmerie. His partner still watches from the door like a spectator to a play.

When they disappear inside, I help Baba to his feet. He says nothing. Not a word. Not even a sound, except for a mild groan. However, his moist eyes tell the story, just as mine reveal my shame. My grip on his shirt loosens, and my fingers ache as they move again.

He looks at me, and I can't tell if the glistening in his eyes is from shame or rage—or maybe both. He bends over to brush off his knees, then straightens. As if he knows what I am thinking, he places a hand on my shoulder.

"Fighting doesn't always involve fists, son."

He gently nudges me toward home, but my hands remain clenched.

7

A Talk in the Dark

As I stare at the ceiling, I hear from downstairs Mama's sobs between Baba's muffled words. I don't see them, but I know my sisters are huddling by the door frame, trying to hear what they are talking about.

Without my brothers here, I have my own room. Just a single bed stuffed with hay, a thin cotton blanket, and two empty beds by the window. Not like Nshan's mattress, which feels like sleeping on clouds. Under my pillow, I feel the lump of my Bible pressing into the back of my skull. Baba always told me about how his father slept with the word of God under his head so God would speak to him in his dreams. This sounds like an easy way to learn Scripture, so I keep it under my pillow every night.

My mind replays the fights between Raz and Mihran, the woman and the Kurdish merchant, my father and the gendarme. The thud of fists on Mihran's face and into Baba's gut. The piercing words from the merchant's table. No group spared in Van. A small part of me feels what Professor Manukian and Uncle Tarzi said is still only rumors: a small band of angry Turks and Kurds who did unspeakable things to our people in the villages. Could someone like Hamza harbor such hate for us? Could he be capable of doing it?

I hear a floorboard creak and turn my head to the doorway.

"Are you awake?" Ani whispers, standing in her white nightgown.

"Of course."

She comes over to my bed and sits at the edge, brushing the blanket flat with her hand. Her long, black hair reaches to her elbows, and even in the faint light, her green eyes shine.

"What are they saying?" I ask.

"It's hard to say. Whatever it is, they seem scared," she replies in a soft voice. Though only two years older than me, Ani always carries a peace with her. Mama always told me that no matter how fussy I became as a baby, Ani could always sing to me, and I would stop. Even now, with all of these rumors and meetings, her voice makes my bed feel like a calming hot spring. Baba had not mentioned anything about the meeting or the gendarme when we'd returned home. Maybe he never will.

"I know about the rumors," she says.

"What rumors?" I reply.

"Everyone knows. I know you went to the church tonight."

My cheeks flush. "Did your boyfriend tell you?"

"No! Arshak wouldn't tell. I overheard Baba mention it after we'd gone to bed."

I do that nervous tic I've always done where I flick my fingers in sequence on one hand. Based on Ani's look, she can see my tell.

"No one would have known if Raz and Nshan hadn't fooled around," I reply with more anger than I truly feel.

"I have a terrible feeling, Suren. One I can't pray away."

"If the Turks try to take our home, then we will fight. Professor Manukian and the *fedayi* will defend us. I will defend you."

From the faint light of the door, I see a tear fall from her soft eyes, which she swipes off her cheek before it reaches her chin.

"What are you two doing?" a harsh voice snaps.

Taline waddles into the room with her pointy finger shaking. Her long hair is wound tightly into a bun even when she goes to sleep.

"They could hear you, and then we lose our cover." She glances at me, sitting on my bed with the pillow crumpled behind my back. "This is all your fault anyway."

"My fault?" I reply with a squeak.

"If you hadn't snuck into that meeting, our parents wouldn't be so upset right now."

Ani stands. "That's not what they are upset about."

"Yes, it is. I heard them say—"

Ani takes a step closer and interrupts her. "The Turks are coming."

Taline pauses. Her face contorts like it does when she gets confused, and the scar on her upper lip lifts like a dog begging for food. I catch a chuckle in my throat.

"What do you mean?"

In her quiet way, Ani places a hand on Taline's shoulder. "I have a feeling."

Taline slaps her hand away. "Unless God comes down from heaven and tells you, we have nothing to worry about. Everyone is getting concerned over nothing. Soon all of these fears will pass.

Mark my words. The Turks and us have not always been friendly, but what you are thinking? Impossible."

As she gives us her opinion, I catch her scratching the top of her forearm, just like when the gendarmes pillaged our house to collect taxes or when our brothers marched away in their Ottoman uniforms.

From downstairs, a low, mournful wail carries up to my room. We sit staring at the doorway as if the sound itself will take shape, walk up the steps, and visit us, maybe bringing our worst fears with it.

Taline scoffs and rolls her eyes. She thrusts herself to her feet and smooths her gown with violent swipes.

"I still don't understand why you have your own room."

Ani stands, placing herself between the bed and our sister. "Now is not the time."

She stares back at her sister with her chin lifted. Taline opens her mouth, probably to insult Ani, but for once, she says nothing. With a huff, she pivots and stomps out the door to their room. The wail from downstairs softens as she shuts the door.

"Why is she so . . . her?" I say without really expecting a response.

Ani faces me, twisting the ends of her long hair in her fingertips, her green eyes shining. "Fear makes us do and say things we wouldn't normally do," she remarks.

"She must be scared all the time," I mutter, clenching my fists around the fringe of the sheet. Ani stays silent and stares out the window.

"Are you afraid?" I ask with a quick flutter in my chest.

She pauses and wipes at her eyes before leaning over and kissing my cheek. As if floating, Ani drifts out of my room and disappears. The dark house falls into an unfamiliar silence, as if the walls, the floor, the bed, even the dishes have taken a long, deep breath. I do the same until I fall asleep, but the echo of Mama's wail still travels through the house.

April 19, 1915

Preparation

8

The Empty Market

On most Mondays, we would be in school learning arithmetic or reading, but not today.

Above the tops of the stone houses, clouds roll in across the spring sky. Raz walks in the middle of our group with his hands in his pockets, kicking at a single rock with each step.

"Mr. Duman better be open. My father is going to kill me if I don't buy some pork for tonight."

Though no one says it, we all know Raz's father sent him to the market to buy *oghi*, the drink that makes all adults clumsy, say foolish things, and even beat their own families.

"It is so quiet," Nshan remarks.

I don't notice until he mentions it. Normally, the buzz of the market can be heard already—a mix of shouting, bartering, laughing in Kurdish, Armenian, Turkish, maybe even Farsi or Greek.

"Have you seen your Turkish friend lately? Maybe he knows something," Raz asks. The way he pronounces "Turkish" stings my ears, but I know better than to pick a fight with Razmik.

"We haven't spoken since the fight behind the church."

"Hmmm," he replies, but I ignore him.

We round the corner to enter the market and stop almost simultaneously.

Only an empty, dusty street extends between the buildings. The stalls no longer crowd the square, no tents or tables filled with textiles or vegetables. A few cats foraging for discarded food stop to watch us.

"Where is everyone?" Nshan whispers.

Raz takes a step forward and growls before asking with a slight tremor, "Now what am I supposed to do?"

I look around, hoping maybe Hamza might be somewhere nearby to ask him why the market that never closes is actually closed. To just see him after the odd conversation outside the cemetery. But I only see dozens of cats lurking around, eating scraps, and the faint outline of where the booths used to be.

Some footsteps clamor from behind us, and we pivot around. The faces of Mihran and a young girl nearly run into us.

"Ahhh!" Mihran shrieks as he almost collides with Razmik. His eye is still bruised and swollen.

"You came back for more," Raz says, puffing his chest up and flexing his biceps enough to show under his shirt.

"No, no, no. I just came to buy some food for me and my sister."

The young girl beside Mihran looks at Razmik with sharp eyes and a furrowed brow. I notice her fists clenching as she stares at him. Her delicate nose and long eyelashes contrast with the rage in her eyes.

"Are you Razmik?" she asks in a piercing voice.

"The one and only," he replies with a smirk, crossing his arms.

The girl stomps forward, fists still clenched, as Raz watches with an amused smile. Before Raz can react, the girl swings her right leg back, fanning her dress out, and kicks forward. Her foot lands right between Raz's legs. His howl can probably be heard in Ayeksan. He clutches his groin and falls to one knee.

"Aye!" Nshan exclaims, grabbing his own groin and wincing. I realize I've done the same thing.

"That's for my brother!" she informs and returns to Mihran's side with a whip of her ponytail. Raz gasps, bent in half with watery eyes.

"Why'd you do that? Now everyone will think I need my twelve-year-old sister to fight for me!" Mihran says, slapping his hand against his face and then wincing.

"Not even a thank-you!" she exclaims with her hands raised.

Nshan points to the girl. "This is your sister?"

Mihran wipes his hand down his face, eyes rolled to the sky. "This is Shushi."

Shushi looks at us with her arms folded across her chest. She examines us through slits as if deciding who she can trust—or if she needs to kick someone else in the groin. In a way, she reminds me of Taline.

Nshan gives a shy wave. As for Raz, he's still having a hard time catching his breath.

"Anyway, where is the market? The American told us to come here and get some groceries," Mihran asks. He looks around at the still street and the lurking cats.

"What American?" Raz asks, still wincing.

"The one that runs the orphanage—" Shushi begins, but then stops.

I shrug. "I don't know. It is always here. No Armenians. No Kurds. No Turks. Nothing."

Nshan clears his throat as he does whenever he plans to say something he thinks is important. "In my opinion, I think it has to do with the Turks."

"That's obvious," Raz mutters, rising from his hunched position. His hands hang loose at his sides as he looks at Shushi.

"That was a free shot," he informs her, then looks at Mihran's swollen face, and the two exchange nods.

"Do you hear that?" Nshan asks.

We pause.

From one of the homes, a door creaks open and a man pokes his head out, looking around the empty street. He sees us standing at the far entrance but seems not to care. He pushes the door open, and four or five men, gripping rifles in their hands with the barrels pointing to the sky, trot across the square. Their chests hold belts with rows of shining bullets. The clink of the metal echoes with every step.

"The *fedayi*," Raz whispers—to himself or to tell us, I do not know.

The soldiers disappear down an alley, and we breathe a collective sigh.

"We should follow them!" Shushi shouts, pulling at Mihran's sleeve.

"Let it snow on your brain," he replies and yanks his arm away.

"It's happening," Nshan says. "The war has come just like Professor Manukian said."

I can feel the blood pumping in my veins and my stomach sizzling. The meeting in St. Boghos comes back to me, along with the words of the fighter from Varak. All the death and pain coming from the west have arrived at our doorstep.

"We should leave," Mihran suggests and grabs Shushi's hand.

Without protest, she follows, and one by one, the others turn and walk back the way we came. However, I stand still.

"Are you coming, Suren?" Nshan asks.

"Go ahead."

Soon, I am alone among the cats in the ghost of the marketplace. The eerie sound of nothing lingers in the morning sun, and I can't escape a sinking sense that even the cats may no longer have a home.

"*Psst.*"

What is that?

"*Psst*. Suren."

I turn to the sound. In the shadows behind an abandoned barrel, I see Hamza, crouched and beckoning with his hand.

A surge of hope flows through me, and I run over to the barrel. Hamza's eyes dart around even as I crouch in front of him. His hair sticks to his sweaty temples.

"Where have you been?" I ask, unsure if I want to know. "So much has happened."

Hamza swallows. "Listen. I should not be here. My father told me to stay away from the Old City, but I had to warn you. He thinks I am doing my chores, so I have little time. Are you listening?"

His eyes glow so intensely that I don't know if I should be afraid or concerned for his health.

"Yes. Yes. I'm listening," I stammer.

"The gendarmes came to the Shamiram quarter and told all Turks to stay away from the city. They assured us we would not be attacked when your people revolt against the Ottoman government. Governor Bey is going to attempt to stop it before it begins tomorrow."

"Revolt?" The word sounds foreign as it leaves my lips.

"Yes. Please don't get involved with these radicals. I don't want you or your family to get hurt."

I can see the sincerity in his face, but I still feel my body clench.

"Hamza, we are the ones under attack."

He reaches out and grabs my hand. "Please, Suren. The Armenians will not win this fight. Please don't do anything crazy. I have to go. I'll try to come back again soon."

My body tenses as he tussles my hair with his hand. Then, in a blink, he vanishes down the alley, back to the safety of the Shamiram.

Alone again, one word rolls over and over in my ears.

Revolt. Revolt. Revolt.

9

The Mountain

Revolt?

Hamza's words still sit in my gut like rotten milk even after I arrive back home. Is that what they are saying in the Muslim part of the city? That we are a bunch of violent, crazy rebels with a death wish?

"Suren, where is the food?" Mama asks, her voice short and direct, hands on her hips.

"The market was closed."

"Don't give me that nonsense!"

"It's true. Nshan and Razmik walked with me. You can ask them."

She stares at me, then looks at Taline next to her. It's difficult to tell if she truly believes me. She exhales a heavy, aggressive sigh.

"What kind of world are we living in where the market closes?" she resolves, throwing her hands in the air.

"Where is Baba?" I ask.

"He's with your uncle."

"Where? At the church?" My voice lifts as I ask.

"I don't know where. But he told me about the other night." Those eyes that pierce like a mother's can make me freeze.

I freeze.

Her gaze stays on me. "Listen, you are not to get mixed up in this *fedayi* foolishness. I want to protect our family's land, but this is madness. The army is far too large, and we have no weapons. Refugees from Varak and other villages flood into the Old City constantly. How do we feed them? How do we . . . ?" She seems to choke on the words for a moment and continues when she gathers herself. "You are just a boy, and you will stay with your sisters and me."

My jaw sets and my arms tense as my voice propels from me. "I can fight!"

Her weight shifts to one leg as she leans with one arm on the counter. Her lips vanish within her tense mouth.

"I don't care if you can. You will listen to your mother and stay here where it's safe."

Each word she speaks prickles my skin. "I am nearly a man, Mama. If my brothers can fight, then I—"

"They won't have you fighting their wars too!"

She slams her hands onto the wooden table as she shouts. Cups of water bounce and spill, and the room turns to stone. I watch the small puddles spread, and Taline shrinks against the far cupboards.

"Anyway," Mama whispers, changing her tone, "I'm going to cook some food."

Off she goes with her busy hands, which she wipes on her apron, though she has nothing on them. Normally, Mama moves with grace and purpose when she begins to cook. But today, she sifts through baskets, boxes, and cupboards as if searching for some lost object.

My instincts want to say something—to apologize or plead my case. To make her see why I need to help the *fedayi*, help Baba. It is my duty. Just like my brothers' duty is to fight in the Great War. But words no longer make sense in this kitchen, in this home, or in this world.

The rest of the morning, Mama bustles around the kitchen: cleaning the cupboards, rearranging the utensils, sweeping the whole house, sitting at the table, then wiping it down, sweeping again. Every now and then, I hear her mutter something to herself—maybe a prayer or a curse to God or the *pasha*. I can't tell.

Aside from Mama's incessant cleaning, the world feels still. I felt it in the abandoned market too. The air seems polluted, and each time I inhale, I can feel the tension stick in my lungs.

In my room, I try to read the Bible as Father Zakarian always preaches about. "God will give you peace if you read his Scriptures," he says almost every Sunday. But I read through all the words Jesus said so long ago—of loving your enemies and turning the other cheek. What happens when you run out of cheeks, arms, or hands? At what point do you give all of your body and your enemies have nothing more to take? It would be nice if Jesus were still here to answer these questions.

I close the thick book with a thud and look out the window of my room. The sun hangs high in the sky, and I hear nothing but the occasional shuffle of boots on the ground running by my window. Our neighbors' shuttered windows block my view, and the suffocating air in my home gnaws at me too much. Placing my Bible in its place under my pillow, I stand up, head to the hall, and climb the wooden ladder that leads to the roof.

A blast of sunlight blinds me for a moment as I lift the roof hatch. Mama always scolds me for coming up here, but the breeze and the view make it worth the scolding. I climb up and stand on the stone rooftop, where small puddles gather on the uneven surface from the light rains.

A cool spring breeze touches my skin and blows my hair across my forehead. Clouds roll in front of the sun, then leave. No birds fly or peck around on the rooftops like usual. But the true reason the roof calls me is the view over the rooftops and bell towers of the city. Mount Ararat's snowcapped peak looks down on us.

The Bible tells us that Noah landed there after the flood. But Baba still tells us of our savior, Artavazd, who is still chained in the mountain by evil spirits. When he escapes, he will deliver Mount Ararat and the Armenian people from their enemies with vengeance. Then Baba would always tell all of us children not to tell anyone. In hindsight, I think he didn't want Father Zakarian to find out he told us stories that weren't in the Bible, even if these are our stories passed down from long ago.

I walk over and sit with my back against the chimney. The blue and gray sky hangs over the Holy Mountain, and, as happens when I am in its presence, the lump in my chest fades and air flows through my lungs as it should. Even in the deathly stillness of Van today, Ararat speaks to me.

"God or Artavazd—whoever wants to chat today—protect us from what is coming."

As I say my prayer, something catches my eye near the reflection of Ararat in the lake. Small black figures, hundreds of them, come single file toward the city's edge. Some ride horses, and others are in vehicles pulling massive, long-barreled guns on wheeled carts. In the breeze, their red flags bearing the moon and star wave. Though I can't make out for sure from my roof, I know deep within me it is the Turks. Hundreds, maybe thousands of them.

I hope my prayers reach Ararat in time.

10

The Decision

At dinner, we sit in our spots. No one ever told us to sit there; it just happened that way. The only seat that we all, somehow, agreed on without really agreeing is Baba's at the head of the table. However, the two chairs for my brothers remain empty.

Mama and Taline cooked harissa with no meat since the market was closed, but we have some leftover kufta from earlier. Sheets of lavash sit on a cloth in the middle of the table. I dip my spoon, and the thick, soupy wheat falls off the side and plops back into the bowl. I catch Taline gazing at me, sharing the same disgusted look.

"Thank you for dinner, my love," Baba says, reaching out his hand and taking Mama's.

She doesn't reply and keeps her eyes on her bowl. Her cheeks seem to hang below her eyes as if she'd failed in some way. A silence lingers over the table. Outside, I can see the lamps being lit.

"How was your day, Baba?" Ani asks, dipping out a dainty spoonful of harissa.

He turns from Mama with a solemn expression. "A good day. Productive day." He seems as if he wants to say more but takes a bite of lavash instead.

The silence returns. We all know what is coming. But why will no one talk about it? It simmers in the air, begging to be heard, but all I can hear is the sound of Baba's chewing and the clink of spoons. My cheeks burn, and the claw in my chest squeezes until I can't hold back.

"I saw the Turks coming from the lake."

Everyone stops chewing and looks at me like my eyeballs have fallen out of their sockets.

"Suren!" Mama and Taline both say. Ani turns her face away and continues eating as if nothing is happening.

Baba releases Mama's hand. "When did you see this?"

"Earlier today. On the . . . roof." I wish I could take that second part back.

I see Mama's look, and I'm glad she's on the other side of the table.

Baba turns his face slowly from me, surveying the faces of the women at the table. The sound of boots running can be heard in the moment of silence outside the kitchen window.

"Is this true, Baba?" Ani asks, twisting her black hair into braids at the end before pulling them out over and over again.

Placing his hands on the table, he exhales a long, almost painful breath and closes his eyes.

"I heard that the Turks are telling everyone in the Muslim quarters that we are revolting against the government," I blurt out.

"You heard this where?" Baba asks.

Though they know Hamza, my lips can't seem to tell them his name. "From the other boys."

"Vartan?" Mama asks, obsessively smoothing her dress.

Baba scans all our faces. "It is true. War has come to Van."

Taline gasps, Ani bows her head, and Mama's lips curl as a mournful cry flies over the table. As for me, I sit with my eyes fixed on Baba.

"The Turkish forces are gathering on the outskirts of the city near the lake. The *fedayi* have scouts watching them from different homes with clear vision and are ready to let us know as soon as something happens."

A pile of lavash ripped into tiny bits piles up in front of Taline. Her fingers hold the two shards that are left. "I've heard of many who have already fled, headed east where the Russians can protect them."

Baba reaches out and holds her hand. "This is our home, and if we will not protect it, who will?"

"But this," Taline says, gesturing at all of us seated at the table, "*this* is our home. These walls are just walls. We can make a new home somewhere else."

He pats her hand, then sits back. "You're right, Tal. We could join the exodus and flee. But what would that prove? That Armenians are cowards? That the Turks can exile us simply because they feel like it?"

"Vartan, stop talking as if you are one of the *fedayi*," Mama scolds. "You have a family to think about. You have children!"

"I am thinking of my children. This land is Armenian land," Baba says, looking at each of us and jamming his forefinger into the table as he speaks. "Centuries before the Ottomans set foot on this earth, this was the Armenian Kingdom. Lake Van was one of the three mighty lakes of Armenia. And it has been stolen from us again and again. If we flee to the east out of fear and abandon the home of our ancestors, then the Turks don't have to kill us to have won. They will say, 'Look at how they run away when we come. Just like we always said.' If we run, they have already defeated us."

Mama covers her face. "Why has God allowed this to happen?"

"I don't understand His ways. But I know He requires us to make difficult decisions, and this is that decision. However, I can't make it alone. You are all smart. I want us to be united in this choice. Do we fight, or do we flee?"

The heaviness of the silence sits like a stone on the table, as if we have a two-sided coin that must be flipped to determine the direction of our lives as a family and as a people. My mind races with the thought of holding a rifle and firing it at a bloodthirsty Turk bent on ending my family. Fighting alongside my Armenian comrades against an enemy who has wanted our demise for centuries. Singing revolutionary songs and charging into battle like Tigranes the Great. Or like my brothers. But in my heart, I feel the coldness of fear.

During the silence, Baba closes his eyes and prays, holding hands with Mama as she wipes at her endless supply of tears. Ani has braided a section of her hair near her right ear, and Taline, always with a scowl, has now torn apart Mama's lavash as well, adding to her pile. As for me, the pressure of tears wells behind my eyes, but I will not let them fall.

Baba opens his eyes and releases Mama's hand.

"Well then?"

A long pause. My courage to vote rises, then falls just as quickly. As the youngest, would my opinion even matter?

"Stay."

The first vote comes from Ani. Her eyes are determined as she makes her decision. Part of me wonders if this has to do with the man she loves fighting in the *fedayi*.

More silence passes before Taline throws the remains of the lavash in her hands at the center of the table.

"Go," she says, then folds her arms across her chest.

"Yes. Yes. We should go," Mama agrees, as if Taline has somehow influenced her to go along.

"I understand," Baba says before turning his face to me. "That's two votes to stay and two votes to go."

All eyes fall on me, piercing into my skin. I can't look anyone in the eye, and the claw squeezes tight around the bones in my chest. I should have voted earlier, and now my fear has made me the deciding vote. I don't want to hold back my tears, but I have to. Taline would never let me forget it. As I feel my teeth clench, I hear Baba's soft voice.

"Choose with your heart, Suren *jan*, and God will guide you."

I close my eyes and take a deep breath. Though I have asked God many times to speak to me, I have been met only with silence. So, God, I ask you now to guide me. Help me make the right decision. Speak to me, please. Tell me what to do.

I wait through an endless moment with my family expecting my decision. But I hear nothing but the creak of a chair, Baba's sigh, and Mama's sniffles. Father Zakarian always speaking about visions and seeing the face of God in difficult times. But God's face doesn't come to me. I see different faces. Familiar faces. I see Nshan and Razmik. I see Mihran and even his little sister, whose name I can't remember. But the face that haunts me is Hamza's.

I open my eyes to the eager faces awaiting my answer. The night air fills my nostrils. I scan each face, then lift my chin as I make my decision.

"We stay."

11

A Song of Memory for Tomorrow

The city streets buzz. Not with the excitement before a festival or wedding, but it sizzles behind everyone's eyes and words—a mix of fear and hope. I saw it at our kitchen table, and I see it now in the faces of all the men sitting around the bonfire in the street, glowing red from the flames.

Of the fifteen men, I know only a few by name, and some I recall from the church meeting. The others must be refugees from the outer villages. Uncle Tarzi sits across the bonfire while I sit close to Baba. Everyone sits on boxes, chairs, and crates—whatever we can find, really. Each soldier keeps his rifle close. Some grip theirs tightly, while others sling theirs across their shoulders.

A few talk quietly, but the only sound I hear is the crackling of the fire and the beating of my heart. Next to me, I see the cold barrel of Baba's rifle across his lap, the metal as black as the night.

I lean close to him and ask, "I thought it was against the law for Armenians to have weapons?"

"You're right."

"Then how did everyone get a gun?"

"Some laws are meant to be broken." Baba smiles and gives me a wink.

I look across the fire.

"Where is my gun?"

He turns to look at me, his eyes stern.

"This is not your fight, Suren. You must stay back and protect your mother and sisters."

"Why can't I fight? This is my home too."

"I know it is. But you will not fight this war."

My muscles tense, and I point at the faces around the fire. "Look at them. Some are no older than me, but they have a weapon."

Baba grabs me by the arm, making me wince.

"I won't lose another son," he whispers.

Behind his beard, I can see his lips tremble, and his stern eyes show me something else.

I open my mouth to argue my case, but pause.

"Promise me," Baba insists.

I can't be sure, but I think I hear a tremor in his voice. He looks at his hand on my arm, then pulls it away in one swift jerk. The way he looks at his hand reminds me of the expression he made when he found out my brothers had been drafted into the military.

He returns his gaze to the fire without waiting for an answer, rubbing the hand that grabbed me as if he were trying to remove something from it.

"You can stay here a little longer, then you must go home."

Silent, I watch his profile aglow in the fire. A tear slides down his cheek. The desire to cry lingers in my throat, ready to push through and make me look weak, but I hold it back because, no matter what Baba may think, I am a fighter—just like the *fedayi*. I'll show him one day.

The sky remains dark except for a few stars between the clouds. A new moon has started, and I can't help but wonder if the Turks decided to attack us for a reason at this time of year—to use the darkness to surprise us and take out all our fighters. I'm not sure when the fighting will start, but I feel deep inside my soul that it will be soon.

Tonight?

Tomorrow?

Now?

Who knows?

A few *fedayi* stand, clutching their rifles to their chests and wearing bandoliers that glisten in the firelight. Some men grab shards of wood from a broken cart and throw them on the bonfire to a spray of sparks. Others sit as still as stone. If the Turks do attack, they may think we are just a group of statues.

A voice lifts up in the quiet—a smooth, nasally tone that startles some of the men, and many of them look up. I see Uncle Tarzi rise to his feet with his rifle slung over his shoulder. His chin is high and his eyes are closed as a song fills the still night:

Bright sun, don't give your light anymore,
But bind a necklace of mourning around your light.
A simoom from the south passed through our country.
It dried up and withered every tree and flower.

Not a soul moves as he sings. I glance at Baba's serious expression, and most of the older men look burdened with memories the young do not have.

A moment hadn't passed, and the poor Armenians
Fell beneath the sword and the terrible mob.
Churches and schools were lost in the flames.
Thousands of Armenians died unsparingly.

There is something familiar about the song. A strange understanding in the sad words that comforts me. Can sadness be comforting like the Psalms? I want to hold on to hope against the Turkish army. To have faith like Abraham or Jacob or Job. If we have faith, then God will surely give us victory. Still, I don't know if God would be a better option than Artavazd.

"Baba," I ask, tugging at his sleeve. He turns his moist eyes toward me.

"What is Uncle Tarzi singing about?"

"He sings of a memory none of us wish we had."

"Is it about Adana?"

Baba nods. "Do you know this story?"

I want to lie and say I do, like a good Armenian boy, but my need to know about Adana takes over, so I shake my head.

"What month is it? April?"

I nod.

"Six years ago in the west, near the Mediterranean Sea, many Armenians lived in the city of Adana. Still, as it has always been, many of the Turks hated us. Kurds too. Why? I cannot say. Maybe it is our God, our clothes, our names. Who can say what fuels hate? Six years ago, the Muslims executed some Armenians. Some of them fought back. But the fire had been lit. Turkish citizens attacked the Armenians in Adana, burning homes, torturing women and children, and slaughtering whoever they found. An unspeakable disease swept through Adana and every Armenian heart in the empire. It left twenty thousand of us dead. Your grandmother was one of those who perished."

"What disease?"

Baba keeps his eyes on the fire. "Evil."

The last word struggled to find its way out of Baba's mouth. Twenty thousand people? I close my eyes to try to imagine it, but my mind refuses. How can someone understand such a number of deaths?

"Did the government punish those responsible?" I ask, feeling the sadness of the melody mix with my rage.

"The Turkish newspapers said we had started it. 'Revolted,' they wrote. The government condemned the citizens' actions, but that was it. Besides, we are separatists who wish to rule over the Ottoman Empire, according to most Turks. They say the Turkish citizens acted in self-defense."

My blood roils inside me. I can't tell if the warmth in my face comes from the bonfire.

"But that is a lie!"

"History is often written by the winners. The truth depends on who gets there first."

I hear Uncle Tarzi's song:

The unfeeling, lawless evil left orphaned
The child from its mother, the bride from her groom.
The shameless Jevad, the vile Adil
Ate and were satisfied by the blood of the Armenians.

My mind shifts to Hamza. What are his people saying right now? Is he listening to the lies they spread or sitting around singing songs about the violent Armenians? I imagine him seated with his family, his father spouting lies about our people, and I wonder if Hamza listens. Really listens. He told me once that Turks sit on the floor when they eat, on a large Persian rug. Maybe the Quran sits open and orders them to kill non-Muslims like us. I wish I had asked him more about what he believes. Maybe I could understand how they think. Maybe understand why they hate us.

Some of the other men begin to join Uncle Tarzi, standing with their tin cups of *oghi* high in the air like a salute. They hang their arms around each other's shoulders. A cup is passed around the circle as the song continues.

> *For three days and nights from within the fire*
> *The enemy's sword and bomb, from outside*
> *Erased the Armenian from the face of the earth.*
> *Blood flowed from our clear rivers.*

The cup reaches Baba, who tilts it back and winces before extending it to me. Even with the smell of the bonfire, I still catch a whiff of a piercing odor. My hand moves hesitantly toward the outstretched cup. Baba gestures, and finally I take it. The chorus builds as I lift the trembling cup to my lips. The vapors sting my nostrils, and like yanking out a splinter, I take a large gulp.

The burn starts in my mouth, then ignites my throat like a torch inside my sternum. The *oghi* settles in my gut, and I hope to keep my supper inside me. What a terrible drink!

The song ends, and the men stay silent, looking at each other and nodding their heads. Baba takes the cup from my hand and stands, raising it high. Sparks are flung into the air as a log pops. He surveys the others' faces.

"Remember Adana."

Uncle Tarzi snatches a cup from the young man next to him and toasts, shouting, "Adana! Adana! Adana!"

Like a bonfire, the name spreads to everyone.

"Adana!"

"Adana!"

"Adana!"

I hear my own voice chanting the name over and over, wondering if those monsters on the other side of the wall can hear us.

April 20, 1915

The Battle Begins

12

Gunshots

The darkness surprises me, and I wonder how long I've been asleep since the meeting around the fire. My Bible under my pillow digs into the back of my skull. After all this time, I still can't seem to memorize Scripture. Are those voices? At first, I thought it was the *fedayi* in the city, but as I stand up and make my way toward the window, I realize it comes from outside the city, near the lake. In Ayeksan.

A few lamps still burn, but over by Ararat, the faint light of dawn is showing. In the windows of the other homes, women's silhouettes listen to what I hear. Straining, my body goes rigid with my hands on the windowsill. My ears tune in to the distant chant, trying to understand. Then, the jumble of words comes together, and my heart sinks as it all starts to make sense.

I sprint from the window and throw open the bedroom door so fast it hits the wall. As I scramble up the ladder toward the roof, I hear the other bedroom door open behind me, and Ani says, "Suren! What are you doing? Get down!"

Before she can finish her sentence, I'm on the roof in the crisp air. The hairs on my neck and arms stand up. Over the roofs of the other homes, the Turkish army stands in the faint dark, torches burning, and their chant reaches my ears strong and clear.

"Allahu Akbar! Allahu Akbar! Allahu Akbar!"

The glow of the sun touches the ridge of the mountains. Gathered around their large guns, the men chant and point their rifles toward the sky. Like a sea of ants, they spread outside the city walls.

"Allahu Akbar!"

The rhythmic call penetrates the air, and my fingers go cold. Some neighbors have also come to the rooftops to see what is happening. Is Baba in the house, or has he joined the others?

From the mass of Turks, a light flashes, and a boom rattles my chest. To the east, the shot hits some buildings in the far quarter outside the city. Men begin shouting inside the city, and like a growing nightmare, the stuttering rattle of gunfire sounds off around me.

My feet stick, cemented to the rooftop. Should I dive for cover? My mind tells me to, but my body resists. Rifle shots fly from outside the city, and my ears swim in an ocean of bullets. Another loud boom and flash from the Turks, and an explosion hits a building past the Tabriz Gate. Next door, I hear a little girl crying for her mama.

"Suren!"

I hear Mama's voice as if in a dream. I know she is there, that her voice cracks with fear, but my mind swirls. Some arms wrap around me and yank me toward the rooftop door, pushing me down the ladder first. Like a machine, I climb down without thinking as Mama follows. Her backside clambers down the rungs faster than I've ever seen her move.

She lands with a thud as Ani and Taline stand near their bedroom door. Mama turns and grips my upper arms, shaking me.

"You stupid, stupid boy. Did you eat your brain with bread?"

I open my mouth to answer, but only a strange moan comes out.

"The war is here. We must stay inside and be safe. Downstairs! All of you! Now!"

Her hand prods my shoulder, and I follow her orders, nearly tripping down the hard steps.

We stagger toward the table as another loud boom comes from the distance. Taline crashes into me. Her fingers dig into my shoulders, but I don't feel the pain I should. The boom of the guns and the pounding of my heart begin to mix together. She whimpers near my ear like a wounded puppy, and her bangs hide her eyes.

Where's Ani? I look around the room and see her standing by the window, peeking through the crack in the wooden shutters. Mama comes down the stairs. Frantic eyes scan the room, and she can't seem to catch her breath.

"Ani! Get away from there!" she shrieks.

When Ani turns toward Mama's voice, fear grips me for the first time. The peace and steadiness I've always found in Ani's eyes are gone. Instead, I see the eyes of a deer looking down the barrel of a rifle. But I must protect them. I promised Baba. I should run toward her, but I just stare.

Men shout and run through the streets, gripping their guns as they pass the window. Gunfire from all sides pierces the air like firecrackers at New Year's, and if I close my eyes, I can picture myself in the streets with Raz, Nshan, and Hamza, lighting wicks with matches and tossing firecrackers into the air.

But I am here. Now, in Van with the Turkish army wanting to kill us, and I must be the man of the house. For Baba.

"My children. Come here, quickly!" Mama urges, waving her hands for us to gather. Taline still clings to me, and Ani rushes from the window into Mama's arms.

"We must pray to God for safety. All of us."

Without waiting for us to bow our heads, Mama's mournful prayer rises above the distant gunfire, crying babies, and wailing women outside our house. Ani and Taline pray fervently, making the sign of the cross over and over again. I try to pray too, try to push the words from my throat and cry out to God for help, just as I had been taught by the Bible, by Father Zakarian, and by my family.

But my lips stay still.

13

The Word of God

The firing stops at sunrise, and the mosque's megaphone blasts the call to prayer near the Shamiram. Some of the *fedayi* still fire their rifles while the Muslims pray until the big guns resume. In daylight, smoke and dust rise in the east beyond the city walls.

"Suren *jan*, come away from the window," Mama orders.

"I want to see what's happening."

"I won't say it again." The tone all boys fear from their mothers makes me drop my head and return to them.

"Straighten up, or your head will fall on the floor," she warns.

I straighten my shoulders and drop into one of the chairs across from Ani, Taline, and Mama at the table. I should be out with the men, defending the city from those monsters. Instead, I'm stuck here watching the women.

"Where is Baba?" I ask.

Mama sighs. "He's doing his part to protect us. We should have left a few days ago. Packed the cart and headed—" She looks at me as if she realizes something too late and stops. I know she thinks I might feel guilty for my choice. I look at her with my head held high.

"I know you and Taline wanted to leave. It would have been the safe choice. But this is our home. Our land. We can't give in to the Turks."

Mama's worn face shows a strange expression—one whose meaning I can't grasp.

"What? Why are you looking at me like that?" I ask, unable to hide my annoyance.

"Nothing. It's nothing."

A knock pounds on the front door. My heart jumps, and Mama gasps violently. She grabs Taline and Ani beside her, pulling them against her with one arm and reaching for me with frantic eyes.

A muffled voice from outside says, "Suren! Open the door. It's Nshan."

I push myself up from the table just as Mama leans across and grabs the hem of my shirt. When I reach back to pull away, I see a fire in her pupils—a fire that, if I disobey her, would make my chances of survival better if I fought against the Turks with a spoon.

"But my friends," I whisper.

"Sit! Just as your Baba wished."

Another knock on the door. "Suren?" Then, "I don't think he's here." Razmik's muffled voice comes through. "We'll come back later. Let's head to the church." The sound of their footsteps disappears amid the rifle shots and distant shouting.

Mama exhales and releases me. I glare at her, trying to pour all my anger through my eyes, but she either doesn't notice or doesn't care. I slink back into the chair.

She says nothing. Not a word. I wait and wait, but all she does is sit and close her eyes for a while before making the sign of the cross.

"They could have needed my help. Maybe they were in trouble," I blurt out.

She sits, calm and patient, listening.

"I know you want to help. But those boys have no idea what they're getting into. They could get killed out there."

"But the guns are firing into Aykesdan, away from the city."

"Where do you think they'll aim their guns next?" Taline interrupts.

"Your sister is right," Mama agrees.

"I'm ready. I can help. So can Nshan and Razmik. We're not children anymore."

Her lips tighten, and she folds her arms. Ani looks at her lap, and Taline stares past me toward the window.

"You are my child, Suren Simonian. And I am your mother. You will do as I say. In this house, we will stay hidden and safe. God will protect us. I don't want to hear another word about it."

"But, Mama—" I begin.

"Enough!" she says, slapping her hands on the table. "You will not leave this house! Go to your room and stay there!"

The anger in her words makes her lip tremble along with her finger pointing toward the stairs. The urge to cry wells up in my eyes, but I refuse to let the tears fall. To cry would be the worst thing that could happen right now. Heat flashes across my cheeks, and my knuckles turn white against my balled fists. Without a word, I stomp across the floor and up the stairs, and slam the door to my room.

Pacing across my bedroom floor, my thoughts become words and drown out the explosions rocking the city.

"She treats me like a little boy. Baba told me to protect them, and I can't do that here. I need to be out there, fighting and doing my part to protect the land, not babysitting my sisters and mother. Nshan and Razmik need me; otherwise, they wouldn't have come over. I'm sure Baba needs me too."

I fall onto my bed and sit at the edge, leaning back onto my hands. As my pulse slows, I feel something hard under my pillow and remember Father Zakarian always talking about finding answers in Scripture. Baba warned against bibliomancy. He said it's a trick the devil plays to convince you of God's will. But if I try it with the Bible, how could it not be God?

I hold the book in my lap, and before I open it, I make the sign of the cross and whisper, "God, show me what to do in Your book."

With my eyes still closed, I hold the edges and fling the cover open to whatever pages will reveal themselves. If God is listening, He'll speak to me and show me the true path. I look down at the first passage my eyes focus on:

> *Children, obey your parents in the Lord: for this is right. Honor thy father and mother; which is the first commandment with promise; that it may be well with thee, and thou mayest live long on the earth.*

This doesn't seem like something God would say. Maybe God the Father, but not Jesus. I close the book, utter the same prayer, and try again. Digging my nails into a different part of the thick pages, I open my eyes and see

> *I myself will fight against you with an outstretched hand and a mighty arm in furious anger and in great wrath.*

I lift my head and make the sign of the cross.

"Amen," I say before closing the Bible and sliding it back under my pillow, a smile stretching across my face.

I walk over to my small window. Smoke rises from some buildings in the distance, and more gunfire fills the air. As far as I can see, our home is out of reach of the big guns. I repeat in my mind the words I read: "I myself will fight against you." If God says it, then it must be true.

14

Taline the Prophet

Around nine o'clock in the morning, Taline proves herself right.

The Turks position a few of their guns and begin firing into the city. Though our house is beyond the reach of their cannons, the blasts rattle the dishes and cups in our home. Babies cry after each blast. Women shriek, including Mama. I try to watch from my bedroom window but can only hear the loud explosions, the returning gunfire, and the shouts echoing through the streets.

At midday, we still have no word from Baba or Uncle Tarzi. No news from anyone except some rumors from ladies so old that they've grown thin mustaches or bulging goiters on their necks. From my bedroom window, I can't see much. The sound of artillery and gunfire becomes like birds in the morning or the trickle of a stream to me. Groups of *fedayi* skitter through the streets, running awkwardly with their rifles from one building to the next. They shout at one another, but between the crying children and gunfire, I can't make out what they say.

I watch the streets, hoping to see Nshan or Razmik again. When I think of how Mama wouldn't let me open the door for my friends, a knot tightens in my heart, and all the angry words I should have said to her replay in my mind. Why is it we can never think of the words we want to say when we need them?

A slight breeze comes from the lake where the Turks have stationed themselves outside the walls. The intoxicating scent of smoke accompanies it—not just from the buildings that have burned but a strangely sweet smell I remember from my childhood. It makes me think of my brothers, wherever they may be. Part of me believes they are dead—maybe even killed by the army they were forced to fight for. I heard rumors from men in the market, right after the Great War started, that Armenians fighting for the Ottoman military would be better off if they were captured by their enemies.

At home, I'm forced to sit and watch, feeling like a coward in my bedroom. If my brothers can be drafted and fight for a country that hates them, why can't I join the fight for my people? For my home? I understand Mama's fear, but why does Baba deny me the chance to be part of history?

I glance back at the door, expecting to see Mama standing there, arms folded and reading my thoughts. I know it sounds foolish, but part of me still believes she is a sorceress. My older brother Narek always said God speaks directly to mothers about their sons. Maybe she knows I believe this and uses it against me.

"Suren!"

I look down at the street below and see Nshan, Razmik, Mihran, and his sister. What was her name?

"Hey! My mother won't let me leave. I would have opened the door earlier, but she forced me not to answer it."

Nshan shrugs. "It doesn't matter. We can't get to the fighting at the front of the city by the lake. The Turks have big guns blowing everything apart."

"Are we winning?" I shout.

"They are soiling their ugly uniforms!" Razmik calls up, raising a fist high in the air.

Nshan pushes Raz's big shoulder, which barely moves. "Don't say that. We have no idea if we are winning or not."

"Well, we will win anyway," he replies.

"Suren, what do you see up there?" Mihran asks. "Can you see if those dirty Turks are retreating?"

I look out over the city. A haze hovers over the rooftops near the city wall. A building, maybe a home, billows black smoke into the air.

"They are holding their position." A swell of pride fills me for sounding like I know what I'm talking about.

Mihran's sister steps forward, her black hair pulled tight and a red scarf tied around her forehead. She cups her hands around her mouth and calls up.

"Are you joining us or not?"

Mihran shakes his head and slaps his palm over his eyes. "Shushi—"

"It's time to fight. We need to do our part," she replies.

She's right. I do need to make a choice. Sitting here, watching from a distance, makes me useless. Am I really defending my home from here? I glance back toward the door, expecting to see Mama there, but I see only my empty room—a room that could soon be blown apart by the Turks' guns or, worse, burned down by the gendarmes still hiding near the Shamiram quarter. I see my Bible, lying open on my bed, and I recall how Gideon with his small army defeated the Midianites. All they needed was faith that they would win.

I turn back and see my Midianites on the other side of the walls. The Holy Mountain looks down on all of us. Maybe God is sitting on top of the snowcapped peak, watching us and seeing if we will make the right choice.

"I'll join you!" I say—not loudly, but just enough. A son, no matter how old, will always fear the power of his mother's ears.

A joyful squeal comes from Shushi. Mihran smacks the back of her head and puts a finger to his lips. Without a pause, she rams a fist into his chest, and he staggers back.

"When can you come?" Nshan asks. Some rifle fire rattles off just a few streets over.

"Mama is always watching, and she will kill me before the Turks do if she finds out. Meet me here tonight."

"What about your father?" Razmik asks.

"He's defending the city. Just like we will soon."

They nod, lift a revolutionary hand like the *fedayi* do, and sprint off down the street. I watch them until they disappear around the corner.

Alone, my chest tightens, and I fear Mama and Baba already know my plans to disobey them. Even with bombs exploding around me, I am more afraid of my parents than of the Turks.

15

Waiting Until Midnight

I gather the bowls and clean up the kitchen after dinner. Mama made *khash*, a disgusting soup of cow hooves. My stomach groans just thinking about it. However, I don't know if it is the anticipation of tonight or the *khash* that makes me feel sick.

It feels like time is creeping by until night comes. After dinner, I pace around the kitchen area, light the stove, and wonder when everyone will finally fall asleep. Taline stormed off to her room during dinner after she blamed me for everything going on. Ani voted to stay also, but Taline blames me. Mama cries and prays before hiding away in her bedroom. Ani sits with me by the fire for a while but doesn't say much before leaving me alone downstairs.

I climb the stairs to my room. Quickly, I cram my cap on my head and slip my arms through my coat's sleeves. I don't have many clothes, but I do have blankets. I draw some from a basket and bunch them under an overlying quilt, trying to imagine what I would look like sleeping in my bed. It takes some time, but I lump the blankets together into the shape of me—a little misshapen around the head, but in the dark, the others won't notice. I hope.

With shaky hands, I open the door. Across the landing, I put my ear close to Ani and Taline's door but don't hear anything—this doesn't mean they are asleep. With urgency, I tiptoe down the steps to the bottom floor. Mama and Baba's room sits off from the kitchen but has no door, and Mama left the curtain ajar.

I inch closer to the opening in the dimming lamplight. Inside, she is lying on her side facing the doorway. With her knees tucked toward her chest, she cuddles something in her arms. Straining in the low light, I can make out Levon's coat and Narek's fez.

As I watch her sleep, holding her sons' clothing, I feel a weight in my chest—a weight I chose to carry. Is disobeying the wishes of each of my parents the right choice? Should we have stayed? Maybe Taline is right. Maybe Ani and I are just selfish for wanting to stay and fight. But this is war—a war against our people. How can I look at myself again if I do nothing? If I don't help my friends?

"I love you, Mama," I whisper.

Then I walk across the kitchen toward the front door. From the window, I hear the faint sound of men's voices. Are they singing?

With my gut burning, I open the heavy wooden door and slip out into the night. I expect to see a gendarme, Baba, or Uncle Tarzi standing there, ready to arrest me, beat me, or both. However, no soul wanders in the streets, and silence crashes in my ears.

April 21, 1915

The Great Resistance

16

Gathering Intel

Outside, the lamps illuminate a path through the streets. I take a breath as if I've forgotten what the air tastes like beyond my house. The stone houses loom above as I turn the corner and head through the district toward St. Boghos. In each window, my eyes deceive me into thinking a face is watching—a face that resembles my father's.

No sounds of bombs or gunfire disturb the night. I imagined the battle would continue until one side prevailed, but it seems both sides grew tired and wanted to sleep. Do they just resume in the morning where they left off? Perhaps all wars are fought this way.

As I walk quickly through the streets, I search for my friends. It took me so long to sneak out of the house that I worry they've all gone home. If their hearts are pounding like mine, I can't imagine how they could sleep right now.

Some lamps glow in the lower windows, casting the silhouettes of families hiding inside, likely waiting for the battle to end. Perhaps the men are near the front of the city, close to the wall, holding their rifles at their sides and watching for any Turkish spies trying to enter.

Around the corner, I see St. Boghos. Unlike before, when we sneaked into the secret meeting, the windows are dim. Maybe some candles are lit for those fighting at the front—candles for Baba, Uncle Tarzi, brothers, or even sisters. Creeping low, I approach the stone wall in the courtyard and watch. Not much moves in the windows. Father Zakarian could be pacing the church as he does when he prays for everyone. Aside from Baba, he is the last person I want to catch me out here.

"You made it!"

A girl's voice sends a shiver down my spine and makes my feet dance. For a moment, I think it's Mama. I spin around and see my friends huddled beside the stone wall behind me. Mihran's sister crouches, trying not to smile.

"Don't do that!" I whisper sharply.

"Oh, shut up. I thought you were tough," she replies, fists on her hips and head cocked.

"Shushi, be nice. How did you get away?" Mihran asks.

"I had to wait until they all fell asleep. I'm not sure how long I can stay out before they wake up."

"What if your mother checks on you at night? You know how mothers like to sneak up on you when you sleep," Nshan says. I see Mihran's face drop slightly at Nshan's remark.

"I stuffed blankets under the sheets to make it look like I'm in bed."

Nshan nods as if he is surprised at my cleverness. I'm not sure how to feel about that.

"So what have you heard? Tell me all you know—" I say, sounding like I do when I receive a gift.

"Those Turks have no idea what hit them," interrupts Razmik before I finish my sentence. He stands up with his fist raised high.

Nshan leaps up and pulls on his massive arm, nearly dangling from it. "Get down! They'll see you."

"Who?"

"Everyone!" he shrieks.

Razmik lowers himself and crouches behind the wall.

"All right," Nshan begins, "from what I can gather, the Turks have been firing bombs across the wall and damaging buildings. Luckily, the *fedayi* successfully moved everyone who lived there away, so no one was hurt. Unfortunately, the people in Aykesdan were not as lucky. All our soldiers have been firing rifles, hiding in different houses."

"Have you seen Ba—my father?" I ask, my skin sizzling with anxiety.

"I don't know. We've been running around the city trying to gather information, but no one will talk to us. They just tell us we don't belong there and to go home."

"Stupid men," Shushi shouts.

"Hey, I'm a man," Razmik replies, flexing his arms.

"Point proven," she says with a faint smile.

I expect Raz's defenses to kick in, but judging by his expression, he doesn't seem to realize she had insulted him.

I point to the church on the other side of the wall. "Are they still meeting in there?"

"Sometimes," Nshan replies.

"We've snuck in before. We can do it again."

Mihran leans in. "Maybe. But you need to be careful."

"Why do we need to be careful? What about you?" Razmik interrupts. Huddled so close, I can smell his sour body odor and see the thick mustache he has grown.

"The only person looking after me is the missionary, and he has hundreds of others to attend to. Shushi and I can do what we want."

He has a point. One of the few benefits of not having parents, I suppose.

"All right. Mihran and Shushi, you can keep watch then. When you notice the soldiers coming to St. Boghos, send one of you to get us, and we'll meet you here," Nshan instructs. His thin finger emphasizes each word like a general unsure of his orders.

Mihran nods. "Understand, Shushi?"

No answer.

"Shushi?"

She has vanished.

"Where did she go?" I ask.

"There she is!" Razmik says, pointing toward the church.

In the night, Shushi's tiny silhouette sprints across the gravel square toward the church.

Deep down, I feel like I've made a huge mistake.

17

The Self-Appointed Scout

Looking across the stone wall, we watch Shushi's thin, black shape scuttle from window to window. She lifts herself on her toes and cups her hands against the dingy glass. After a few seconds, she hops down and sprints to the next one.

"Has she always been so, so . . . ?" Nshan searches for the right word.

"Annoying?" Mihran asks and answers at once.

Without realizing it, my fingertips begin to sting from gripping the wall so tightly. "What do we do if she gets caught?" I ask.

"Leave her," Razmik replies, folding his arms across his massive chest and chuckling to himself like he tends to do when he thinks he has said something clever.

Under his breath, Nshan makes a strange whimper. The only other time I heard him make that noise was when a large, stray dog bit his arm last year.

"Should one of us go get her?" I ask.

No one says anything. Our shared expression makes it clear that no one wants to volunteer. Not even Raz.

So we sit and wait.

To our left, we hear men's voices and the crunch of their boots on the ground not far off. My eyes shoot toward Shushi, near the front of the church, looking into the last window. It feels like we all hold our breath at the same time. In a strange way, I feel that if I stop breathing, our hearing would become superhuman. However, I'm not sure how this helps Shushi.

"If she gets caught, she's on her own," Razmik whispers.

"She won't get caught," Mihran says confidently.

The three *fedayi* pause near the front doors of the church, reaching into their pockets with their rifles slung over their shoulders. My eyes dart back and forth from Shushi to the soldiers. A small light comes from the men, and based on their strained necks, they must be lighting cigarettes. Shushi runs across the gravel field without a sound, and the men don't notice.

In no time, she reaches the stone wall, climbs over with Mihran's help, and slides down onto her backside. While the others look at her, I hear footsteps approaching.

"They're coming," I crouch down and whisper through my teeth.

"Who?" Nshan asks.

"The *fedayi* over there."

We all scurry over to the stone wall and slam our backs against it. I press my back into the stones with my arms spread out, trying to flatten myself like a rug, just like when we used to hide from Baba, hearing him counting down and trying to find us. I always felt like I had to pee, no matter if I had gone before or not. Actually, I feel like I have to right now.

We hold our breaths again as the crunch of their steps grows louder. The smell of tobacco wafts above us as they walk past. It seems like an eternity before they continue along the short wall and disappear into the streets. A collective exhale escapes from all of us.

"Shushi, you're asleep in a donkey's ear! How could you do something so stupid?" Mihran growls. He grabs her by the arms and gives her a shake.

She squirms out of his grip like she has done it a thousand times, standing up with her chin out. The knot of her black bandanna juts behind her head.

"Don't be angry with me just because all of you were too scared to do it," she snaps back. Her dark eyes scan all of our faces. I don't know whether to be upset with her or admire her.

Mihran's eyes narrow. "There's a fine line between being brave and being dead."

Shushi steps forward to meet him. "I'd rather die being brave than cowering behind a wall."

Mihran grits his teeth and opens his mouth to respond, but Nshan cuts in.

"OK. OK. She's back now, and nobody saw us. No harm done."

"For now," Razmik comments.

Nshan shoots him a stern look. I never understood how little Nshan could always correct Raz and never get beaten for it. I doubt I would have the same success, and I know for sure Mihran wouldn't.

Turning his gaze back to Shushi, Nshan stands like a disappointed father. In all the excitement, his glasses have slipped down and cling to the end of his nose. A small part of me feels compelled to push them back up.

We all look at Shushi, but she is too focused on adjusting her bandanna. Her tongue sticks slightly out of the corner of her mouth as she concentrates. A few seconds later, she notices us.

"What?" she asks, palms up and head cocked.

"Well," Nshan says, gesturing with his hands, "what did you see?"

"Oh," she pauses for a moment, "nothing."

All of us exchange baffled looks. Mihran drops his face, shaking his head.

"See? I told you we should have left her."

"Shut up, Raz!" Shushi snaps and steps forward. Big Raz, despite all of his big talk, flinches, covering his groin with his hands.

I can't help but wonder if I should be sneaking around with my friends after all.

18

A Turk at My Door

After slinking about St. Boghos, we agree to meet tomorrow night by the church to see what else we can find out.

I walk home alone through the lamplit streets, unsure of the time or how long I have actually been out. Thoughts of my mother yanking the sheets off my bed make my gut sour. I know without a doubt a beating would be around the corner.

The crisp night air is silent except for some distant singing. I'm certain they are men's voices, but I can't make out the song. Through the open windows, I smell various meals cooking. Some wealthy homes still have lamb or pig roasting. We are stuck with disgusting *khash*. My mouth waters, and a part of me wants to sneak over and steal a tiny piece from my neighbors. Just a small one. God wouldn't blame me for that, would he?

Around the corner, I see my home at the end of the street and scan the windows for any lights. All dark and quiet. I exhale, feeling relief wash over me. Still, I keep my eyes open. If Baba, Uncle Tarzi, or anyone close to the family sees me, my future missions are over.

I pause at the door, pressing my ear close to the wood. No voices. No sounds. They must still be asleep. As I place my hand on the door, I hear something behind me. Could it be a cat?

"Suren!"

I freeze. Baba's caught me. It's over. I won't be able to sit for a month.

"Suren, it's me," the voice says.

I turn around and, in the shadows of the street lamps, make out Hamza's floppy black hair and faint mustache. My body begins to thaw. It has been only two days since I last saw him, but it feels much longer.

I tiptoe away from the door and meet him across the street, checking the windows to make sure my nosy neighbors do not see me.

"What are you doing here?" I ask.

"I came to see if you're all right."

"I'm fine."

"Have you seen the others? Raz? Nshan?"

I check the door behind me before speaking. "I just met them by St. Boghos. We plan to meet again tomorrow. Are you joining us?"

Hamza looks at his feet. "Father doesn't know I'm here. If he finds out, I don't know what he would do. You know how he feels about . . . everything."

"Is there fighting in your quarter?"

"No. Nothing. But everyone is acting strange, as if nothing is happening here. No one talks about it, and when I try to bring it up, everyone just ignores me."

A small flare of anger flashes inside me. "Why would they pretend nothing is happening? My mother buys food and clothes from them in the market. They've known us for years."

Hamza glances around. "I've been talking with others in the Shamiram."

"About what?"

Hamza looks around. "How we can help. Not all Turks believe like the *pasha* do."

I examine Hamza in the dark and can't help but remember what he said at the market two days ago.

"Why would they help us? We're just a bunch of rebels to them." The biting words slip from my mouth, and I don't try to stop them.

Hamza looks back at me. "Suren—"

"Do you believe we are rebelling against the government?" I ask.

He pauses. "I don't think this is a fight the Armenians can win."

I cross my arms over my chest, hiding my clenched fists. "What should we do, then? Sit back and let them kill us?"

"They won't kill you. Just do what they ask. It will be better than going to prison. Or worse."

I roll my eyes. "Do you know what is really going on? What is happening in the villages?" My hands move as I talk, as if this will help Hamza understand the situation better.

"I don't know why the government wants to deport your people." I once thought he believed the lies the government told about us, but his words suggest that he is just ignorant.

"We are Ottomans too, Hamza! My brothers are fighting for this country. Maybe they died for this country too. Still, they want to send us into the desert. The same country murdering people in villages! They want to take our homes where we have lived for centuries. What would you do if they came to take everything you own?"

He says nothing. All I can hear is my heartbeat and the song of the *fedayi* in the distance. Hamza looks around, as if the words he wants to say are hidden somewhere in the street.

"You are my friend. My oldest friend, and Allah willing, I want to help," he says.

My cheeks flush, and I wave my hand at my friend. "You are just a Turk. You'll never understand."

The air grows thick, and the sounds of the night seem to grow louder in the silence. A baby cries. A donkey brays around the corner. Two cats screech and hiss at one another somewhere in the darkness. I can feel Hamza's gaze on me, but I won't look at him.

"I will pray for you and your family. From the Aegean to the Euphrates," he finally says, his words tinged with hope, expecting me to reply.

I sigh and, without looking at him, respond, "Blood brothers."

When I glance toward the sound of his fading footsteps, all I see is an empty street and darkness all around.

April 22, 1915

Hiding in Shadows

19

Father Returns

Something shakes me awake. I open my eyes and see Mama leaning over me.

"Are you going to sleep all day?" she asks, pointing toward the window.

Sunlight paints the walls and the end of my bed. Is it still morning? As the grogginess fades, I hear the gunfire has started again. Part of me hoped it was all a bad dream and the Turks would be gone.

"Get up," she says, pulling my blanket off.

I rub my eyes and prop myself up on my elbows. Mama stands, watching me as she folds the blanket.

She knows. She must know. Why else would she stare at me? She must have heard me talking. This is all Hamza's fault.

"There is some breakfast downstairs. Let's go," she finally says and turns, leaving me wondering if my secret is still a secret.

I get dressed and wash my face in the basin before going downstairs. When I reach the bottom step, I see Mama at the stove ladling food into a bowl. At the table, Ani and Taline sit on either side of Baba, who leans over his bowl, shoveling spoonfuls into his mouth. Bits of food cling to his beard.

"Baba!" I exclaim, and he lifts his eyes to me. A gentle smile spreads across his face.

He beckons me over, and I stand at his side. He smells like a bonfire. The sleeves of his once-white shirt are stained with dirt—maybe old blood. His grip tightens around me as he pulls me close, kissing my cheek.

"Suren *jan*. My son," he murmurs. The way he says my name feels different, just like how he calls me his son.

"Have you been doing what I asked?" He looks up at me, and I pause. My stomach drops, and I want to speak, but I can't. The only response I can give is a nod.

He nods back and pats my arm.

"What is happening near the front of the city? Are the *fedayi* fighting bravely? Have the Turks retreated yet?" The questions pour out of me.

"In time, in time," he replies and returns to his bowl.

Mama joins us at the table without a word. We watch Baba eat, waiting for something, though none of us knows what. News, maybe? Ani bites her lip and braids the ends of her hair. She makes the same face when she wants to ask something but is afraid to. I've only heard Ani shout a few times in my life, but she might at any moment.

A loud boom echoes outside, and Baba flinches, flinging a spoonful of food into the air. It lands on the floor behind him, and looking at all our alarmed faces, he chuckles and smiles, though his eyes say something else.

He slides the bowl forward and wipes at the bits in his speckled beard. It hasn't been long, but it looks like more gray has peppered his beard since I last saw him.

Mama rings a damp rag with her fingers a moment before she stands and walks around to clean up the food splattered on the floor. Mama used to sit and read before my brothers left. Now, the only time I see her still is when she sleeps.

"Baba," Taline says, wrapping her hands around his arm. "What is the news out there?"

His sleepy eyes look to her, and even though Taline can be the worst sister, she knows how to make her eyes turn into an inviting lake that Baba can't resist. As I expected, he reaches up and strokes her cheek, and I see the red cuts on his knuckles for the first time.

"I suppose you all want information, yes?"

We sit up in our seats, and Ani leans forward, still biting her lip. Mama is now in the kitchen again, cleaning something I cannot see.

Baba lets out a sigh. "Do you want the good news or the bad news first?"

"Good news!" Ani blurts out, then slinks back, covering her mouth.

Baba smiles as if it takes all his strength. "Good news, yes. The good news is the city is still ours. Our positions around the walls have held despite the Turks firing their big guns and cannons at us, but not one enemy soldier has set foot in Van. It is beautiful to see all Armenians—rich, poor, farmers, leaders, men, women, even children—all come together to protect the land. By God's grace, we will stay strong. Not one Armenian has died, but some have been gravely wounded. However, the *fedayi* have killed many Turkish soldiers. You will probably read about it in the papers. The military command plans to disperse reports about the fighting so everyone will know."

Ani leans back in her chair.

"What about Uncle Tarzi and Aunt Yeva?" Taline asks.

He turns to her. "Yeva can take care of herself. She is helping with the wounded. Tarzi? He will do what he wants. If there is proof that God exists, it is because your Uncle Tarzi is as old as he is."

We laugh together at the table, and it feels refreshing. For a brief moment, it feels like the war had never come to Van. It was just a memory or a bad dream, and we were laughing about how it never really happened. But another loud blast from the cannons and gunfire brings the battle back to our minds.

Baba's smile fades, and he looks toward the window, hearing some Armenians shouting and firing their rifles. I feel a desire well up inside me to do my part at the front.

He turns back to us at the table. Mama faces the corner, and from how she stands with her hands to her face, I know she has started to cry.

"I would be out there now if I weren't such an old man," he mumbles, "so I will sleep here tonight before returning to our positions at the front. Comrade Manukian's orders."

Two thoughts strike me as Baba speaks. One is that I still can't believe the man who taught me literature is now known as "comrade." The more pressing thought is that Baba staying here tonight creates problems for me sneaking out to meet my friends.

As if just noticing, Baba sees Mama by the window. Slowly, he pushes his chair back and walks toward her, placing his scratched hand on her shoulder as she jerks away from him. He whispers something in her ear, and she shakes her head, moaning low.

I look at my sisters, who just stare back at me. I expect to see Taline's bitter glare aimed at both of us. Of course, she blames us. But her eyes are not bitter or angry. She bites her lower lip and scratches the top of her forearm just like she did when we spoke in my room the other night. For a moment, I want to reach out and hold her hand.

A loud clang comes from the kitchen, and Mama stomps toward the bedroom. Baba looks after her, hands raised and eyes wide. He sees us watching him, and the moment feels endless. Without a word, he follows her into the bedroom. He pulls the curtain closed, but I can still see them through a slit on the side.

"Suren," Ani whispers.

I turn to her, and she shakes her head in two quick twitches.

Behind the curtain, the sobs and hushed voices hang over us like a cloud. A single tear slips from Taline's eye, and she wipes it before it leaves her chin.

20

The Princess and the Peasant

The afternoon drags on.

My parents move in and out of the bedroom like ghosts before vanishing again. Ani reads by the stove, but every time I look at her, she is tapping her foot and twirling her hair incessantly. Still thinking about *him*, I suppose. Taline stays in her room.

Most of the day, I sit on the roof, feeling the tiny pebbles dig into my palms as I watch the battles. The Turks' cannons blast into buildings, and smoke coils into the afternoon sky—all under the distant gaze of Mount Ararat.

From my roof, I can see the monastery on Aghtamar Island. As a boy, I swam at the shores of the blue lake all day with Baba, Mama, and my brothers. Sometimes Hamza would join us. Baba would stand waist-deep in the cool water with me on his shoulders. The breeze brushed against my damp skin as he held me by my ankles. He pointed toward the island in the distance, past the fishing boats, and told me how the island got its name. How Tamar, a princess, fell in love with a peasant who lived on the island. At night, he would swim across the lake, guided by Tamar's lamp on the shore, just to be with her. But one day, her father discovered their secret and extinguished her lamp. Without her light to guide him, he got lost in the dark water and drowned. Later, when they found his body on the shore, it looked like the words "Oh, Tamar" were frozen on his lips.

I don't know why I thought of that story just now. It's just an old tale like Artavazd or Vishap with their dragon-like heads stirring storms over the lake. Do Armenians even believe in the old stories? Not with Father Zakarian urging everyone to follow God. But what if God is just a new myth we cling to? Shame washes over me just thinking it.

As I pick up little pebbles and toss them off the roof, I consider how I will sneak out tonight. With Baba home, it will be much more difficult. What if he doesn't fall asleep? A sinking feeling makes me believe I may have to stay in this prison tonight. Nshan and the others will think I lost my courage. Especially Shushi. She scares me more than anyone else.

From up here, I see smoke rising from different buildings burning near the front. Some *fedayi* on rooftops near the police station lie flat, but I still see their red *arakhchi* on their heads, and I wonder if that makes them an easy target for the Turks. The thin points of their rifles are just visible from my position.

I lay flat on the roof with my *arakhchi* securely on my head, eyes narrowed down the barrel, finger on the trigger. Each shot sends a bullet into the body of a murderous Turkish soldier. One down for the homeland.

One of their rifles fires several rounds, and my mind shifts back to reality. The gunshots remind me of Hamza. How could he think we would not win? The Turks have tried to exterminate us for years, and we're still here. Fighting on our feet. Coming together as one. His words churn in my mind. When you know someone as long as you can remember, their words can be like sweet food or a sharp knife. Many Turks in the market stopped selling to Armenians long before this happened, but I never imagined Hamza would be like them. Maybe not completely. He did risk coming into the city to see me. But . . . I don't know. Am I just an infidel to him? A dog he might feel sorry for?

"Suren!"

Baba's voice calls from the window and jolts me. I scramble to my feet and hurry down the ladder. My heart races. I need to be on my best behavior.

21

Dissension in the Ranks

With Baba in the bedroom, every shadow, creak, or cough makes me jump. I expect him to appear everywhere, looking at me with those disappointed eyes that still haunt me from when I punched Taline in the nose last year. She may have deserved it, but when the blood poured down her lips and chin, regret hit me as hard as I hit her. Baba's eyes, a mix of anger, disappointment, and sadness, did more damage than anything I could have done to her.

The cool night air feels nice on my damp skin. Had I been sweating that much just sneaking out of the house? The door shuts silently, but it still feels too loud for me. The nagging sense that someone's eyes are on me bothers me.

I twist around and scan each shadow, every nook of the buildings, but there is nothing.

Part of me wishes Hamza were here, waiting for me. Instead, there are only prowling cats whose eyes glow as they slip between the lamps.

I run toward St. Boghos. I hear babies crying in the houses I pass, and *fedayi* trot by without glancing at me, their ammunition vests jingling with each step. I recall the gendarme from a few nights ago and wonder if he is still roaming the city or if all of them fled to the Shamiram quarter with the other Turks. Or maybe they joined the Turkish forces outside the city.

The church comes into view, and the light from the rows of votive candles glows through the windows. I inspect the wall, straining my eyes for Nshan, Razmik, and the others. Maybe I should have stayed home. They would understand—a scolding for a day or two. But sneaking out several times? This could end very badly.

I hear a hiss. Near the wall, I see Mihran crouched and waving me over. My head swivels as I awkwardly crouch-run to my friends. They all look at me as I collapse onto my backside against the wall.

"Are you all right?" Nshan asks.

Unlike before, it takes me a few seconds to catch my breath. "Yes. My father came home yesterday, so it made getting here more difficult. Any news?"

They exchange glances, and Nshan says, "I overheard my parents discussing things this morning. They said there have been some wounded, but no Armenians have died. Some Turkish spies trying to sneak into the city were shot, and though many buildings are destroyed, the Turks have not made progress. Even some women are fighting on the front lines."

"Women?" Razmik exclaims. "They give women guns but won't let us fight even though we're almost finished with our schooling?"

"What is that supposed to mean?" Shushi interrupts, standing up with her fists clenched.

"Not again," Mihran mumbles, shaking his head.

"Women should be helping in other ways. Men are supposed to do the fighting."

Even in the dark, I can see Shushi's rage burning. "And what should they be doing?"

"You know," Razmik begins, looking for agreement from us boys, "cooking, watching the children. Women's things."

"How about I show you why women can be fighters?" Shushi growls.

"Sit down, little girl," Razmik says, dismissing her with a wave.

"OK. That's enough," Nshan interrupts, stepping forward as if he could stop either of them from throwing punches. Shushi's eyes bore into the side of Raz's head.

"Nshan is right. We've been sneaking around all this time, and we need to find ways to fight back. We all stayed, and if we are just going to meet by the church every night and argue, we might as well go back to our beds while we still have them."

I had never heard Mihran talk so much. To be honest, I don't really know him at all except that he hates all Turks as much as they seem to hate us.

Nshan nods. "Yes. Mihran has a point. The question is, how do we get weapons, and will the *fedayi* let us fight?"

We sit in silence. I'm sure we all know the answer to the second question. Maybe Razmik knows where some rifles are stashed, but how to get them is another matter. The night air is quiet except for some distant songs; however, I can't tell if they are Armenian or Turkish. After a moment, Shushi clears her throat.

"OK. Here's what we can do. First, we sneak toward the front position near the wall where all the action is. From there, we wait until we find some *fedayi* who drank too much *oghi*. Once they pass out, we take their guns."

A strange pause hangs over everyone for a moment. The boys exchange glances and then start to nod.

"That's not a bad idea," Mihran says, "but what do we do once we get the guns?"

Shushi shrugs. "Shoot Turks."

"That would get us guns, yes, but it would also be illegal. I heard my parents discussing how unarmed Armenian citizens were disarming others for their own protection. The Military Council strictly prohibited this."

Raz stares at Nshan with a blank expression. "Prohiga-tits?"

"What?" Nshan replies, squinting. "Pro-hi-bi-ted. It means it's not allowed."

"Oh," Raz says. "So why didn't you just say that?"

Shushi laughs like one of the coots that fly around the lake, and soon, I'm laughing at her laughter.

Raz glares at both of us. "What's so funny?"

I shrug and point to Shushi. Raz stands up, towering over her tiny frame. Though he appears ready to fight, she doesn't seem to care.

"What?" Raz snaps.

"Nothing. It's nothing," she stammers, wiping tears from her eyes.

He looks around at all of us, his face somewhere between a scowl and on the verge of tears.

"We're wasting time. I'm tired of waiting for you idiots. I'll find my own guns."

Without a pause, Razmik stomps off between the dark buildings away from the church. Nshan follows, calling after him to wait. Shushi wipes her eyes and walks behind them. Mihran and I tag along at the rear. The more I think about it, maybe we shouldn't have guns.

22

A Stranger in the Shadows

Our feet crunch on the gravel as we walk through the alleys. Most of the windows we pass are dark, and there's not much sound except for the growing chorus of *fedayi* around the city singing of Armenia's glory. I can't make out the words, but I know the melody. My brothers used to sing it whenever Mama and Baba asked. I can still hear their voices and harmonies in my ears.

Razmik has calmed down somewhat, but Nshan still clings to his arm like one of those Spanish matadors I have read about trying to soothe a bull. However, Raz continues to glance back at Shushi, whose whistling echoes off the buildings.

"Shushi!" Mihran half yells, half whispers, "Stop that. Everyone can hear you."

She turns her head as she walks, sticks her tongue out, and whistles just a bit quieter. Mihran slaps his forehead, a familiar gesture around her.

He sighs and says, "I'm sorry about my sister."

"You don't have to keep apologizing for her," I reply.

"I know, but she's my responsibility. I'm all she has."

An ox in a small stable lets out a deep low and shakes flies from its ears. I want to ask Mihran how he ended up at the missionary school. It's a simple question, but I hesitate. All I can picture is his red, swollen face from his fight with Razmik. It seems so long ago now, even though the bruises and cuts are still fresh.

I keep an eye out in the shadows in case someone who knows the Simonian family sees me and reports to Baba that I'm roaming the streets at night.

"It's so quiet at night since the battle started," he comments.

"Yes. I wish I knew what was happening at the front lines."

"As long as they are killing those monsters, I don't care."

His words drip with a foreign hatred. I don't know how to respond at first, but then I ask, "Are they really monsters?"

Without hesitation, he replies, "Yes. All of them."

"They can't all be evil. Hamza is not like them." A hint of doubt creeps in, and I wonder if he truly is like those outside the city gates.

"Why would you be friends with one of them?"

"Because . . ." I pause. Why am I pausing?

"There's no good reason. That's why you can't think of one," Mihran says, as if his words are truth. "You can't trust a Turk. If you do, their words will drip with honey while they slip a blade in your . . ."

His voice trails off. In the lamplight, I notice a scar near his temple.

"When did you get that scar?" I ask, pointing at his head.

He rubs his fingertips on his temple and then looks at his finger as if expecting to see blood.

"It's old. But it still hurts sometimes."

"How did you get it?"

He doesn't answer for a few steps. "Has Razmik calmed down?"

"Uh, I think so," I reply, unsure if he is avoiding the question or if he really cares about Raz's feelings.

Nshan, Raz, and Shushi freeze up ahead. Mihran and I join them. Nshan tilts his head to the air.

"What do you hear?" Shushi asks in a whisper.

Before he can answer, a shape creeps around the corner. The silhouette of a rifle casts onto the side of the building.

"Quick! Hide!" Nshan says.

We all dart in different directions, ducking behind barrels and carts. In the fragments of lamplight, we sit breathless, watching as the figure moves down the street toward us. I try to see in the dark where the others are hiding but can't find them.

"What do you see? Who is it?" Mihran whispers, gripping my forearm.

As the figure gets closer, slinking against the houses and staying close to the shadows, I catch a glimpse of their clothing—a uniform I recognize from sitting on the rooftop.

I look at Mihran, hoping my expression doesn't reveal the fear surging inside me.

"It's a Turkish soldier."

Saved by a Cat

Mihran and I crouch behind an oxcart. I lift my head enough to watch the figure creeping along the street. He stays close, dipping under windows with his rifle ready.

"What do we do, Suren?" Mihran asks.

"Give me a moment," I say, though I have no idea what we should do. I strain to see where the others are hiding, but all I see are shapes in the dark.

"See if you can find Nshan and the others," I tell him.

He starts to stand, and I grab his arm and pull him down.

"Look for them with your eyes!" I snap, pointing two fingers toward my own eyes.

He nods and searches while I check on the soldier. He stands about thirty meters away. In the dark, his body looks like a demon. The tan uniform stands out against the gray houses. My thighs burn from crouching, and I grip the rough edge of the oxcart. Should we run? Fight? If we fight, with what? The questions fire off like firecrackers in my head.

"There they are!" Mihran whispers, pointing and shaking.

I follow his finger to the faint outline of Raz, Nshan, and Shushi cowering behind a mound of hay with a pitchfork sticking out of it. Could that be a weapon? The Turkish soldier comes closer, and I hear the jingle of his ammunition belt. I can't help but think of my parents mourning the loss of another son at this moment.

Mihran's head swivels between the soldier, the others, and me, like a bird watching for a hawk. "Should we run? Or just hide here?"

His questions grate on my nerves, and with my heart pounding, my body feels like a bomb about to explode. I strain to get the others' attention, but from what I can tell, they are huddled together talking.

"Wait," I whisper, keeping my eyes on the soldier in the shadows. I run my tongue over my lips and feel the fine cracks. Have I drunk any water today?

The soldier slinks closer now—just one building over.

Any closer and he might see Mihran and me behind the oxcart. If not him, the owners may open the door and find us. I start to speak, but a sudden noise startles me—an eerie, high-pitched howl from the other side of the street. The familiar sound of two cats fighting echoes in the dark.

The soldier stops and presses himself flat against the wall. The silhouette of his head swivels up and down the street without pausing. A frenzy of hissing and spitting rises again, and a woman from one of the homes shouts at the cats. At this, the soldier turns and runs from us down the street. His footsteps clop on the rocky dirt until he disappears.

I stand up, feeling my muscles come to life again. I can hear Mihran breathing as if he had just surfaced from a long swim.

The others come out of hiding and join us on the other side of the oxcart.

"I've never loved a cat so much," Nshan says, but his joke falls flat like most of his attempts.

"Was that a Turkish soldier?" I ask.

"I think so," Raz replies.

Nshan shakes his head. "I'm not so sure. From our side, he seemed much younger. It may have been a gendarme still hiding in the city."

Mihran huffs. "Probably wants to be a hero." He sounds brave now that the Turk has fled.

"Well," Shushi says, throwing her hands up, "let's go after him."

Raz smacks her shoulder with the back of his hand. "Are you crazy?"

"I thought you wanted to fight?" she snaps back.

"Shouldn't we tell someone?" I interject.

Nshan nods. "We need to tell Professor Manukian or someone important. Maybe the Military Council."

We all stand around as if the unspoken question hangs in the air. Who do we tell?

"Does anyone know where the military command is?" Mihran asks.

Standing in a half circle, we stare at each other as if we have the answers for one another. Raz scratches his scalp and looks up toward the cloudy night sky. Deep in thought, Nshan rests his chin on his hand and stares at the ground. I wonder what I look like to them.

Shushi, standing rigid and uneasy like a child trying to hide something behind her back, lifts her hand. Her dark eyes dart around the semicircle at our faces.

"What is it?" Mihran asks, a hint of annoyance in his voice.

She lowers her hand. "I might have an idea of where the military command could be. Maybe," she squeaks in a timid tone, so different from her usual confidence.

Mihran narrows his eyes and crosses his arms. "And how would you know where the military command is?"

Shushi surveys our faces. Normally, she seems much bigger, but with her hands behind her back, she appears to have shrunk. "Because I might have been there before?"

Mihran grits his teeth, gripping the sleeve of his shirt. He says nothing, and Shushi's lips twist into an exaggerated smile before repeating, "Maybe?"

Caught

As we follow Shushi through the lamplit streets, I check every doorway and shadow, expecting to see the Turkish gendarme's young face staring back at me. Even in the dark, he seems familiar. I can't be sure, but the way his shoulders hunched is striking. Until a few days ago, a gendarme was present on every corner. Some just walked by, but others, especially the young ones, enjoyed demanding bribes or roughing up old Armenians—like the one with the pointed mustache a few nights ago when all of this began.

The group remains mostly silent, with only our footsteps echoing between the buildings. A nagging feeling settles in my chest. In all the excitement, I have lost track of time. For all I know, the sun could rise at any moment, and Baba or Mama will find my bed stuffed with pillows. I can already picture them sitting at the table when I sneak into the house, waiting for me with that familiar look of parental disappointment.

I walk beside Nshan as we follow Shushi, Mihran, and Razmik. For once, the trio ahead isn't arguing or, in Mihran's case, apologizing.

"Do you know where she is taking us?" I ask.

Nshan pushes his glasses up the bridge of his nose. "Not entirely. I overheard my father talking with others about the fighters being spread out in different homes. However, I don't know whose houses. I assume they are near the city wall."

"Your father doesn't ask you to leave the room when they discuss the conflict?" I ask, trying to hide my jealousy.

"Never! He always taught my siblings and me about knowledge. He said, 'To know that we know what we know, and to know that we do not know what we do not know, that is true knowledge.'"

I think about the quote for a moment, then ask, "What does that mean?"

He shrugs. "I'm not sure. But I know it's saying that knowledge is important."

We turn down another street, and the muffled sound of voices comes from somewhere nearby.

"Almost there," Shushi shouts. In an instant, Mihran puts a finger to his lips and shushes her.

"What do you think, Suren?"

I pause at Nshan's question, as if jolted awake. "What do you mean?"

"Do you believe knowledge is better than ignorance?"

At school, Nshan always asked these kinds of questions—the ones that made professors smile and praise him. They love thoughtful inquiries while the rest of the students sat dumbfounded and annoyed.

"I don't know," I reply.

He scurries closer and looks up. While all the other fourteen-year-old boys have sprouted taller, Nshan seems to have stayed the same height.

"Come on," he insists. "You have opinions. Share them! Just like Professor Manukian used to tell us."

The muffled voices grow louder ahead. I think I hear someone playing an oud.

"I think knowledge is better. Maybe. I'm not sure," I reply. The words come out clumsy and disorganized.

"Why?" he asks, nudging my ribs with his elbow. I resist the urge to nudge him back harder.

"Quit nagging me," I blurt out.

"Suren," he says in an almost pleading voice, "if you can't explain what you believe, then what is happening right now, not only here but all over the world, will just continue. The Turks believe what the *pasha* tell them. Only a few know what they truly believe, and some may lose their lives over it."

His intent eyes glint behind his glasses. The ever-studious Nshan rarely shows this much passion. The same nervous energy I feel before exams surges through me as Nshan's probing gaze holds me. The faint smell of smoke from the last fires around the city drifts on a soft breeze. I don't have the thoughts or words to answer Nshan, but I open my mouth, feeling a slight terror at the unknown words I might unleash.

"We're here!" Shushi shouts.

I turn away from Nshan and look to the trio ahead. Shushi stands with her foot perched on a crate, pointing forward. The hair once tucked under her bandanna now flutters around her face in the breeze.

Razmik and Mihran start laughing and pointing. Of course, Shushi hears them, and even in the dark, her face almost looks red.

"Why are you laughing? I told you I knew where it was."

"We're not laughing at that," Razmik says through a chuckle.

"You look like you just found the Holy Grail," Mihran comments.

"Yeah! That's it. Or the Fountain of Youth, like the Spaniards."

The two buckle over with laughter. Nshan, despite his stoic demeanor, can't suppress a few chortles.

She stomps her foot on the dirt, bends down, and in one smooth motion, throws a small rock straight at her brother. A deep thud, and then Mihran howls like a wounded dog. The sound travels through the night air. Now Razmik laughs at Mihran, until he yelps as another stone hits him square in the back.

"Shushi, stop!" Nshan cries, raising his arms as shields and turning his face aside as he approaches her. Razmik circles around, reaching for the bruise forming on his back while Mihran staggers, holding his still-healing nose. I have heard of the circus but never been to one. Still, I imagine this is what it may be like to watch the clowns.

"Hey, what are you kids doing here?"

A deep voice interrupts the scene, and a figure walks toward us from one of the open doors. Several other men stand in the doorway with rifle barrels raised.

I may have forgotten how to breathe.

As the figure approaches, all sound in the street fades into a buzz like a swarm of gnats. Even Shushi doesn't move. Our faces remain fixed on the black figure growing taller until its shadow looms over our terrified faces.

25

The Professor

"I know your faces. Well, some of you anyway," the looming figure says in a voice I have heard many, many times before.

"Professor Manukian?" I half whisper, half cry out.

"Nice to see you again, Suren. Who else is with you?"

He surveys us huddled together on the street.

"*Parev*, Professor," Nshan says quietly.

"Nshan Bedrosian? Sneaking around at night while a war is going on? Doesn't seem like you. And I see Razmik Adomian. Have you grown taller since I saw you three eavesdropping on our meeting at St. Boghos?"

Raz smiles and puffs out his chest. "Maybe a few centimeters."

A man shouts from the doorway, holding a clear bottle by the neck. "What is going on, Aram? Are they spies?"

He lifts his hand without turning around. "Everything is fine." The man shrugs and closes the door behind him.

In the lamplight, Professor Manukian's face comes into focus. He looks older, but I cannot tell if it is the darkness playing tricks on my eyes. His pointy mustache seems fuller than I remember.

"Professor, should they be drinking? What if the Turks attack?" Nshan asks.

The professor chuckles and runs his fingers over his mustache. "No one fights at night. We may have some spies trying to sneak into the city, but we have lookouts to prevent that."

In my mind, I think they must not be very good at their jobs.

"Unless they are schoolchildren," he remarks with a wink.

My body relaxes, and all the tension in my back, legs, and jaw melts away.

"Who are these two?" he asks, pointing at the others.

Shushi steps forward, jamming her thumb into her chest. "I'm Shushi."

Mihran slumps forward and pulls at his shirt. "I'm sorry, sir. She's my sister."

The professor examines them for a moment. "And what is your name?"

"Mihran," he replies, clearing his throat as he speaks.

"I've never seen you at the Yeramian. Where do you attend school?"

A loud uproar comes from inside the building, but the professor doesn't seem to notice and keeps his eyes on Mihran.

Mihran drops his head to his chest, staring at his feet. "We attend the, uh, missionary school, sir."

Professor Manukian's expression softens. "I see," he says, rubbing his chin as if trying to make a decision. He looks around the street, at the windows, the doors, and even up into the night sky at the few stars peeking through the clouds.

"So, young men and lady, I assume some of your parents are unaware you are roaming the streets at night. It is very dangerous this close to the front. Just a few buildings down are the Turkish forces and their cannons. They have reasons for their rules to keep you safe, and I support those rules."

"But we can help! We're almost finished with our schooling," Razmik interrupts, stepping forward. He is nearly as tall as the professor and half his age.

"I'm sure you can, but this is not the same as working for your family."

Nshan steps forward. "We saw a Turkish soldier in the city."

The professor pauses. "A soldier?"

Nshan scratches the back of his head and squints. "It could have been a gendarme. Maybe. It was dark."

"Are you sure?" he asks.

"Yeah, I saw him too," Shushi says, stepping forward.

The professor studies each of us, the same look most adults give teenagers when trying to determine if they are telling the truth. The faint smell of cigarettes drifts in the air, and a rumble of voices comes from the lit window behind the professor.

He exhales a long sigh. "Come. Tell me more inside," he says, gesturing for us to go ahead.

Without hesitation, Shushi pushes past us and marches toward the closed door. The rest of us exchange uncertain glances and follow the direction of the professor's hand.

After entering the stone building, we stand in a large room where the air is thick with smoke. Men with gray beards and smooth-faced *fedayi* in uniforms crowd around a wooden table, pointing at a map. Lamps and candles flicker, and a haze of smoke hangs in the stuffy room. Nearly everyone besides us has a cigarette dangling from their lips. The clamor makes my head spin, and the urge to cough tickles my throat with every breath. Even when the other boys sneak cigarettes after school, the smell turns my stomach.

To my surprise, a few women sit around the burning stove, smoking and taking shots of *oghi* with the men. They wear the same uniform as the *fedayi*. How can they be allowed to fight? I bite my lower lip as I watch them laugh with their rifles propped beside them. Someone bumps me, and I see Shushi head straight for the women.

"Boys!" I hear Professor Manukian shout over the chorus of deep voices from one of the back rooms. He gestures for us to join the men at the table, where several maps are spread out. The men don't notice us at first, but when they see the professor, they stand tall and salute.

"At ease, comrades. I want you to meet someone." He extends his hand, drawing us closer to the large table. Cups, bullet shells, and cigarette ash surround the maps of the city. Raz and Nshan crowd me, their hot breath warming the backs of my ears.

"These are some of the brightest and finest of my former students from Yeramian. This is Nshan, Razmik, and Suren. And their friends, though I can't recall their names."

Mihran steps forward and waves awkwardly.

"I'm," he starts, but his voice cracks, and he stops. "*Parev.* I'm Mihran Altunian."

"And I am Shushi Altunian!" she shouts, pushing past us and nearly knocking Mihran and me off our feet. She turns around, points a finger at her brother, and whispers through her teeth, "Don't apologize for me."

The professor chuckles and places his hands on his hips. "So it seems."

"*Pari yegak*," the men mumble through their beards. Of the five, only one or two glance at us. Luckily, none is Uncle Tarzi, but he could be nearby, and my secret mission will be over for good.

"This is my second in command, Charo," the professor says, patting the large man on the shoulder.

The older, gray-bearded *fedayi* with wrinkles at the corners of his eyes looks at the professor and says, "No offense, but we have more pressing matters than meeting some of your former students."

"Exactly," the professor replies, pushing the small lenses of his glasses up the bridge of his nose. "Nshan, tell Charo what you told me outside."

Chin up, Nshan speaks like someone running for governor of Van. "As we patrolled the city tonight, we spotted a Turkish soldier or gendarme roaming the streets under cover of darkness."

The old *fedayi*'s expression grows serious. "A Turkish soldier?"

"Yes," Razmik interjects.

Charo turns to the other fighters and whispers something before looking back at us. "Where did you see him?"

"Between here and St. Boghos," Nshan replies.

All eyes fix on Charo, who points at two younger *fedayi*. "You two come with me."

Without another word, Charo and the men head toward the door. The remaining men regard us with slight smirks. The professor chuckles again and places a hand on Nshan's shoulder.

"You know, boys—" he begins.

"And me," Shushi interrupts.

"And Shushi. Battling the Turks requires more than just guns and cannons. It takes all of us doing our part." He leans over, grabs a glass of *oghi*, and drinks it down.

"One of our biggest issues is communication. For our fighters near the Tabriz Gate and Amparag, we need to relay messages from military command. Since you've proven your worth, I believe this would be the right job for you."

"Really?" Shushi gasps.

"What do you say?" he asks.

We exchange glances without answering. The thought of being part of something so important and being asked by the one leading the Armenians against the Turks sends a surge of excitement through my blood. But then I think of Mama and Baba.

"It's an honor to protect the land," Nshan replies with a salute.

"Excellent!" the professor replies. "For tonight, go home. Rest. Meet me here tomorrow at dawn."

Raz, Nshan, Mihran, and especially Shushi bubble with excitement as they weave through the fighters and women, then spill into the night. I'm not sure why the professor wasn't upset that we knew the military command's location, but being invited to join the resistance made it all worthwhile. Still, I stand with my back to the table, the weight of my decision heavy in my gut.

"Suren? Dawn isn't far off, and you need your rest. Everything all right?" the professor asks.

I turn around, my eyes on the floor. "Thank you for the offer, sir, but I have to decline."

He pulls out a chair, sits, and gestures for me to join him.

"There's no shame in being afraid," he assures me.

"No, sir, it's not that."

"What is it then?"

I take a deep breath. "My parents don't know I'm out here. If they find out, they might lock me up until the battle is over."

The professor leans forward, the air in the room feels heavy.

"Your father is Vartan Simonian, yes?"

I nod. "My uncle is Tarzi Simonian. He's not here, is he?"

The professor smiles. "No, he's stationed by the Tabriz Gate. A proud Armenian, your uncle is."

"A little crazy too," I mumble.

"Yes," he says, smiling. "That too."

He lifts a smoldering cigarette from the bowl and takes a drag. As he speaks, the smoke seeps from his mouth like dragon's breath.

"Your parents love you, which is why they want to keep you safe. I have no children, but I don't fault them for their decision. However, sometimes the choices we make out of a good heart are not the right choices. You must ask yourself what it is that you feel God wants of you. What Armenia needs of you. I could talk with your parents, if you'd like."

He pauses. The idea doesn't sound terrible. Better he do it than I.

"But," he continues, "you know that is not how it should be done."

His compassionate eyes peer over his small glasses, and though the thought of telling my parents what I've been up to makes me want to vomit, I know the only way to protect my home and family is to win the battle at home first.

April 23, 1915

The Big Guns

26

Childish Games

A loud bang wakes me. Somehow, I managed to sleep with my arm underneath my body, and now my hand feels dead. I pump my fingers until the blood returns, bringing with it a stabbing pain that prickles across my skin. Then another pain hits me.

I'm already late for my first mission.

A deep throb rests behind my eyes. I can't recall what time I came home from the military command or how I even made it to my bed. Outside the window, the sun touches the rooftops. Faint shouting from across the city carries into my room. I wonder if Charo and the others found the gendarme we saw in the streets.

Wearing the same clothes from yesterday, I quickly pull off my shirt and trousers and find some fresh clothes. Mama will definitely notice otherwise. Downstairs, I hear voices and wonder how long I slept. If Mama keeps finding me sleeping later and later in the morning, she will get suspicious. Mothers just know. Maybe they are all born with the ability to talk directly to God like the old prophets. More mothers would have been prophets if they weren't so busy with children.

My legs feel heavy, but I smile and try to skip down the steps. Downstairs, Baba sits at the table reading a sheet of paper and sipping coffee from a small cup. Mama stands by the stove, holding the handle of the *jazva* over the flame and stirring the dark coffee. Though I hate the taste, the fresh smell always reminds me of home.

Both of my parents seem lost, as if they are staring at what is in front of them without really seeing it. Mama's eyes are fixed on the *jazva*, while Baba pores over the piece of paper. Not until I stand next to her does she notice me and startle.

"Oh! Suren *jan*. *Pari looys*."

"*Pari looys*," I repeat and hug her.

I walk over to Baba, who takes small, noisy sips from his cup. He glances up at me as I pull out a chair.

"How did you sleep?" he asks, still focused on the paper.

My gut sinks. Is this a test to see if I will lie to him?

"Good. Good," I mutter. "What are you reading?"

He sighs and takes another sip. My stomach growls, and I can't recall the last time I ate anything besides the *khash*. I grab a boiled egg and a piece of lavash from the plate and begin to crack the shell.

"Communication numbers six and seven from military command. Looks like the *fedayi* have to take it easy on the *oghi* and wine."

He winks, easing my nerves a bit. I think of the others, probably sitting with Professor Manukian at military command and being trained on what the *fedayi* are asking of them. Even Shushi is there, and she's crazy.

"Communication number seven has some good news. Several Turkish soldiers have been killed, and positions throughout the city are being held. A gendarme was wounded, and we confiscated three hundred cartridges from some fleeing Turks. Not bad for a day's fighting, yes?"

"The gendarme! Did they find him?" The words leave my lips before I even realize I've said them.

Baba raises a bushy eyebrow at me.

"Good news?" Mama interjects from the stove. "What kind of world do we live in where people being killed is good news?"

Baba ignores her and watches me for a moment. His eyes probe every twitch of my muscles or blink of my eye. A rush of heat floods my skin. He lifts his empty cup and looks inside, staring intently at the grounds. My heart is relieved that his focus is somewhere else.

He tilts the empty cup toward me, revealing the black swirls of sludge at the bottom.

"What do you see?" he asks.

"I'm not a child anymore, Baba. I don't feel like playing this game."

"Come now. Tell me what you see."

I look in and let my eyes relax. The black smears and clumps swirling around the mug are just smudges. Nothing forms into an image.

"A bird," I reply, just like I did all the other times he shoved the morning cup into my face.

Bringing the cup back, he squints and turns it around a few times. "You see a bird?"

I nod.

He looks at it again. "Maybe." He pauses, then asks, "Is the coffee ready?"

Without a word, Mama brings the *jazva* and pours the dark drink into his cup.

An itch deep inside me wants to ask my parents the fateful question. But, as I've done for the past few nights while trying to fall asleep, all the scenarios replay in my mind. The one where they look disappointed but understand, or the one where Mama uses the *jazva* to beat me for disobeying and sneaking out like some hoodlum. Each silences my mouth every time I open it.

I hear footsteps and see Ani coming downstairs, looking as tired as I feel.

"*Pari looys*, Mama," she says and kisses Mama on the cheek.

Mama lifts her chin and inspects her face. "Are you sick?"

"No. Just tired."

A brief cough fills the air, and Baba clears his throat. "I must report back tomorrow. The fighting has slowed, but it will continue."

Just like that, the moment vanishes. I could never tell either of my sisters before I tell my parents. Taline would rat on me the moment she heard. Ani probably wouldn't, but I can't risk it. I can hear the doors and windows of the house shutting on me, locking me in for the rest of the day.

After all the waiting and hoping, I've failed my first mission as a *fedayi*.

27

Ani Strikes a Deal

On the edge of my bed, I sit as still as an owl and listen for the sound of nothing. Fighting has continued throughout the day but not as intensely as the first attacks a few days ago.

Most of the morning, I sat on the roof and watched the city. My mind imagined Nshan and the others standing in the military compound, backs straight, in new uniforms, saluting Charo or the professor as they received orders for the day. Carrying messages? Surveillance? I guess I may never know. The bigger question in my mind is whether they would even want me there. Maybe they think I deserted. Ran away like a coward.

In the afternoon, another communication from Military Council reported some Turks killed and a few Armenians wounded. One who may lose his leg, according to Aunt Yeva.

I pause and hear nothing in the thick darkness. All is clear.

I mold the pillows and blankets under the sheets as if sculpting a masterpiece, then place one of my caps where my head should be. In the dark, it resembles my black hair as long as no one comes too close.

Carrying my shoes, I tiptoe down the stairs. I check the bedroom curtain, see that it's shut, and open the front door. Quickly, I slip out, looking back into the room one last time.

My back collides with something, but soon I realize it is not something but someone. My heart leaps into my throat, and I whirl around, preparing to run or throw a punch.

"Don't say a word, Suren Simonian."

Ani's big, round eyes stare back at me in the night, and I slap my palms over my open mouth to stop myself from making that weird noise I make when I'm startled.

Under her headscarf, her eyes dart from side to side before staring at me and asking, "What are you doing out here?"

I drop my hands. "What am *I* doing out here? What are *you* doing out here?"

She straightens from her hunched stance. "That's none of your business."

"Then it's none of your business why I'm out here too."

We stare at each other for a moment before we both realize my back is to the front door. Ani grabs my arm and pulls me behind our oxcart, even though we have no ox to pull it. We startle a sleeping cat that bangs into something and runs off into the night.

Ani holds my shoulders. "All right. We both agree not to tell each other why we are sneaking out of the house. So how do you want to do this?"

"This?" I ask. "I know why you are out here."

She looks at me with a suspicious expression. "And why is that?"

I roll my eyes. "To see your sweetheart."

Not very often do I see Ani glare at me, but tonight, her eyes dig into mine before a fist lands on my shoulder.

The surprise hurt more than the actual punch. "What's that for? I'm right anyway."

"Yes, but that's not the point," she whispers, pointing her finger centimeters from my nose. "You can't tell anyone. None of your little friends. Especially not Taline."

"OK."

She sighs and adjusts her headscarf, which had loosened when she'd punched me. "And if Mama or Baba catch you sneaking out of the house, you won't say anything, right?"

"Only if you do the same," I counter.

She extends her hand, and we shake on it. I turn and head down the street, and just before I round the corner of the house, Ani quietly calls my name.

"Suren."

I stop and look back.

"Be careful."

Accepting the Mission

The smoke fills the night as I reach the military command building. From outside, voices clamor behind the walls. I stop at the door and push down the nervousness in my chest. Will my friends be upset with me for not showing up? What about the professor? The unknown waits for me inside, and I know I cannot, will not, run away a second time.

I knock and wait. A moment later, the door cracks open, and a sliver of light comes through. A *fedayi* with a curling mustache peeks out. His face is stern and emotionless.

"What do you want? Why are you here?" he snaps.

"I, I, he told me to come," I stammer.

"Who?"

"Professor Manukian."

His eyes narrow to slits as he slings the rifle off his shoulder, holding it ready with his finger near the trigger.

"Don't move," he orders, then leans back and shouts something behind the door. Does he not remember me? I was here last night. Or has the professor ordered them to keep me away since I have no honor?

I wait outside in the crisp night air. Through the crack, I try to peek in to see if anyone I know is inside—maybe Nshan, Mihran, or even Shushi. Only glimpses of *fedayi* pass back and forth. I should have stayed home. I don't belong here. I can't even stand up to my own parents. How can I defend this city against Turks who use more than words to control me?

The front door swings open.

"Come in. Quickly!" he orders.

I scurry into the large room, and the heat from the stove and the mass of bodies hits me as I remove my cap. Several people crowd around the large table. Lit lamps illuminate the maps sprawled out on it.

The professor leans with his elbows on the table and his head hanging. I move closer, feeling my knees tremble with each step. Cigarette smoke and the musky bodies nearly choke me. The group of men doesn't notice me, and I stand just far enough away to hear them.

"Aram, what do we do? Hundreds, maybe thousands of them are flooding in from the villages."

The professor keeps his face down and sighs. "Let me think for a moment."

Charo pushes himself to his feet. His round belly hangs over his belt as he adjusts his trousers. He points at the map.

"My heart goes out to those coming from the villages. But there is a reason the Turks are allowing them to come. If we let them in, we will be overrun. There is not enough food or water. We will make ourselves vulnerable to attack. Who knows? Maybe Turkish spies are hiding among them."

"Most of them are women and children, Charo," Aram interjects.

"Exactly. It's the perfect strategy. Hit us where we least expect it."

The professor lifts his head as the others around the table begin to talk at once. The voices flood the room and build into a frenzy, louder and louder, until the professor lifts his hand and slams it three times onto the wooden table. The voices fade away.

"Everyone out! Charo, you stay. The rest of you give me a moment to think."

They exchange glances before filing out of the room one by one. I don't see Nshan and the others, and a part of me feels relief.

With the other *fedayi* gone, my presence feels exposed, as if I am standing naked. Charo sees me first, taps the professor on the shoulder, and nods his large head in my direction. When the professor turns and sees me, he smiles, but not out of happiness.

"Come here," he orders softly.

I approach as he points to an open stool at the table.

"Sit."

Charo rolls his eyes. "I'm getting a drink." His round body lumbers past me into another room, leaving the professor and me alone at the table. In the other room, someone plucks at the strings of an oud without melody or rhythm.

The professor pulls a packet of cigarettes from his coat pocket and places one on his lips. He rummages through his pockets until he finds a match and lights it in a flash, puffing until smoke fills the space between us. He offers it to me, but I shake my head.

He says nothing. Is he angry? Disappointed? Indifferent? His face seems obscured by a mask. Leaning forward, he rests his elbows on the table and smokes, staring at the wall adorned with portraits of the family this house once belonged to before the Turks arrived.

He points his cigarette at the photos. "Perhaps it would have been easier if we had all left like them."

The father and mother with a young girl look back at us, empty and almost disapproving. He says nothing else, sitting in silence, rapping his knuckles on the table.

The tapping becomes an itch in my throat, building until I can't take it anymore.

"I'm sorry I didn't come this morning. I meant to. Really. But my father was talking about different things, and then my sister came. I tried, but—"

"What do you think, Suren Simonian?" he asks.

"I'm sorry, sir?" I respond.

"This business of resistance. Fighting an immense government meant to exterminate us from our home. What do you think of it?" He blows out smoke that coils over the maps.

"I think it is evil, sir."

He lifts his eyebrows. "Evil?"

"Yes, sir."

"And what is that?"

I pause. I'm not sure anyone has ever asked me what evil is. I think about Father Zakarian's sermons before I answer. "Evil is the devil's work, sir. Stealing our home and murdering our people is evil."

The professor ponders my answer for a moment. "That sounds like something a priest would say."

My shoulders drop. "Father Zakarian may have said that."

The professor chuckles. "I wish I could see the world as a priest does."

I scratch my scalp, trying to understand what he means. Does he want to go to St. Boghos now, or does he want to be a priest?

He exhales smoke and then snuffs out the end of the small cigarette into a clay bowl littered with butts and ash.

"Have you spoken with your friends yet?"

"No, sir."

He nods. "I guess you'll have your chance to explain yourself. They were quite disappointed you didn't show up this morning. Especially Mihran."

"Mihran?" I ask, surprised. I didn't know Mihran liked me all that much.

"I sent them all home to rest and get some dinner before returning here. Tonight, you all have an important task."

"We, sir?"

"You still came. Even under the threat of your parents finding out. As your teacher, I should not permit this." He winks as he says the last part. For a moment, the tension in my shoulders eases.

"Actually, your fellow comrades should be here soon."

As if planned, Nshan, Raz, Mihran, and Shushi enter the room. I want to jump up and greet them, but shame weighs me down. They come forward, and the only one who seems glad to see me is Mihran. A wide smile spreads across his face.

"You came!" he exclaims.

Razmik grunts. "Better late than never."

The professor stands. "Now is not the time to dwell on the past. I have a mission for you." He looks at me. "All of you."

"Yes, sir!" they all say together. I stand as Professor Manukian begins to tell us our mission.

"Now, I need you to deliver—"

A commotion of voices and banging doors comes from the other room. A young *fedayi* bursts through, interrupting our meeting. Winded, he shouts between breaths, "Sir! We found him."

"Who, comrade?"

"The gendarme, sir. The one they told us about," he says, pointing at us.

The professor looks at us and then returns to the messenger. "Where is he?"

Sweat drips down the messenger's temple. "In the Ohanian home. Charo is already there."

A grave look comes over the professor. "Take me to them. Quickly."

He turns back to us. "Stay here until I get back. I won't be long."

In no time, we are left standing around the table, staring after the *fedayi* and professor as the oud player in the other room plucks notes out of rhythm. An awful melody for an uncomfortable moment.

29

Brainstorming

"Where were you?" Shushi asks, punching my bicep.

"Yeah, we were counting on you to come," Nshan comments, arms folded.

"I'm sorry. I tried to make it here this morning. But my father . . . and then Ani. I tried . . ." The words stumble out as if I've never used them before.

"I told you all he wasn't cut out for this," Razmik announces, his fat head held high. I've never punched anyone, but if I were to punch someone, it would be Raz. I may regret it, but at least it would be deserved.

"Look. I'm sorry. I'm here now. That should count for

something," I plead. Nshan and Raz avoid looking at me, and Shushi is now distracted, reading the maps and humming a song to herself.

Mihran steps forward and stands next to me. Facing the others, he says, "I'm glad Suren is here. He wants to help and he won't let it happen again, right?"

In this moment, Mihran no longer seems like the orphan boy from another place. In fact, it feels like he has never lived anywhere else.

Nshan and Raz exchange a glance. An unspoken agreement must be passing between their minds like the gypsies who passed through the Old City in the summers.

"All right, you're back in the Big Guns," Nshan replies.

I pause. "Wait. The what?"

Shushi pipes in from behind us, rolling her eyes. "That's our new name."

"The name of what?" I ask.

"Our group. We are the Big Guns," Nshan says.

"The Big Guns?" I exclaim. "But we don't even have any guns. I've never shot a gun in my life, and I know you haven't either."

Nshan rolls his eyes and shakes his hands at me. "No, no, no. It doesn't mean we literally have 'big guns.' It's a metaphor."

"So," I begin, "we have symbolic big guns."

Nshan nods. "In a way, yes."

I look to Mihran, who shrugs and whispers, "I don't get it either."

"It's a good name," Nshan argues. "It's American. I think."

"I voted for the Brain Bashers," Razmik interjects.

Nshan shakes his head. "We talked about that, Raz. It's not realistic. You're the only one capable of doing any bashing."

"Well, I didn't vote for the Big Guns," Shushi says, standing on a chair and towering over us. "My suggestion is . . ." she pauses for effect, "the Night Rats." She sweeps her hand across as if the name belongs on a marquee.

We all pause and look at her, perched with her hands out and a hint of pride on her face.

"Shushi, that is the most terrible name I have ever heard," Mihran remarks flatly.

She scowls at him and then turns to us. "I don't care. It strikes fear into the hearts of the Turkish murderers."

Nshan politely replies, "It makes us sound like pests."

Her head tilts to the left as she looks up. "That's a good thing, right?"

We all stare at her blankly. Mihran hangs his head and sighs, as usual.

Shushi stomps her foot. "Fine. See if you can find a better name."

"Is Brain Bashers still on the table?" Razmik asks.

"No!" everyone else says at once.

The twang of the oud from the other room continues, and I can't help but feel that each pluck of the string is a needle in my ear.

"Anyway, what did Professor Manukian have you do earlier?" I ask.

"First, we cleaned up that room over there," Shushi says, pointing at the kitchen where the oud player keeps trying to play. "Then, we . . . sort of waited here."

"That sounds like a mission my mother would give me," I reply.

Back home, I imagined many scenarios about what I missed, and now, standing in this stuffy house, the truth feels far less exciting than my imagination.

"Maybe there will be other missions once we prove ourselves," I suggest with a shrug.

The others don't say much but nod as if they agree.

On the table, a plate of dried goat meat sits among some maps of the city. A few *fedayi* relax on benches, resting their heads against the cold walls. Their rifles lay across their laps, and one of them, a man slightly younger than Baba, has a thick beard and a red-stained bandanna wrapped around his forehead. I feel like I've seen him before—perhaps in the markets selling olives? I can't be sure.

"So what do we do now?" Shushi asks.

An awkward pause fills the space. The oud player's incessant plucking stops, and the silence feels soothing.

"Wait?" Nshan asks, half asking.

We agree, and Mihran and Nshan start whispering while Razmik picks up a knife stuck in the table and begins whittling a wooden spoon into a small spear. Shushi walks into the other room, and the oud comes to life again. I can't help but feel Shushi is responsible.

I sit at the table and look at the maps showing all the churches and schools in the different districts of the city. The smell of dust and the laughter of my classmates come to me just by looking at them. I even find my home and the market. Close to Ayeksan, the Tabriz Gate is marked boldly. Then I see the Shamiram on the other side of the cemetery. The Muslim quarter. I miss Hamza and wonder if, no matter the outcome, anything will be the same.

A bang hits me like lightning as the wooden door crashes into the wall. The sleeping *fedayi* startle awake and spring to their feet. Their guns drop to the floor, and they scramble to pick them up.

Professor Manukian and Charo march into the room and toward the table where I sit. Neither looks at the others as they approach. I am so surprised that I don't even stand and just look up at them from my chair. Am I in trouble? Did Baba find out and come to military command to take me home?

Professor Manukian's chest rises and falls. Heavy breaths push through his nose a moment before he stares hard into my face and says, "Come with me."

"All of us?" Nshan asks.

"No," he answers. "Just Suren."

I stand on shaky legs with an unsettled gut. With each step, my mind swirls, searching for reasons why they want me to go with them. All the while, the off-key and out-of-rhythm oud player plays my funeral song.

Outside, I walk with the professor, Charo, and two other *fedayi* into the streets. Other than the occasional gunshot nearby, the night feels calm and still. The shadows of cats dart across the road at our footsteps.

An ominous cloud hovers over me as I walk between the two men. No one speaks, and Charo takes puffs from a fat cigar tucked between his fingers. The invasive smoke blows across my face, but the aroma is strangely sweet. Maybe I am growing up and considering trying coffee tomorrow morning.

"Where are we going?" I muster the courage to ask. The words almost crash in my throat like a derailed train.

No one answers. Not even the professor, who always answers. It must be difficult to ignore me since he is a teacher. I've never known one who didn't want to give an answer.

We pass the oxcart where we saw the gendarme last night, and I guess we are going to St. Boghos. For a secret meeting? Or are they keeping the gendarme locked up in one of the confessional booths? I can't imagine Father Zakarian torturing information out of a Turkish policeman, but war makes men do things they wouldn't normally do.

The old church sits straight ahead. The two *fedayi* are ready with their guns as they walk. Both remind me of my elder brothers—at least my memory of them before they were forced to enlist and fight in the Great War. Only God knows where they may be, above ground or below.

"This way," Charo mumbles with an exaggerated wave. "Hurry up."

I try to catch a glimpse of their faces as we pass the dim lamps, but I see only shadows. Why do they want only me and not the others to come? I'm the last person who should get special privileges or assignments.

The long walk finally reaches the back door of St. Boghos. We pause at the crowded landing, and the two *fedayi* stand on the steps, facing the courtyard where we boys used to hold our fights. That seems like ancient history now.

Charo leans forward, cigar in his lips, and whispers into Professor Manukian's ear. He nods and then turns to me with his hands on his hips. His long mustache spreads across his face, and in the faint dark, it feels more intimidating.

"Tell me about your brother," he asks.

"My brother? Why?"

"This is very important, Suren. Tell me."

I take a breath. "Which one?"

"What?"

"Levon or Narek?"

The professor looks at Charo, who shrugs.

"Both."

With their eyes on me, I realize I haven't talked about my brothers in what feels like months. "They were, are, much older than me. When the Great War started, they enlisted and joined the Turkish forces. Baba told me everyone believed the Ittihad would be different, and they wanted to fight as Ottomans."

"Do you know where they have been stationed?" the professor asks.

"No, sir. We have never received a letter or notice from the government. They are like ghosts."

A cool breeze blows against my damp scalp. The professor looks over my head into the distance, his eyes seeming to search for something out there. The *fedayi* behind me puff on cigarettes, and the smoke blows toward me so strongly that it stings my nostrils.

"Sir," I ask. "Why am I here?"

Without answering, he stares at me with an odd shift in his eyes—something like pity or uncertainty, but I can't tell which.

"Have I done something wrong?" I ask, but my voice comes out almost pleadingly.

He sighs and then nods at Charo, whose bulky body opens the rear door of St. Boghos. The heavy glow of candlelight at the altar shines out onto the stair landing. The professor lifts his hand and ushers me into the church. The faint memory of the Big Guns' first secret mission before the Turkish army arrived floods back to me: the smell of incense and the faces in the pews. But more importantly, I still don't care for the name "Big Guns."

Inside, I see Father Zakarian in his white robe. His white beard catches the light from the crowd of candles glowing in the dark. With his back to me, seated on the edge of the altar, is the familiar black uniform of the gendarme. I assume they want me here to identify whether this is the same spy we saw a few nights ago. I can't see his face, but I expect his features to be swollen and his eyes black and blue from the beating the *fedayi* gave him.

The rear door slams shut and echoes through the stone walls of the sanctuary. I jump at the sound, and Father Zakarian looks at us. Then the gendarme shifts, looking over his shoulder. A wide, toothy smile spreads across his face. A familiar voice comes at me through the stale church air.

"Miss me?"

My body freezes. Could it really be?

As his droopy eyes and white teeth catch the candlelight, the gendarme stands, and I can see the ghost of my oldest brother standing in front of me.

30

A Familiar Face

Levon's soft eyes look at me, waiting, maybe wondering why I am standing here with a stupid look on my face, as if I've seen someone come back from the dead.

"What are you doing?" he asks, hands out. "Come here."

His familiar tone awakens me. Like out of a dream, my legs come free, and I run forward, wrapping my arms around him. Unlike before, he smells different, like cigarettes and dirt. Similar to *oghi*, but as if it leaks out of his skin.

He places a hand on my head but says nothing.

I stand back and look up at him—not as far as I used to, but he still stands taller than me.

"Look at you," he exclaims, running his fingertip across my fuzzy upper lip before I slap it away. "Turning into a man already."

I chuckle. "Maybe you can tell Baba and Mama that."

Up close in the candlelight, the creases around his eyes seem deeper, perhaps from the heavy bags under his eyes. A star-shaped scar sits just above his right eye, and I can't recall if he had that before he left to fight in the war.

"I can't believe you're here. We thought you were—" My lips can't seem to form the word.

He nods. "How is everyone at home? I want to make sure they are OK."

"They are fine. Well, as fine as they can be with everything happening."

Levon looks at the professor and Charo, who linger by the altar, arms crossed and whispering. With a firm hand, Levon turns me toward them and raises his voice, saying, "See? I told you I was a Simonian."

The professor steps forward. "As you can assume, we had to err on the side of caution. These are dangerous times, and with you sneaking around the city in a Turkish uniform . . ."

Levon examines his dusty uniform. "You have a point. May I see my family now?"

The professor glances at Charo and then looks past us to Father Zakarian, seated on the first wooden pew. His extravagant robes drape over the edge, and he seems to sag in his seat, drowning in those religious clothes.

"One of the sheep has returned to the fold," he replies weakly.

"Oh, for God's sake, Father, spare us the Scripture. Yes or no?" Charo growls.

Father Zakarian sighs. "Go with God."

"Thank you!" Charo barks before turning to leave through the back entrance.

My eyes meet Levon's, and even in church, we both chuckle. For a moment, it's as if we are back in the old days before the war, before the Turks shot cannons into our home. The only thing missing is Mama smacking the backs of our heads.

The professor follows Charo out the back door, but the two *fedayi* linger on the landing outside. The tired figure of Father Zakarian nods at us slowly, as if trying not to fall asleep.

"Thanks, Father," Levon remarks. The old man rises and turns down the aisle, his long robes dragging behind him.

Once Father Zakarian reaches the back of the church, Levon says, "He might see God sooner than the rest of us."

I laugh, not because it's funny, but out of instinct. Levon always had a way of lightening the mood, no matter the situation. I never thought I'd have the chance to laugh at his bad jokes again. Silence settles around us, and the faint mumbling prayers of Father Zakarian echo from the rear of the church.

Levon scans the stained glass of Jesus on the cross, and I watch him drift off into his thoughts. Something in his eyes tells me all I need to know, but I can't quite grasp it—like the equations in arithmetic back at school that I could never solve.

"Levon?" I ask.

He doesn't respond. Same eyes in the same place.

"Levon," I repeat, a little louder.

His wide eyes snap to the sound of my voice. No sound or words, just those wide, darkened eyes.

"Y-Yes. What is it?" he says, as if coming out of a daze.

I want to ask about Narek. Where is he? Has he seen him? Is he wounded somewhere? Or worse, is he dead? But the trickle of sweat down his temple and his wild eyes keep the question locked away for now.

Instead, I smile and say, "I'm glad you're here."

He smiles and places an arm around my shoulders.

"Let's go home. I've been dying for some good food."

I don't have the heart to tell him about the *khash*.

April 24, 1915

The First Mission

31

Family Reunion

"Do you think Mama will scream when she sees me?"

A toothy smile flashes under Levon's mustache as we approach the front door of our home. I shrug without answering.

Outside, the lamps have died away, and dawn peeks just behind Mount Ararat. Now, I stand outside our door with my brother, facing the truth I must tell my parents. All the sneaking out and lies will surface. They must. There's no other explanation for why I would be out in the streets at night. With Levon next to me, dancing on his heels before the door, I feel like a criminal headed toward the executioner.

"Should I knock or you?" he asks.

"I don't think it matters. Just walk in," I reply.

"You're right. You're right," he mutters to himself. Narek was always more nervous and jittery than Levon. Like Hamza, everyone loved him, especially the girls. It's strange to see him so anxious about meeting his own parents after a few months.

He exhales, then nudges my shoulder. "You go first."

I roll my eyes and push the door open.

The door swings inward, slow and creaking. Levon stands behind me. No one is at the table yet, but Mama stands at the kitchen window, rubbing her hands together as if kneading dough. The door blocks him from Mama's view as she turns at the sound and sees me. Her heavy eyes fill with confusion at the sight of me in the doorway.

"Suren? What—why aren't you in your room?"

The questions in her eyes lift as she says the words, and then her eyes carry the very real sense of punishment soon to come.

"I, I." My tongue has quit. It must know the battle is over before I do.

From behind me, I feel Levon's arm brush against my side as he steps into the room. I thought he had followed me, but I guess he lingered just outside. Mama's deep-set eyes turn to Levon, and her hands cover her mouth as she drops her towel. An expression of terror crosses her face, probably at seeing only the Turkish uniform and not who wears it. The *jazva* on the wood stove boils over and hisses.

"*Parev*, Mama," he whispers.

As she lowers her hands, I see her lips mouthing something I can't quite make out before she rushes forward, nearly knocking over one of the chairs, and wraps her arms around Levon.

Tears slide down her cheeks as she repeats his name over and over. For the moment, a sense of relief washes over me. Maybe, just maybe, they won't ask where I've been.

Baba emerges from the bedroom downstairs, his hair disheveled and his eyes puffy from sleep. His sleeping frock bunches around his waist.

"What's all this about?" he grumbles.

Mama releases her once-missing son and turns toward Baba. Levon smiles his toothy grin and opens his arms wide.

"I'm home," Levon shouts.

"Am I still asleep?" Baba mutters to himself as he takes unsteady steps toward Levon.

I see tears welling in Baba's eyes before he reaches Levon and grabs him tightly by the shoulders. His wet, squinty eyes examine Levon's face. Have I ever seen Baba cry before?

"My boy. My boy. My boy," he repeats under his breath, then cups Levon's head in his big palms and kisses his cheeks.

Baba sees me off to the side and reaches out his hand. I take one step before he yanks me forward into his side, engulfing both of us.

"Praise God!" Mama sings, clapping her hands. "Ani! Taline! Come downstairs!"

With my face pressed against our bodies, I hear the shrieks of my sisters as their embrace hits us, and I can no longer tell who is who among the sobs, laughter, songs, and mumblings.

Hot and crushed between my family, only two thoughts swirl in my brain: Have I escaped my punishment, and, most importantly, where is Narek?

Levon's Journey

Soon after Levon and I returned, Mama came alive. She asked him if he was hungry and started to make a meal with whatever we had, whether he answered or not. Mostly lavash, but our neighbors brought over a bag of unripe plums, which she was quite happy about.

"The first bite reminds me of spring when I was a girl sitting by the lake," she says.

We sit around the table. Levon, as if he never left, sits in his usual spot. Each chair has its original owner except for one. But no one seems to want to ask about my other brother, or maybe they are afraid of the answer.

Everyone watches Levon as he rips strips of lavash and tosses them into his mouth, chewing and smacking the way Mama hates. But today, I don't think she cares.

"Where have you been all this time?" Taline asks.

Levon holds up a half-eaten plum as he answers. "We were supposed to be stationed at the front in Egypt. But after several changes, our regiment took a train toward the east, right on the Persian border. Most Armenian volunteers were treated poorly by the Turkish soldiers. They made us clean latrines and gave us meager rations. Some were even disarmed and beaten while they mocked our God. But since I was placed with General Nazarbekoff and other fighting Armenian soldiers, I escaped their games. When the tracks ended, we marched for several days to Salmast. Before the fighting, it reminded me of home. We swam in the large, blue lake. But then the Russians came."

He pauses, slowly chewing a strip of lavash, staring at the bread as if hypnotized.

Baba interrupts, "How did you make it home?"

He returns to us. "After a month of fighting, we moved south toward Urmia, fending off attacks, losing men, trying to stay warm. I lost track of time. The days and months all seemed to blend together. But we received a message for our unit to return west. They never told me where, but after we joined another regiment, they said we were going to Van. Why, I asked, and after bribing a Turk with my day's rations, he said we were going to take care of the Armenians. How did he put it? 'Answer the Armenian question.' A shiver ran through my bones when I heard that. So, we marched west. Each day I thought of all of you. Thoughts of home. And my swollen feet from all the marching every single day."

In one quick movement, Levon swings his foot up, and his heel lands on the table with a thud. Mama and my sisters jump with a gasp as he wiggles his calloused and dirty toes. Taline and Ani giggle while Mama hits the back of Levon's head with a towel.

"No! No! Get your filthy foot off my table," she says, trying to hide a smile.

"Let him be," Baba urges with a laugh. Levon removes his foot and places it back on the floor.

"Nothing changes," she mutters, letting a slight smile turn the corners of her lips.

Levon coughs and then continues.

"As I was saying, we were headed to Van. To home. Along the way, the regiment approached smoke in the distance. It was just south of Arjesh. It seemed to take forever to reach the smoke, and then we saw—"

Outside, rapid gunshots echo through the streets. Men shouting and a loud boom follow, and Levon's shoulders tense. His pupils widen. Ani and Taline give an uneasy glance at Baba, who rests his hand on Levon's shoulder.

"It's all right, my son. You are home. What you saw can remain in the desert."

The almost unfazed joy Levon always had no longer seems to be a part of him. More like an actor playing a familiar role he was once famous for. I'm sure everyone else notices it like I do.

Levon tries to smile again but drops his gaze to his lap. In a faint whisper, he mumbles, "So many ghosts. So many." I want to be confused. To have no idea what he might be talking about. But I know deep inside exactly what he means.

Baba keeps his hand on Levon's shoulder but looks across the table at me.

"Do you know where Narek is?" I ask.

Mama and my sisters scold me with harsh whispers like a flurry of bullets.

"I am just asking what we all want to know."

Levon closes his eyes and takes a deep breath. Then he raises his face and looks at all of us. His eyes soften, and he shrugs.

"I don't know. Once we were forced to enlist, they split us apart. Have you not heard from him?"

Baba removes his hand. "Until now, we assumed Suren was our only son."

Levon scratches his scalp, covered by his thick, black hair. "Maybe he deserted. Like me."

A solemn silence falls over the table. Any trace of forced joy slowly fades from Levon, and only the faint sputter of gunfire fills the space. He blinks at every distant shot.

"I'll make some tea," Mama suddenly informs us and heads to the stove, fiddling with the kindling.

Baba stands. "That's a good idea. Let's allow Levon some time to rest."

One by one, Ani and Taline stand up and join Mama in the kitchen. I keep my eyes on Ani, hoping to catch her attention and ask her without asking that our pact still stands.

"Suren?"

Baba speaks my name in that fatherly tone that sends terror through me.

"Yes," I reply.

"Come with me outside."

He opens the front door. Light spills across the chairs, the table, and reaches me and my pounding heart. My eyes meet Ani's. Her gaze is stern, as if trying to remind me of our agreement from the other night. I rise and take unsteady steps toward my father waiting outside.

33

Confession to a Different Father

This is the day of my execution. I know it. I can feel it.

Outside, Baba stands with his back to me, looking at the tops of the buildings in our neighborhood. Not all homes are two levels, but most rise into the sky, and an army of clouds passes slowly overhead. A white and black cat sits atop some wooden crates stacked in front of the empty house across the street, staring at me with unblinking eyes.

Will he speak first and put me out of my misery? I'm sure he wants to give me the chance to confess what I have been doing at night, but no matter how quiet he is, I will make him ask. I won't volunteer my own punishment.

The sun breaks through and warms our skin. Baba's back remains turned to me, and my mind returns to Narek. Has he died? Is Levon telling the truth? Why didn't he fight to stay with his brother when they enlisted? I'm glad Levon has returned, but the joy in my heart feels incomplete—a half joy, in a way.

The sound of whistling comes from Baba. Whistling? I don't need a melody right now. Maybe this is part of his mind game to trick me into confessing. The tune is familiar—one from Sundays at St. Boghos.

Baba continues to whistle and strolls with his hands behind his back. With each step, he kicks out the tips of his shoes as if he is just taking a leisurely stroll. Even the sudden crack of gunfire doesn't stop him.

The more he whistles, the more a fire burns inside my gut, and the only way to put it out is to confess. Spill my guts like I'm in the confession booth with Father Zakarian again. "Forgive me, Father, for I have sinned." But Baba is no priest. I won't tell my secret. Never.

He stops whistling and turns slowly toward me with a slight smile on his face—a smile I haven't seen in many days. The words shoot out of me like vomit.

"I've been sneaking out of the house at night."

Facing me, he stops. The whistle vanishes, and I feel desperate for it to return.

"I'm sorry, Baba. I shouldn't have, but—" Pressure fills behind my eyes, and I fight back tears.

He sighs. "Is this how you found out about Levon?"

I nod, unable to speak. Should I tell him about Ani? She is the only sister who likes me, and losing her trust would feel like losing a sibling again.

The sun no longer warms me but burns me. Baba just stares. I keep fiddling with the edge of my jacket. When will he say something? Punish me already.

"How long have you been sneaking out?" he asks, crossing his arms over his broad chest.

"Once. Maybe two or three times. A few," I stumble through these tiny lies like a wounded animal.

A strange smile lifts his cheeks. "So I suppose those times I checked on you sleeping, I was actually checking on your blankets?"

For the life of me, I cannot understand why a father would smile when his son has disobeyed him. "Yes, sir."

He shakes his head, and a subtle chuckle escapes him. "You are my son. There's no doubt about that."

My eyes widen. "You're not . . . angry?" I ask, a hopeful lilt to my voice. A long thread unravels from my jacket. I must have been pulling on it this whole time.

"Oh, I'm disappointed. But your grandmother always said she hoped I would have a son who put me through the same misery I put her through."

Baba strokes his beard, lost in a memory. He doesn't flinch when gunshots ring out in the morning sun. But I realize I don't respond either, as if it always was. One half of me feels relief, but there's a chance Baba is so excited knowing Levon is alive and home that nothing could dampen his happiness.

"I assumed you had been sneaking out when I saw you in the same clothes as yesterday."

"Do you think Mama knows?" I ask. Disappointing a father and disappointing a mother are two very different betrayals.

"Ha! Of course she does," he replies. "All mothers have a direct line to God. If I noticed, she certainly did."

I'd held out hope she might not have noticed. But Baba is right. Each word feels like a punch in my gut. I don't know whose wrath I fear more.

"So what are you going to do?" I ask.

He adjusts his sleeping frock as he walks over to me. Normally, he would never leave the house in that outfit. The light catches the gray in his beard. He exhales deeply through his nose and says, "I understand why you disobeyed us."

"You do?"

"You are a Simonian. A son of Vartan. Your family fought in the Hamidian massacres. Your brothers volunteered to join the Ottoman army. I don't have to tell you about Uncle Tarzi. I can't keep lying to myself that you would just sit back at home and not try to do something even if I told you not to. I had to try at least. But your mother's fear is so strong. I had to protect her as much as I had to protect you."

I'd never thought of my father as so understanding. At times, I wondered if he even saw me for who I was or if I was just the baby of the family who needed others to look after him. But standing outside our house, in the midst of a battle to save our land and lives, I know that he sees me. He knows me.

"Does this mean I get to stay with the Big Guns?" I ask.

"The what?" he replies.

It still sounds stupid, and I feel my face flush.

"I mean, do I get to help in the fight?"

The calluses of his palm scratch against the fabric of my shirt, and he looks down at me with soft yet sad eyes.

"Let me talk with your mother."

He musses my hair with his big palm as he passes me.

"Now," he says, opening the door, "help her with the dishes."

An Undeserved Gift

The events of the morning swirl in my mind as I walk toward military command.

Baba and Mama spoke in the bedroom the entire morning. From shouts to whispers, the conversation resembled my nerves. After breakfast, Levon slept in my bed for hours without stirring. Even when I snuck in to change my clothes for the day, his snores drowned out all of the fuss I made. I should be exhausted right now, but I couldn't sleep if I tried.

While our parents had their "discussion," as they usually called it, Ani looked at me with a feverish gaze. I knew what she wanted to know, but with Taline around, I couldn't just tell her, so

I nodded, and she seemed to relax, knowing her secret was safe. However, now that Baba and Mama know my secret, it will only be a matter of time until Ani's secret is known as well.

I helped my sisters pick up the plates and put away the dishes. Keeping myself busy helped ease my mind and distract me from the words behind the curtain. I had this odd, ridiculous belief that if I did my chores, all of the lying and disobeying of the past few nights would be forgiven a little more easily. If I stacked the firewood, swept the floor, made my bed, and read chapters of the Bible, then my parents would no longer want to punish me now that I am a reformed sinner.

When the curtain snapped open, Mama came out first. Her red and puffy eyes locked on me as I finished sweeping around the stove. She walked toward me, lifted her hand, and slapped me on the crown of my head. Then, almost as if it were part of the slap, she pulled me into her and squeezed. The hug was so tight and so long that I could feel her heartbeat against my cheek. Then she released me without a word.

I can still feel her heart as I walk down the corridor toward the military compound. The sun drapes like a shawl across my shoulders in the cool spring air. Normally, on a day like this, I'd be in school, working on mathematics, or running down to the lake to fish for *tarekh*. Instead, I am walking toward gunfire and smoke at the front lines of the place I call home.

Some cats scatter from behind an overturned oxcart spilling hay onto the street when I see a face appear. I stop and squint, lifting my hand to shield my eyes against the sun, and see the dark, familiar eyes of Hamza.

He waves me over, and I head into the shadow of the building to meet him behind the oxcart.

"Suren, I heard Levon has come home," he says.

As I crouch, I can see his cut lip and swollen, bruised right eye.

"Yes, he has, but what happened to you?" I ask.

Hamza touches around his eyes as if he forgot part of his face had been smashed. "It's nothing. Just some of the boys in the Shamiram giving me a hard time."

"It looks like it hurts," I remark.

"Only if I touch it. Makes me look tough, yes?" he replies, pouting his lower lip to show me.

"Why did they do this?"

"Because of this," he says, rolling his eyes toward the buildings, the bits of rubble in the streets, the smell and trail of smoke in the air.

"You shouldn't be here."

"And you should?"

"This is my people's fight. Of course I belong here."

Hamza glances around. "Did Levon say anything about Narek? Is he alive?"

I shrug. "I don't know. Every time someone asks him, he seems to go somewhere else in his head, and it can be hard to bring him back."

Running footsteps echo in the street, and we duck down as a group of *fedayi* trot past us. Gunshots sound off in the distance. Some dogs howl somewhere in the city. As the men round the corner, we straighten up.

"I'm surprised everyone is still here," Hamza remarks, wiping the back of his hand against his forehead.

Heat rushes into my cheeks. "Why are you surprised?"

He looks at me. "A few thousand Armenians against the Turkish army seems like poor odds. I thought most had fled east."

I adjust my cap. "Well, when you corner a dog, it will bite back."

Hamza bites at the cut on his lips. The wound reopens, and he sucks at the blood.

Part of me feels relief to know Hamza is OK. Well, mostly OK. But as he looks down the street toward the rising smoke and gently runs his fingers over his prayer beads—his Muslim prayer beads—I see the Turk in him. Dead eyes. Deceiving smile. Silent prayers to Allah to rid Turkey of its Armenian "problem." Just like a Turk to think we could be so easily exterminated.

My jaw tenses as we sit in silence. Hamza turns to me and says, "I'm happy to see you are OK."

I spit to the side. "Maybe you should head back to your quarter with the others. It's safer there."

The words slip out like snakes from the weeds—cold, bitter, and foreign words I've never shared with my best friend. Even during the times when we punched and pinned each other, never did such a tone escape my lips. In his eyes, I see he feels the frigid words too.

"I only want to help. My father would kill me if he knew I was here. You know how he feels about Christians. It's not easy being friends with an Armenian when I am a, a—"

The sparks inside my chest ignite.

"Not easy? You treat me as if I am the problem when it's your people who are slaughtering mine in the desert. Your people sit right outside those city walls with cannons and soldiers trying to destroy our home. To destroy us! You come here like some hero to save me. But I don't need saving from a Turk."

Hamza's mouth hangs slightly open. His dark eyes stare into mine, but I stare back. I won't let him intimidate me. None of them can use fear anymore.

"What happened to you, Suren?"

I stand up, looking down at Hamza for once. "I am a *fedayi* now."

Below me, Hamza rises slowly to his feet. Our faces draw close enough for me to sense the smell of pomegranates on his breath. I clench my fists, expecting a punch or maybe a shove into my chest. But it never comes. His bloodied lip quivers. Out of anger? Out of hurt? I can't tell.

We lock eyes like fighters before I feel his hand lift mine, and he shoves something into my palm.

"You need this more than me, *giaour*," he says.

I hear a small tremor in his voice before he pushes past me, nearly knocking me backward into stacks of wooden crates. I glare at him as he storms off and disappears around the corner. My heart pounds as regret and pride rage inside me.

I feel something rub against my leg: a stray cat. A loud purr hums in the air. Looking down, I open my palm and see Hamza's prayer beads—small, black olive seeds tied together with twine, still warm and stained with his blood.

35

First Mission

I am still thinking about Hamza when I reach military command. The women and children spying from the windows must think I'm insane for talking to myself as I walk.

I knock on the door, and a *fedayi* opens it. I know better than to wait for him to ask who I am, so I stand straight, salute, and say in a stern voice, "I am here to report to Prof—I mean, Aram Manukian."

He startles back a bit and then lets me in. Confusion spreads across his face, so I walk past him before he can ask any questions. The others sit around the large table. Shushi swings her feet just above the ground while Razmik taps his legs with his fingers, scowling as always. Nshan is the first to see me and stands up as I approach.

"Where have you been?" he asks.

"Yeah," Shushi chimes in. "Why did the professor want you to go with him and leave us behind?"

Soon, they all crowd around me. Voices swirl, and their eager eyes pin me against the far wall. I try to speak, but they bombard me with questions until I blurt it out.

"My brother. He's alive!"

The frenzy of questions stops.

"Narek?" Nshan asks.

I shake my head. "Levon."

A slow smile forms on his face, and he falls forward, engulfing me in his arms and squeezing tighter than I imagined little Nshan could. Soon, they all pile in for a stuffy and uplifting embrace. When they finally let go, I brush them off and take a deep breath.

"Do you remember the gendarme we saw in the street? The one we told the professor about? That was Levon. He heard about what the Turks were planning, and when his unit was being sent back to Van, he deserted and snuck his way back into the city."

All their mouths hang open as I speak. When I finish, Nshan asks, "Did he say anything about Narek?"

I shake my head. "I know Narek was much kinder to you than Levon was."

Nshan's lips curl down, and he nods.

"Anyway," Mihran interjects. "We have big news."

"Tell him, Nshan," Razmik urges, landing a thick fist on Nshan's arm. He winces and rubs his bicep as he talks.

"Professor Manukian has assigned the Big Guns as messengers."

"What does that mean?" I ask.

"Military command writes out messages, and we deliver them to the various outposts at the front."

"Really?"

They all nod, eyes on me. The low murmur of voices bustling through the room bounces off the walls and into my ears.

"Does your father know what you've been up to?" Nshan asks.

I nod in a daze. "I told him. No more problems with me being here now."

"Good!"

I glance around the room. *Fedayi* drink and eat from bowls of whatever can be found. I hear one complain about the new food rations. Some have red-stained bandages around arms, legs, and heads, their eyes staring off into nothing. The rifles lie across their laps.

The door flies open and bangs against the wall. Charo and some other *fedayi* stomp into the room toward the map table where we stand.

"Move!" Charo barks, and we scatter.

I crash into Nshan, nearly tumbling onto the dusty floor. The *fedayi* in their dirty uniforms and disheveled hair crowd around the table and slam their weapons onto the wood. Charo always seems upset, but his snarled lips and wrinkled brow make him seem even angrier than usual.

"Sir?" one of the *fedayi* asks. He looks no more than eighteen.

"What?"

"Many of the men fighting at the front of the city have not had food in days."

"You think I don't know that?" Charo snaps. "Look around. Do you see much food here? We've tried to reach Aykesdan to send more, but the Turks are blocking the access road. Until we get those Turkish pigs removed from the key access points, we need to ration what we have."

"But, sir, even with the rations—"

Charo's fists crash onto the table. The weapons and cups rattle and startle everyone.

"You want food?" Charo barks, grabbing one of the rifles from the table and throwing it into the hands of the young *fedayi*. "Go kill the Turks blocking the Tabriz Gate. Dismantle their machine guns. Let the food pour from Aykesdan back into the city. You'll be a hero. I'll personally have a statue made in your honor."

The young *fedayi* stands with the gun in his hands, eyes wide and mouth open. Charo grimaces, and I can now smell the faint odor of sweat, gunpowder, and *oghi* on him. The tense moment fades as the young *fedayi* drops the rifle and looks at his feet.

Charo smirks and then looks around the room a moment before his eyes land on Nshan and me. His fat finger points at us.

"You two. Come here."

We walk over, stumbling over each other. Charo yanks a chair from the table, spins it to face us, and then drops into the seat. His ammunition belt clinks, mixing with his grunts. He reaches into his shirt pocket and removes a folded, stained piece of paper. We look at it without a word.

"Take it!" he shouts. A surge flies through my body, and I snatch it from his hand before Nshan even decides to move.

"Deliver this to the hospital in sector one. Find Melkon Hakamian—he's part of the Red Cross committee—and give him this note. Do *not* read it. The less you know, the better."

"Yes, sir," Nshan replies. He turns to look at the others.

"Uh, sir?" I ask. Charo turns around, facing his broad shoulders back at us.

"What?"

I feel my lips tremble. "Where is the hospital located?"

He points. "Past the mosque. It's the old Isajanian home."

"A home, sir?" I ask before realizing I should have kept it to myself.

"Yes, a home. Understand? This isn't a government-run army here. You're in military command, yes? This was the home of

Prelate Vartabad before the Turks came. So deliver the damn message or I'll find someone else who asks fewer questions."

He never raises his voice, but the stern and terrifying calm in his words makes me want to run out of the building. I shove the note into my trouser pocket and pull Nshan toward the door. Before leaving, I glance back at the others watching us.

I nod to the other members of the Big Guns and then exit the building.

36

A Presence in the Mosque

Outside, the clouds cast a gray haze over the city. Maybe it is smoke from the burning buildings or from the cannons. Nshan walks next to me without a word. Normally, I can't get him to stop talking about the recent tax imposed on us or a deep question about Plato's politics. Today, it's difficult to tell which is gloomier: the sky or my friend.

We pass the dome and spires of Topchu Mosque. Neither of us has ever been inside. Though I have never asked, I doubt my parents would let me or my siblings even enter a place like that. Not even with Hamza, though he attends the mosque to the south near the Shamiram quarter.

I point toward the large dome. "Do you think any Turks are hiding in there?"

Nshan looks up from his feet. "I can't imagine any would be devout enough to pray in the Armenian sector. Or even stick around the Old City right now. I haven't heard a call to prayer in a few days."

The ornate mosque doors line the front of the building behind a row of pillars. Engravings are etched into the dark wood, and one of the doors sits slightly open. I tap Nshan on the shoulder.

"Have you ever been inside?"

He squints at me. "No. Have you?"

I smile.

He looks back at the front of the mosque. "What if someone is in there?"

"You said it yourself. Who is stupid enough to attend prayer in the enemy's territory?"

Nshan smiles back, and it feels as if we are young children again, plotting to steal a pomegranate from Old Man Altan's fruit stand.

We approach the mosque and walk cautiously up the steps. A loud boom echoes in the distance, and we pause, scanning the empty streets. We grab the heavy iron handle and pull the partially opened door, which lets out a long, slow groan. We stop halfway—just enough for our thin bodies to slip through.

Inside, the hall opens into a spacious room. High windows let light flood the area, and long rows of rectangular rugs with Persian patterns line the floor. I take a step in before Nshan whistles at me.

I turn back, and Nshan places his shoes on a long shelf near the door.

"There's no one here, and we're Christian. What does it matter?" I ask. This is not my religion, so I tell myself I can speak loudly, but I whisper despite myself.

"It's still a holy place to someone," he replies, standing in his bare feet on the tiled floor.

This is stupid, but I walk over, remove my shoes, and place them next to Nshan's. With our shoes side by side, I notice how clean the leather is on his shoes while mine reek of dust and age.

Together, we walk across the cool tile until our feet touch the seemingly endless rows of prayer rugs. The room has a faint smell of incense—not fresh, but as if it has settled into the rugs and tiles over centuries. The gray dome curves overhead, upheld by pillars near the front of the hall. I stop in the center, my eyes fixed on the ceiling as Nshan drifts on.

A soft silence rests in this hall. Could it be God? Could God dwell in a Muslim place of worship? Maybe Allah and God are brothers who don't always agree. Maybe one is Turkish and the other Armenian. Like me and Hamza. Muslims and Christians have spent all their time fighting and killing each other. Even now, outside the city walls, their faith and our faith aim guns at one another. So why such peace inside the enemy's temple?

When I look straight again, Nshan stands beside me, gazing up at the tall dome's ceiling as I had been.

"It's not what I thought it would be," I remark.

"What did you expect?"

My eyes scan the room, taking in the line of rugs, the raised wooden platform similar to the one Father Zakarian uses, and the windows lining the walls.

"I don't know. Posters warning parents about evil Armenians who might eat their children?"

Nshan stares back at me, his lips tense as my smile fades.

"Sorry. Bad joke."

I glance down at my bare feet on the soft carpets, and Hamza walks into my mind.

A soft but human sound bursts in the silent hall.

"What was that?" Nshan asks.

"It sounded like a sneeze."

Our eyes meet, and Nshan's eyes reveal what I am just realizing.

"We need to get out of here," I say, pulling Nshan by the arm.

"Wait. Wait."

His eyes are fixed on the raised wooden platform. Slowly, he starts creeping toward the front of the hall.

"Nshan! Where are you going?" I whisper as loudly as I can.

Without looking back, he gestures for me to follow.

"Nshan!"

What is he doing? There could be a gendarme hiding in here. I'm sure he wants to stay hidden and might kill us to save himself. Knowing I can't let Nshan die alone, I follow. By the time I reach him, he is already standing beside the wooden platform. He takes a deep breath and steps forward, searching behind the wide base.

Nshan stops.

"What is it?" I ask.

He looks at me and crouches down, extending his hand toward someone or something hiding under the platform.

"It's OK. We won't hurt you."

I join Nshan and follow his gaze to whoever he is talking to. A young girl huddles close to the side like a frightened animal. Her cheeks are smeared with dust and grime, except for the tracks cleaned by her tears.

She stares at Nshan and me with a blank, terrified expression.

"We are here to help," Nshan repeats, but she doesn't reply.

"Try Turkish," I suggest.

He repeats what he said, and the girl sits up. Her almond-shaped eyes dart back and forth between us and the door leading to the courtyard.

"What is your name?" Nshan asks in Turkish.

Then she jumps up and dashes across the hall, disappearing outside. The wooden door bangs against the hard walls and echoes through the solemn space.

"Should we go after her? She could be a spy," I ask.

Nshan shakes his head as he rises and pushes his glasses back up onto his face.

"Not all victims in this battle are Armenian."

"But she's a Turk," I argue.

He walks toward the door where our shoes sit on the bench. Bending down, he picks up his neat pair.

"Come on. We need to deliver that message."

37

The Hospital

Nshan remains silent as we pass a building where many wealthy people lived. One of the upper windows has been blown out. The stones from the wall sit in piles underneath, surrounded by broken glass.

From home, the fighting seemed distant, but here the blasts from the cannons and artillery sound as if they are around the corner. Every other building is silent and empty, with holes blown through the outer walls, where I can see tables and beds inside one of the bedrooms. No matter where we turn, all I can smell is smoke.

"Where is everyone?" I ask aloud, not expecting an answer from my friend.

"They've probably fled. Ran to other parts of the city or left Turkey altogether, I would guess. I heard my father mention it the other night."

I take a step and hear the clink of metal under my feet. Something pushes against my sole, and when I raise my foot, shiny bullet casings scatter across my path toward the hospital. Strangely, they glint in the bits of sunlight and almost resemble confetti after a celebration. I look up, and Nshan looks down at his feet as well.

Ahead, we see the hospital, though it looks just like another home, except for the word "HOSPITAL" written sloppily in white paint on the front door. Outside, two wooden rocking chairs sit empty, covered in dust.

Nshan pounds on the door, and a ghostly howl emerges from behind the walls. Muffled voices clamor before an older man wearing a bloodstained white shirt stands before us.

"What? Who are you?" he asks, lifting a red-stained kerchief to wipe his sweaty forehead.

For a moment, I forget why we are here until Nshan speaks up.

"We come from military command to deliver a message."

The old man examines us under his bushy eyebrows. His face is covered by a heavy speckled beard, and his hair, or whatever remains of it, sprouts above his head, flying in all directions.

"A message? Who is it for?" A moan comes from behind him. I look past the man in the doorway but see nothing.

"Melkon Hakamian," Nshan informs.

The man extends his hand and flexes his fingers at us. "Hand it to me."

Nshan looks at me, and I shrug. I don't know for sure, but he must be Melkon Hakamian. Reaching into his coat pocket, Nshan slowly pulls out the message, but Melkon snatches it from his fingers.

A man's voice crying out for his mother rises from one of the back rooms, but Melkon seems unfazed as he scans the paper. Are we supposed to wait? Nshan doesn't know either; I can tell. I try to read Melkon's expression, but he is like one of the old stone statues up the hill from long ago.

"Akh!" Melkon suddenly shouts, crumpling the paper in his fist. As he looks over our heads, grumbling under his breath, it seems he just now recalls we are standing in front of him.

"Come inside, and I will write a response back to them," he half invites, half orders. He walks back inside, and we follow up the few steps into the hospital.

A painful smell hits us the moment we step inside. Both of our hands fly up to cover our noses. It reminds me of when a rat died behind the wood stove in the summer, but different—a stench of a different kind of animal.

Aching moans come from the back room—two, as if they are singing the same awful song. Melkon sits at a small table with a large bowl full of kitchen knives, saws, and forceps. Each instrument is littered with blood and bits of what appears to be meat. Clear vials and needles, some empty and others half-filled, are spread across the tabletop.

My eyes fix on the bowl as the moaning song continues in the other room. Melkon mumbles to himself, but I can't hear his words through his thick beard. A woman's voice interrupts.

"It's all right. It will be all right," she repeats in a soft, reassuring voice.

"I don't want to die," the man pleads, half singing in his moaning song.

Nshan stands near the entryway to the back room. The color has drained from his face. I leave the bowl and come to his side.

I see several beds—three or four—and each bed holds a body.

A woman wearing a bloody apron attends to the man singing and crying about not wanting to die. Other men lie still, and I fixate on their chests, waiting to see if they rise. Are they alive?

Dead? One has his eyes wrapped in cloth, blotches of blood where his eyes should be. Another has a red bandage covering his elbow where his forearm used to be. The smell from before intensifies, and one injured *fedayi* in the back bed has black flies buzzing around his swollen leg.

A hand lands on my shoulder, and I jump. I turn around, heart racing, and Melkon looks down at us.

"Not used to this much blood?" he asks.

The color still hasn't returned to Nshan's face, and I wonder if he will faint. Saliva fills my mouth, and the threat of being sick hits me, but I take a deep breath through my mouth.

"No, sir. Not like this."

He grunts. "This is what happens when men fight one another. Not boys."

Nshan starts to sway, and Melkon grabs him by the shoulder.

"Here," he says, handing Nshan a folded note. "Take this and go sit down before I have another patient on my hands."

With the note in his fist, my friend stumbles to the chair against the wall and collapses, leaning forward on his knees.

The woman sits by the frightened *fedayi* and holds his hand. He's no longer moaning or expressing his fear of death. Instead, he lies with his eyes on the ceiling, listening to the nurse hum a gentle melody.

Melkon pats my shoulder and then heads toward the beds, checking on the motionless figures. How could one human do this to another? But I know the Turks view us as nothing more than rodents—a pest in need of extermination.

I think these things as I watch the wounded *fedayi* and hear the nurse's haunting songs. The more I listen, the more I feel fire rising in my bones, flowing through my veins, pooling in my fists. Even when my mind returns to the terrified Turkish girl in the mosque, I feel only burning heat.

As if on cue, the hospital building rattles as more cannon fire falls on my people, and the wounded soldiers' moaning begins again. Dust floats down from the ceiling, caught in the sunlight from the open windows. Above a wounded man's bed, I see faces looking out from a frame—a family, stoic and observing how their home has become either a hospital or a cemetery.

May 4, 1915
The Tabriz Gate

38

The Gift of Time

"I dreamed last night that a Turk tried to break into our home."

Levon looks up from his meal at me.

"Did you shoot him?" he asks.

I take a bite of my scant meal and chew before answering. "Yes."

"How did it feel?"

I pause and chew for a moment. "I don't know."

Levon's stare digs deep into me—so deep I can feel it in my chest. The only sound is the chewing between us.

For once, I wish Taline or Ani were home to help with him. Most nights, he wakes up screaming, and I try to calm him down. Twice, he wrapped his hands around my throat until he realized it was me. One night, I awoke to see him standing at the open window, staring into the darkness. Even when I called his name, he didn't answer and simply stared outside, as if he saw something I couldn't see.

The front door opens, and Baba walks in. He comes over, takes a piece of lavash, then looks at me.

"Are you ready? We need to go."

"Yes, sir," I reply, shoving the last of my food into my mouth. I respond this way so often I sometimes say it to Mama without thinking. Levon doesn't move and stares ahead as I head toward the front door.

Baba pauses, looking at his eldest son. His lips part as if he wants to say something to Levon, but after a moment, he closes them and turns to me.

"Have you seen your sisters?" he mutters.

"No, sir. Not this morning anyway."

"Finish your food, and then we need to leave," he says, and I stand up to follow him out the door. As I pass Levon, his hand springs out and grasps my arm, squeezing tight. I look down at him, and his dark eyes stare back. He pulls me lower, causing me to hunch awkwardly, and whispers, "You can never take it back. Once it's gone, it's gone forever."

I don't know how to respond. His eyes drift from me, and his grip lightens enough for me to slip my arm away. I watch him for a moment before placing my bowl in the kitchen and leaving.

Outside, the spring air has warmed over the last few days. Like on most days, a lingering smell of smoke hangs over the city from the fires set by both *fedayi* and Turkish gendarmes. The other night, I awoke to see light illuminating the open window. I rose from my bed and walked to the window to see the orange glow of burning buildings in the distance. The flames danced across the city, consuming homes and stores I had known my entire life. Still, there was a strange, captivating beauty to it all.

"Any news from the different sectors?" I ask Baba.

He shakes his head. "Many men and women have been wounded from the bombings."

"Is Uncle Tarzi one of them?"

"I don't think so. Even if your uncle were wounded, he'd still be cursing the Turks with a gun in one hand and the other in a sling."

I have to laugh because the truth can be humorous sometimes.

"So you are a messenger now?" His voice lilts as he asks.

"Yes. Usually, Nshan and I go together to deliver messages to Melkon at the hospital."

"That is important work. Just be careful. The Tabriz Gate is a dangerous place right now."

I never told Baba about my first visit to the hospital. I also never told him that the next day, that same bed was filled with another wounded man.

"Yes, sir."

We turn the corner on our route to military command. Unlike when the fighting first started, the cannon and artillery fire have become louder. When men shouted in the streets, it felt like a distant dream, but now their words are clear.

Without warning, Baba stops and rubs his chin.

"What is it?" I ask. "Are you hurt?"

Baba looks at me with a stern face. "Listen, Suren *jan*. The fighting is getting closer. There were never strong odds in our favor against the might of the Ottoman military. But I want you to listen. If the fighting reaches our home, I want you to take your brother, your sisters, and your mother to the Americans. The Turks would never attack an American building. You'll be safe there."

"But you'll be there too, right?" I ask.

Baba sighs, and his eyes look at me as if he is wrestling with what he wants to say and what he should.

He searches in his coat pocket and pulls out my grandfather's watch. Holding it by the chain, Baba examines it and then extends it toward me.

"That's grandfather's watch," I reply.

"I know," he says, taking my hand and placing the watch in my palm.

"I, I can't take this."

Placing his other hand atop mine, he answers, "I haven't been able to give you much in this world. Consequences of a barber's salary, I suppose. But what I do know is that I can give you one thing, and that is time."

Why does he say this to me? Nothing will happen to him. He's a Simonian, just like me. It's a miracle Levon returned to us, and I'm sure Narek will also. God protects those He loves, just as Father Zakarian tells us at mass. But in Baba's eyes, maybe he has forgotten this important truth.

I take the watch and examine the clock face. How many times have I seen Baba clean it? I look up into my father's face and say nothing. All I can do is nod.

We don't speak much during the rest of the walk, and when we reach the entrance to military command, several *fedayi* gather around, smoking and chatting among themselves. I can tell from the way their heads hang that something has happened. To the side, some young children, maybe eight or nine, bring heavy bags in their hands and dump the contents into buckets.

Baba stops close to the men and asks, "What is all this? Why are you standing around out here?"

An older *fedayi* with a rifle slung over his shoulder replies, "The Turks have pushed past the Tabriz Gate, but we've held them.

The hospital had to be moved further into the city, but as some of us were moving the wounded, one of their shells struck the outside of the home. One of the wounded men did not make it."

Baba nods gravely. "I'm sorry to hear that."

A younger man beside the older one blows out some smoke and then says, "The good news is we killed two Turks."

The older *fedayi* turns his head to the younger. "There is no good news in this."

At this, the younger *fedayi* says nothing and turns away, dawdling over to some other groups.

The older *fedayi* continues, "As expected, we are running out of bullets. Luckily, the children are helping with that."

He points with his chin at the barrels by the house. I walk over and see hundreds of misshapen bullets without their shells. Bits of dirt and dust litter the bucket.

"But these bullets have already been shot," I remark.

"The blacksmiths melt them down and put them in old shells so we can reuse them. Unlike our enemy, we don't have an endless supply from the government," the older *fedayi* replies. "The real problem is finding gunpowder."

Baba smiles. "The federation is full of surprises."

Among the bustle of the loitering *fedayi*, the door opens, and a voice yells out, "Messengers! Messengers!"

Without a word, I push my way through the bodies toward the entrance and enter military command. Inside, it is not as crowded, but bodies still walk from room to room. At the table, Professor Manukian and Charo stand around the maps. From somewhere inside, Nshan, Razmik, Mihran, and Shushi all arrive at once. As I approach, I catch a little of what the two are discussing.

". . . is getting low, and the refugees from the outer villages keep pouring in. How can we feed them? Not to mention trying to keep order from those criminals stealing weapons from other

Armenians and looting abandoned homes. We don't have a proper judicial system to—"

"Let me take care of the looters," Charo answers. "What do we do about sector 1?"

Before Professor Manukian answers, he sees us and straightens from hunching over the table.

"Good. You're here. There's been a change of plans. All of you are to take this message to the new hospital and to those stationed near the Tabriz Gate."

"The Tabriz Gate?" Mihran asks.

"That's what I said. Deliver it to those stationed in the tower."

We all salute, and the professor hands Nshan the messages. As instructed, he folds the letter three times and slips it into his pocket.

The professor's eyes narrow, and he looks into each of our faces with a seriousness that paralyzes us.

"This is important. These *must* be delivered. If one of you fails to do it, then another must get the message delivered. At all costs."

I swallow, and the lump in my throat feels like it's choking me. Is he telling us this because he thinks we have a chance of . . . dying? He finally breaks his stare and turns back to the maps.

"Dismissed," he says and then continues to discuss issues with Charo.

Without a word, the Big Guns file out of the room, across the hall, and into the streets. Among the many faces lingering outside, I don't see Baba, and a haunting regret fills me. I reach into my trouser pocket and hold the watch.

I never told him goodbye, and I wonder if I'll ever get the chance again.

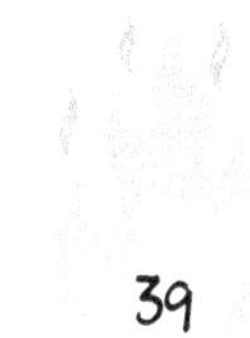

39

The New Nurse

Once we pass the noise of military command, Mihran is the first to break the silence.

"Is anyone else confused? Why is Aram sending us to the Tabriz Gate if the Turks have broken through and are in the city?"

Razmik chimes in. "Don't worry. If any Turks come, I will hold them off and you can run away."

Shushi rolls her eyes and scoffs. "How are you going to fight off the whole army, Razmik?"

"Why are you so annoying?" he snaps. It's difficult to tell if these little spats they get into are because they like or hate each other.

"If Professor Manukian is asking us to deliver these messages to dangerous places, they must be vital to the fight," Nshan says. "We should be honored that he trusts the Big Guns with such an important mission."

A collective groan rises from everyone.

"Oh, come on. I thought you all agreed on that name."

"You did, Governor Nshan," Shushi replies. A few days ago, she jokingly gave him that nickname. Even though she mocks him, I think he secretly likes it.

"Anyway, these messages are important, and it is our duty to deliver them."

"Can't *Ashkhadank* just print the messages?" Mihran asks.

"Put them in the newspaper? If a Turk sneaks in and finds a copy, what then?" Nshan answers.

Mihran drops his head, keeping his eyes on his shoes.

"He said to deliver it at all costs. I just wonder what those costs might be," I say to anyone willing to listen.

We continue on in silence. The cats who normally frequent this part of the city no longer meow in the streets or lounge on doorsteps. For now, the streets feel still and eerie.

We pass the Topchu Mosque, and Nshan avoids looking at it. However, I can't turn away, and the little girl with soft eyes comes back to me. She could have been a spy. Why wouldn't the Turks use children to succeed, even if it meant harm to them? The Tabriz Gate fell shortly after. She might have had something to do with it.

The new hospital sits a few buildings down from the mosque. Paint drips down the edges of the letters "HOSPITAL" on the front door. Even from outside, the bustle of movement and voices can be heard. Nshan and I approach the door. It feels disrespectful not to knock, but Melkon told us several times to just come in.

"It's best to wait out here. Sometimes Melkon gets cranky with too many visitors in his hospital," I tell the others.

Razmik folds his arms, eyeing me as if he wants to rearrange my face. Mihran nods, rubbing his hands together and glancing around while Shushi throws her hands up in the air and mutters what sounds like curses under her breath.

"It won't take long," Nshan assures.

We both pause for a moment and turn back.

"Mihran, make sure they don't kill each other," Nshan orders, pointing at Shushi and Raz.

He shrugs. "You're on your own."

Inside, the large living area is filled with wounded *fedayi*, more than during our other visits. A strange odor of alcohol and blood hangs in the air. Some men cry out in high voices as a nurse wraps a tourniquet on someone's leg. I see Melkon's back as he holds forceps and digs into the abdomen of an unconscious, shirtless soldier on the bed. A half bottle of vodka sits on an end table with bloody rags.

I lean over to Nshan. "Should we wait?"

"Let's give him a minute."

The *fedayi*'s hair lies flat against his wet forehead. His eyes are closed, and sweat drenches his pillow. Melkon removes the forceps from the *fedayi*'s side, lifts a small piece of metal with them, examines it, and then places it on the bedside table.

He looks at the nurse across from him and says something. Without hesitation, she begins to bandage the wounded man as Melkon straightens.

"Sir," Nshan says, raising his voice just enough.

From the corner of his eye, Melkon sees us and approaches, his hands red and sticky as he calls for the message. Nshan pulls the paper from his pocket and places it in Melkon's wet hand. With a sigh, he walks over to a chair, eases himself into it, unfolds the paper, and begins to read the message.

As we wait, I survey the new building and the many wounded *fedayi*. Some lie in beds, more severely injured, while others sit in wooden chairs, clutching an arm or resting their wrapped heads against the stone wall. Near the back, a figure lies under a white sheet.

Across the room, I see a young nurse tending to a *fedayi* in one of the beds. Something about her looks familiar—the way she brushes at her cheek even though there is nothing there. I walk a little closer to try and see her face. Maybe I can recognize her. From school, perhaps? As if she senses my presence, the nurse looks up, and I see her dark, stern eyes lock with mine.

"Taline?"

She rarely smiles, and I can't tell if she is surprised, annoyed, or some combination of both. She finishes mending the wounded *fedayi*'s bandage, stands, and walks toward me, weaving between beds. I recognize her dress as the one Mama sewed for her last summer. At her wrists, the white chemise is stained with dried blood.

Before she reaches me, I whisper, "What are you doing here?"

"Oh, so just because you're a man means you can help, but a woman can't?" she snaps, folding the ends of her sleeves up her arm.

"That's not what I meant. It's dangerous. The other hospital was bombed, and the Turks have taken over the Tabriz Gate."

She folds her arms across her chest. "I can't do much sitting at home. Levon scares me, and Ani disappears without anyone knowing what she is doing. Mama weeps and prays all day. I needed a purpose. You said so yourself: We might as well fight if we are not going to leave."

For someone who always follows the rules, seeing Taline sneak away from home and fight in the resistance feels like a dream. I glance around as if Baba or Mama might show up in the doorway.

"Does Baba know you're here?"

She shrugs. "No, and you can't tell him. His thoughts on women fighting come from the old way of things. He'd never understand."

"He might."

She gives me a typical Taline glare.

"Does Mama?"

"Maybe. I don't know if she cares as much."

"How long have you been sneaking out?"

"Two days."

"Baba was asking where you and Ani were. He could show up here if the command sends him. What if Aunt Yeva sees you?"

"Who do you think recruited me?" she smirks.

We both share a laugh. A comforting warmth covers my skin, being able to share something other than arguments with Taline.

She steps closer and grabs my shoulders like she did when I was smaller. "Suren *jan*, don't worry about me. I'm older than you, remember?"

For the first time in many years, I see Taline. All of the fights and arguments and mean glares. Those times when she ordered me around and criticized everything I did or said. Maybe I misunderstood her. Maybe we misunderstood each other.

Without hesitation, I spring forward and wrap my arms around her, holding her tight. Her arms stick out awkwardly at first. Then she slowly puts her arms around my back and squeezes. Her thick hair tickles my nose, but I don't rub it away.

"Suren," Nshan calls from across the room.

I turn around, and Nshan waves the folded message from Melkon.

"Time to go," I say to my sister.

"Good. I need to get back to work anyway," she remarks with a smile so slight it lifts the corners of her lips, but I am still not convinced she is really smiling.

I smile back anyway and join Nshan.

"Suren," she calls after me.

I turn around, and she points a finger at me that looks just like Mama's.

"Don't do anything stupid."

40

At the Gate

The smoky air feels fresh and cleanses my lungs after the burn of alcohol in the hospital.

Taline, a nurse? The idea makes me laugh inside. I have compassion for the wounded *fedayi* she will care for. If anyone can insult someone while caring for them, it will be my sister. It's strange I don't see Ani, though. I know she has been sneaking out to meet her fiancé. Well, who she wishes was her fiancé, but he hasn't talked with Baba yet. Maybe she's aiding the resistance in some way, but I can't imagine her with a gun or knife. I hope she is safe.

Outside, Mihran and Razmik sit on the steps as Shushi holds a handful of small rocks and throws them at a piece of wood.

Nshan checks his pockets for the message. Reassured, he pats it gently.

"Part one accomplished," he says.

"Finally!" Shushi blurts out, throwing her handful of stones at once.

The boys stand, and we all face each other. Our eyes look to one another in an uncertain game of who will take the first step.

"Well, on to the Tabriz Gate," Mihran states in a shaky voice. Nobody makes a move. A breeze whisks through the streets, blowing dust into the air. Shushi stares at us for a moment.

"Let's go, boys!" she barks, then turns on her heel, walking east toward the not-so-distant crack of rifles.

We look at one another. We could never let a girl lead us on our mission. If we all survive this, no one would let us forget it. Mihran shrugs and mouths an apology to us.

"Don't apologize for your crazy sister," Razmik says.

Mihran nods, and, one foot after the other, we march toward the one part of the city from which we may never return.

Not much is spoken between us as we walk through the empty streets. Above us, the roofs of several buildings have been blown into rubble, which litters parts of the street. Chunks of stone and bits of wood make it challenging to walk without twisting an ankle or tripping. No cats. No birds. No voices of any kind until we hear a voice call down from one of the open windows.

"Stop!"

We all freeze and look up. A *fedayi* leans on the windowsill with his rifle aimed at us.

"What are you doing here? There's a war going on."

"Stop that! We have an important mission."

All of us hiss at Shushi.

Nshan adjusts his glasses and holds up his hands. "We have an assignment from military command. We are messengers."

The *fedayi* screws up his face. He calls back to someone in the room and has a quick conversation before returning to us.

"Who is the message for?"

"Those in the tower at the Tabriz Gate."

The *fedayi* cocks his head at us as if we're not in our right minds. Then he says something to the person behind him. Soon, another face appears in the window, wearing the same bewildered expression.

"Military command sent you?" the other *fedayi* asks.

"Yes," several of us reply.

"You are just children," one remarks.

"That's right. We are the Big Guns!" Shushi shouts. A collective cringe spreads through all of us, except for Nshan, who I'm sure is beaming with pride behind his glasses.

The two *fedayi* glance at each other, more confused than impressed.

"The big what?" the other calls out.

"Nothing! Never mind!" Mihran interjects.

Shushi glares at Nshan. "I told you. We should have gone with 'Night Rats.'"

The two *fedayi* exchange a look and whisper before returning their attention to us.

"May God be with you."

We wait for them to say something else—maybe more information or a warning. It is such a strange way to end a conversation with teenagers. God is always with us, so even with the Turks moving closer, why would He abandon us now? I look back at the *fedayi* in the upper window as they watch us head down the street.

The morning sun's shadows fade as noon approaches. Razmik pulls at his collar and grumbles about the heat; he is always hot. Even in winter, he must be sweating.

"There it is," Shushi says, motioning to a taller building—not much taller, but the closest thing to a tower in this part of the Old City. I sense Mihran tense up beside me. I place a gentle hand on his shoulder.

"It will be OK," I assure him, but inside, I don't fully believe my own words. Does that make me a liar?

We continue on, passing an abandoned pottery shop. Aside from a few bowls, most pieces have been shattered, possibly by looters or cannon blasts. Even in the street, the broken shards push into the soles of my feet, and I can feel every fragment crunch with each step. So many beautiful things are now broken and scattered.

We cut through an alley toward the tower, which leads us right near the building.

"What if we run into Turkish soldiers?" Mihran asks, pulling at Nshan's shirt.

"They haven't made it this far," he replies.

"They said the Tabriz Gate had fallen. They could be in the tower for all we know. How do you know?"

Nshan doesn't answer and twists his body out of Mihran's grasp.

As we turn the corner at the end of the alley, we see two figures standing in front of the door. My heart jumps until we see their friendly uniforms. One leans slightly against the stone wall while the other sits with his head hanging between his bent knees, taking drags from a cigarette. A few rifle shots rattle off, followed by shouting, but the *fedayi* don't move.

Mihran is nearly on my back, and his fingernails dig into my shoulder.

"Would you stop it?"

"Sorry," he apologizes.

"Don't walk too fast. We don't want to scare them," Nshan advises, then looks directly at Shushi. She rolls her eyes in response.

One by one, we walk out from the alley toward the *fedayi*. The standing one, the younger one, lifts his head and sees us. He raises his rifle and slams the butt into his shoulder, the barrel aimed at us.

"Stop right there!"

The other *fedayi* raises his head. His mustache is so full and bushy that you can't see his mouth. He doesn't jump to his feet or move. He simply stares.

We raise our hands as the young *fedayi* takes cautious steps toward us. I can see that his uniform is dusty and possibly stained with blood. Was it Armenian or Turkish blood?

"We are messengers," Nshan says in Armenian, hands raised. It sounds like he is rehearsing a play when angels visit shepherds to announce the birth of Jesus.

"Are you the new ones?" the older *fedayi* asks, still sitting and smoking.

"New ones?" Mihran gulps.

"Yes," Nshan the Governor replies.

The *fedayi* pointing the rifle at us looks to the other, waiting.

With a groan, the other gets to his feet, cracks his back, and strolls over toward the younger *fedayi*. With a slow hand, he places it on the gun's barrel and pushes it down.

"I assume you have a message for me?" he asks.

Nshan, hands still raised, says, "Military command said I am to give it to those fighting in the tower."

The *fedayi* takes the last drag from his cigarette and flicks it into the dust. "You found them. Except for Payel, who is doing reconnaissance. Let's go inside, and then you can decide if you can trust me with the message," he says, slinging his rifle over his shoulder, then walks toward the door.

With no other options, we follow Nshan into the tower.

41

The Tower

Inside, the room resembles other homes converted into military posts. The tables have empty bottles, overturned cups, and a bowl overflowing with cigarette ashes. Even in desperate times, while the dry taste of lavash worsens, there is never a shortage of *oghi* and cigarettes.

A loud boom blasts outside, causing the walls to shake. Bits of stone and dust trickle from the ceiling and rattle the dirty plates stacked on the floor. The older *fedayi* turns and watches us, inspecting our reactions. A loud gasp comes from one of the others near the doorway—my guess is Mihran. Though I can feel my legs tremble, I keep a stern face.

From one of the back rooms, another *fedayi* emerges, drying his hands with an old shirt.

"Mardik, who are they?" he asks, pointing at us with his chin. His face is youthful but not like Levon's or Narek's.

"Messengers," the other replies.

"New ones?"

"What happened to the old ones?" Mihran asks from the back, but the *fedayi* don't seem to notice.

The older *fedayi* nods. The young *fedayi* approaches us with his hand outstretched and shakes our hands. His palm is still damp. He looks over our heads at Shushi, Mihran, and Razmik near the door.

"Are they with you?" he asks.

"Yes," Nshan answers, and I pray to God, if He is still listening, that Nshan won't mention our nickname.

"Excellent!" he exclaims and walks over to the others.

"You two. Come with me," the older *fedayi*, Mardik I assume, says to us. "Hovhannes, make sure these others are comfortable."

Hovhannes, just like the famous writer, salutes and ushers the others toward a table where several flies buzz around some old food.

We follow Mardik up the stairwell as it winds around the corner. A cold draft blows down the stone steps, cooling the sweat at my temples. As we reach the landing, I expect to see more light, but the room is as dark as the stairwell. My eyes adjust, and I can make out a bed with no blankets against the far wall, along with two wooden chairs near a window. An old rug hangs over the opening. The smell of cigarettes and dust lingers in the stuffy room, along with the faint, sour stench of urine from a cistern in the corner. Above the bed, the floor of an old oxcart props against the wall where chunks of stone have been blown away.

Mardik walks to the window, sits in one of the chairs, and lifts an edge of the rug to look outside. He lets the rug fall back into place and gestures for us to join him.

Shafts of sunlight filter through the edges, illuminating the dark rug's border. Nshan takes the other wooden chair, and I lean against a desk pushed close to the wall. When I place my hands on the wood, a sharp pain stabs my palm. I lift my hand and see a small splinter embedded under my skin, and I look down at the desktop.

A long, pale line slices up the surface like a stone skipping across a lake. I follow the trail, which angles toward the wall, and see a hole etched into the stone—the size of a bullet. As if on cue, another blast shakes the building. Up here, it feels like the bomb landed in the bed next to Mardik.

"They are closer now. Before, it was just a few bullets, but now that they've breached the Tabriz Gate, they must have rolled the cannons into the city. Come, have a look."

He lifts the rug just enough to look through with one eye. Nshan hunches over, holding the side of his spectacles with one hand. Mardik watches Nshan with a similarly examining look. After a moment, Nshan leans back, and I walk forward.

Without thinking, I start to pull back the edge of the rug before I feel a slap on my wrist. Mardik eyes me with a serious, disapproving stare.

"Do not open that further unless you want a bullet in your eye."

A knot forms in my throat and sinks to my gut. I nod and, with a dose of extra fear, sneak my eye through the crack. The fresh air outside, still tinged with smoke, cools my face.

From up here, the view extends out to the city walls. Mount Ararat rises in the distance. My eyes scan the skeletons of other buildings still black and smoking from fires.

"The Turks burned our homes?" I ask.

"Yes and no," Mardik replies. "When we can no longer hold a key position, we burn it down. If we can't have it, neither can they. See those over there? We burned those spots so the Turks couldn't have them."

Farther on, across the wall, Turkish cannons line the trenches. Poking up like ground squirrels, the heads of Turkish soldiers dot the horizon. I imagine if I had a rifle, I could shoot the hat off each head like targets at a fair. But I've never shot a gun before. I try to count the soldiers I can see, but I lose track.

"There are so many."

"And more within the city walls," Mardik adds. "Ready to hunt Armenians down. It makes sense that the national animal of the Turks is the wolf."

My eyes lift to the white summit of our Holy Mountain. Noah's ark is said to have landed on its slopes, but my mind returns to Artavazd—the prisoner locked inside the mountain, waiting for his chance at revenge. I imagine the top of the mountain bursting open, Artavazd rising with his sword in hand like a giant dragon, descending on those hiding in the trenches and devouring them.

Mardik releases the edge of the rug, and my view disappears. He clears his throat as I stand up. "How about that message?"

The room goes dark again, and Nshan pulls out the message from his pocket. He hands it to Mardik, who takes it without haste and slowly unfolds the paper. His relaxed black eyes scan the words, then he refolds the message and sets it on his lap. He stares at the rug hanging in the window as if he can somehow see through it.

"Is there a message you want us to bring back?" Nshan asks.

Mardik shakes his head. "No need. We are to burn this tower and retreat."

42

The Last Song

The loud stomp of footsteps carries up the stairwell, and Mardik sits up in his chair. At the landing, I expect to see one of the *fedayi* from downstairs, but instead, I see the thin figure of Mihran. I can hear his shaky voice echoing through the room.

"Come quick! One of the *fedayi* is out in the street."

Before I can register Mihran's words, Mardik jumps to his feet, lifts the rug's edge, mutters something under his breath, and shoots past us.

"Stay here!" he orders and disappears down the stairs. Mihran watches him and then steps into the shadowy room with us.

"What's going on?" Nshan asks.

It takes Mihran a moment to catch his breath. "I don't know. Hovhannes was sitting with us, looking out the windows, talking about a poem he was writing for Armenia. Then he stopped, looked out the window, stood up, and ran outside. We tried to call after him, but he said something about a child."

More footsteps can be heard in the stairwell as Razmik and Shushi come into view.

"He's off to fight!" Razmik shouts.

"I don't think so, Raz," I remark.

"He said something about a girl," Shushi says. "But honestly, she can probably take care of herself."

Nshan points toward the window. "Maybe we can see what's going on."

All of us crouch around the dusty rug hanging in the window. Our bodies cram together, and I can smell Mihran's stinky feet and Raz's bad breath. And smoke? Have they been smoking downstairs?

Shushi grabs the rug and begins to roll it up, but I slap her hands. She punches my arm in response. "The Turks can see us," I say. "Do you want to get shot?"

The sunlight shines through the crack right on her face, and I sec her eyes—not the defiant eyes she usually shows but the wide, frightened eyes of a little girl. Though I feel the same fear as is in her eyes, I swallow hard and reach out for her hand.

"It will be all right," I assure her.

Through the cracks, I can see the street below among the damaged homes.

"There! Look!" Mihran shouts, pointing at something in the street.

Below us, we see Hovhannes. With his rifle slung over his shoulder, his tense face focuses on something we cannot see—something behind a pile of rubble, wood, and stone.

"Why doesn't he have his rifle ready?" Razmik asks.

No one answers.

"What is he looking at?" Shushi asks, leaning into me enough almost to push me over.

The muffled voice of Mardik comes from behind us, yelling something at Hovhannes, who keeps looking back as if he is being pulled both ways. From up here, he looks younger than he did downstairs.

Mardik keeps yelling, but Hovhannes crouches down next to the wall and holds his hands out, gesturing as if calling for a dog. None of us speaks. I don't know if any of us are breathing either. The room simmers in silence, and the heat of our bodies makes the moment feel like we are on the street with him.

Hovhannes keeps coaxing toward the pile of rubble until a shape comes into view. Not much, but enough for us to see a small girl poke her head out. My heart thumps against my bones.

"Nshan," I whisper.

When he turns to me, I point toward the rubble. He squints, holding the side of his glasses. His mouth drops open, and our eyes connect. Her face, cowering behind the wooden platform on the prayer rugs, returns to me like an old dream.

Mardik's voice fights against the reassuring words of Hovhannes, still crouching and beckoning. The girl seems to creep forward a step and then retreat back to the rubble. Back and forth, back and forth, like a cautious cat accepting food from a stranger. Two steps forward, one step back. It takes an eternity before she leaves the rubble and stands exposed in the street—a small figure among broken stones, shattered wood, and ash.

Mardik must have changed positions, because his words are clearer.

"Hovhannes, get back. That's an order!" he commands. His voice sounds strained and anxious. The young *fedayi* no longer looks back but leans forward like a runner getting ready for a race.

"Don't do it," Mihran whispers to himself.

I take a quick glance at the city and the wall. Do the Turks hear this? I think I see dark shapes maneuvering between buildings on the street or darting across the rooftops. Did a soldier just stand near the trenches? I can't be certain. I bite my tongue to suppress the urge to call out to the men on the street.

The others gasp, and my eyes fly back to Hovhannes and the girl. He's abandoned the safety of the wall and is running exposed in the street toward the girl, who freezes. In one motion, he scoops her into his arms and turns, shuffling back toward the tower with the girl clutched against his chest.

But then he stops.

A single rifle shot cries across the city, echoing off stone, walls, and bone. Hovhannes arches his back as if poked with a stick, but he still holds the girl, falling to his knees. The girl's scream mixes with Mardik's shouts as she jumps from Hovhannes's arms and runs off down an alley, disappearing once again.

"Damn it, don't move. We'll get help. Just hold on," Mardik assures.

From his knees, Hovhannes leans and falls like a felled tree onto his side. In the dirt, a dark pool mixes with the dust of the street as he lifts his shaky hand to the sky.

"Stay still," Mardik orders.

The young *fedayi* reaches down and touches the blood spreading on his chest. He stares at his red fingers, trembling.

Then we hear his voice—a song. The words carry on the breeze that has returned and drown out the cries of victory from the trenches. I try to find where the shot came from, but can I trust my eyes?

Armenian youths, move soon.
Never fear, wave your swords.
The hour of holy freedom has come.
It's not time to live, walk away soon.
Let's love unity, let's not do bad things.
Let us, Armenians, have sacred freedom.

As the final words leave Hovhannes, his raised fist drops and lands at his side, bouncing off the ground. The dust around him turns to dark, bloody mud, reminding me of the prayer rugs from the mosque. From the window, the peak of Ararat, our Holy Mountain, rises above, looking down, as silent as we are.

Where is Artavazd?

More importantly, where is God?

43

The Body

"Is he dead?" Shushi asks.

No one answers for a moment, but then Nshan whispers, "I think so."

Mihran stands and walks to the back of the room, facing the far wall. I look at Nshan, and he looks back at me with his mouth hanging open. Shushi squeezes my arm. Perhaps she was squeezing it the entire time, but I never felt it. Razmik, fists balled, punches the hanging rug, causing it to flap in the window frame.

"Why did he try to save that girl? Such a stupid thing to do," he growls, and his big frame stands, pushing back on the wooden chair so hard that it crashes onto the floor.

Shushi leaves and joins her brother, and I hear them whispering behind me. But Nshan and I keep our eyes fixed on the body in the street.

"Why don't they check on him? He could still be alive," I say aloud.

"It's too dangerous," Nshan replies.

The body doesn't look dead. I don't know what I imagined a lifeless corpse to be, but Hovhannes, lying peacefully on his side, is not what I pictured.

"Nshan," I whisper.

He shakes his head.

"It was her."

"I know," he replies, keeping his eyes on the body.

"If we had—" I begin before Nshan's hand flies out and covers my mouth. His round, stunned eyes look at me through the smears on his lenses.

"We don't know that."

I want to bite my lip, but my guilt bubbles up and out of my throat. I push his hand down. "We could have taken her somewhere. Got rid of her somehow."

"Suren, she's just a little girl."

"But Hovhannes would still be alive."

Nshan removes his glasses and rubs his eyes. "We don't know that. He made a choice, and it was the wrong one."

Outside, some voices seem to be arguing before I see Mardik and the other *fedayi* run over to the body. Each grabs a leg, and together they drag Hovhannes back toward the building. The weight of his body leaves a dark trail in the dust.

Downstairs, I hear Mardik giving orders, grunting, and the sound of items being thrown around. We all look toward the stairwell and, one by one, descend the steps. I am third behind Raz and Shushi when I come around the corner. Mardik leans over the dirty body of Hovhannes laid out across a long wooden table, one arm hanging off the edge.

The other *fedayi* sits in a chair near the window with his head in his hands. He may be crying, but I can't tell. Mardik doesn't react to us as we enter the room. No one wants to get too close to the body, so we linger a couple of meters away.

For some reason, I take short steps toward the table. The others try to pull me back, but I keep moving forward. The still, lifeless face, the eyes that seem to have lost their color, look back at me. It's strange to see a face with no soul—no twitch or blink. The cheeks are deflated, and hollow eyes stare at me, gazing at nothing.

Mardik leans on the table, looking at his comrade as if he believes he can will him back to life. Maybe he is praying. But seeing Hovhannes's still face and blood-soaked clothes, I doubt even God could bring him back.

In a way, I feel like I'm watching this body on the table from outside myself. I wonder if Mardik feels the same. The face begins to morph and change, the features shifting slightly until it no longer belongs to the *fedayi* I hardly knew. Now, on the table before me, I see the lifeless face of Narek.

Watching myself from outside my body, I see my face turn green. My mouth floods with saliva, and a wave hits me like a punch in the gut. I sprint from the room, pushing past the others and into the street.

Just as I think the nausea may pass, I empty my stomach into the dust.

A Bitter Conversation

Silence accompanies us on the way back to military command. What words are there? What good could come from them? Even when we pass the Topchu Mosque, Nshan won't look at me.

After we deliver Mardik's message to the professor and inform the command about Hovhannes, the room falls silent. Even Charo doesn't curse the Turks for what they've done. Though it is only the afternoon, the professor tells us to go home and be with our families. Mihran and Shushi just look at each other. They have only each other and a home shared with dozens of orphans to return to.

As we step outside, some young boys hand out repurposed bullets to *fedayi* returning from the front to reload.

We stand around, unable to speak about what we just witnessed. As the silence builds, Nshan blurts out, "See you tomorrow," then walks north, with Raz following.

Mihran, Shushi, and I stand a few meters away from the haggard *fedayi* at the barrels of bullets. In each face, the hope I saw in their eyes earlier seems muted, but there's still a fire I can't quite describe. Nothing they say shows me this, but it's something I can feel.

"Should we go back to the orphanage?" Mihran asks.

"I hate it there," Shushi snaps, crossing her arms and staring away from us.

"The Turks won't attack anything to do with the Americans. It will probably be safer there," I say.

Shushi spits. "I still hate it there."

I consider heading home, but pause.

"Come to my home," I offer, wondering if Levon will be in one of his moods.

Mihran cocks his head. "Are you sure?"

I nod and then look at his sister. "How about that, Shushi?"

She sticks her chin up as if thinking it over. Then she says quietly, "I guess so."

Though her stubbornness annoys me, I find something I like about her.

We walk back along the streets toward home. Mihran talks and talks, but I don't really hear him. I respond with grunts and nods, but my mind is back in the tower, replaying the scene over and over. The shouts of Mardik. The gunshot. Hovhannes twisting and falling. His haunting song. A song it seems he sang directly to me. Those still, glassy eyes that see the unseen.

"Suren. Suren!"

Mihran's voice pulls me back to reality.

"What?" I mutter.

Mihran's concerned eyes lock on me as he points toward one of the abandoned shops. I follow his finger to a figure. The weight of the prayer beads pulls at my pocket as my stomach churns.

"It's just Hamza. You and Shushi can go ahead. Wait for me outside."

"Are you sure?" Mihran asks.

I nod, and Mihran glares at Hamza waiting by the half-open door of the abandoned shop. He grabs Shushi's hand to pull her down the street. Before he leaves, he leans toward me and whispers, "Remember, he's a Turk."

Mihran glares in Hamza's direction until they round the corner out of view. Glancing around, I jog over to the abandoned shop and slip through the door.

Hamza stands away from the window, close to some shelves ransacked since the siege. His black hair sticks to his sweaty forehead, and an overturned shelf sits between us.

"What are you doing here, Hamza?" The echo of our last chat comes to me in the stuffy old shop.

He wipes his brow with the back of his sleeve. "I heard the army broke through the wall."

"You heard right," I answer. Part of me is glad to see him; the other part is uneasy, haunted by Hovhannes's song still ringing in my soul.

His eyes scan the barren shelves, overturned tables, and ripped fabric scattered across the floor.

"Old man Jorin would be upset to see his shop like this," he remarks with a smirk.

Jorin's wrinkled face transports me back to simpler times when Hamza and I tried to sneak sweet bread from the grumpy old Kurd. But my guilt often stopped me.

I can't suppress a chuckle. "He would be scolding his son for not bartering with the looters."

For a moment, the battle, Hovhannes, the divide between our cultures lifts. But as our laughter fades, reality settles back in.

"I think Mihran hates me," Hamza says.

"Of course he does," I reply. "His parents were murdered by your . . . by Turks."

He drops his gaze to the floor.

"Do you?"

I pause. "Of course not! It's just different," I stammer.

He reaches for his prayer beads, which he used to keep around his wrist, but instead rubs his chin, now a bit stubbly.

"Is it different?" he asks.

"Hamza, look at this place. Everything has changed. You just don't see it in your part of the city."

"We both live in the same city, though."

A flash of anger rises in me. "Our worlds are far apart."

He steps forward, and his foot hits the fallen table. Without a pause, I flinch, and we freeze, staring at each other with our hands raised as if we need to defend ourselves.

Hamza looks at his hands, then lowers them. "I'm not like them."

I want to trust his words, but all I see is the Turk in him. Each tiny bit of his people shines through his features: the way he lets his hands hang, his hair, his nose, his eyes. His prayer beads burn in my pocket, and the impulse to throw them at him overwhelms me.

"I need to go home while I still have one," I tell him bitterly.

"All of this is madness. Many Muslims in the Shamiram are fleeing the area. Rumors of the Russians coming and this battle in our city. Everything is falling apart. Allah forbid anything happen to you or your family."

He waves his hands as he speaks. His voice, usually smooth, sounds stretched thin.

"Allah? Why do you talk about Allah when his followers want to eliminate us?" I snap.

"Your God and my God are not so different," he replies calmly.

But I am not calm. A growl escapes me. "You have lost your mind!"

"No, I haven't. Both Allah and your God teach love for others. How can you not see that?"

"Look around, Hamza! I watched a *fedayi* die today. One of my own. He died trying to protect a young Turkish girl and was shot for it by your people. He died singing for freedom for us while it was your people who took his life, following the orders of your God. Our Gods are not the same."

He stands looking at me. Are his eyes growing moist, or are the shadows of the shop playing tricks on me? My breath pounds in my chest, and an electric buzz ripples across my skin.

"Everything is different now," I say, as much for myself as for Hamza to hear.

"The world is different, but we aren't."

I lift my eyes from my feet and stare straight into his. "I am different now. How could I not be?"

Hamza steps over the broken table and debris and comes closer until he stands in front of me. His large hands grip my upper arms and give me a soft shake. I can still see the remnants of his bruises and cuts from our last visit.

"Even if everything changes, we are still brothers."

My lips tense. Our old saying is now a burden to speak. My hands ball into fists as I reply in a dead voice.

"I already have brothers."

I push him away, and he stumbles back, kicking at the debris on the floor. I catch his shocked expression, a look I'd seen only when his grandfather died three years ago, and turn, feeling his eyes on me even though I refuse to look back.

When I step out the door and into the street, I hear him call after me. He doesn't shout in anger but says the familiar words in a calm voice.

"From the Aegean to the Euphrates, Suren. Always."

I don't look back.

45

Checking In with Ani

Hamza's words cling to me as I head home. We've never been in a fistfight, but I almost want to punch him. I guess he can't help being a Turk, but sometimes he seems blind to my life.

"Suren?"

Ani's voice makes me jump, and I glance up from staring at my feet. Mihran and Shushi both chuckle and point at me. Do I look that strange?

"Who are you talking to?" Ani asks, adjusting her headscarf and tucking the sides behind her ears.

"No one. What do you want anyway?"

"To talk," she says, tilting her head slightly toward the other two lingering outside the door.

"Oh," I mutter. "You two go inside. Mama will probably be making some food. I'll be there in a minute."

Mihran and Shushi open the door and walk through. Mama's welcoming voice calls to them, and soon they disappear behind the closed door.

Ani pulls my sleeve, leading me around the corner beside some empty barrels. Gunshots ring out in the distance.

"What? What do you want?"

She pauses, her piercing eyes digging into me without saying a word.

"Did you speak to Hamza?"

I can't hide my surprise. "How do you know that? Are you sending out little spies to watch me?"

She lets go of my arm and straightens. "I can tell."

I stare down the empty street. "He's just another Turk."

"You know that isn't true," she says, her voice above a whisper.

"What have you been doing anyway? I think Taline suspects something."

Ani smiles. "I'm doing the same thing as you—fighting for my home."

I scoff. "Do you have a gun?"

She shakes her head. "There are more ways to fight than with guns. Sometimes forgiveness can be the best weapon."

"Well, whatever you're doing, don't get hurt," I half order, half plead, pretending to ignore her last comment.

She places her hand on my cheek, and I feel the anger and heat in my skin begin to fade. Maybe this is how she resists the Turks—with her mystical peace powers. A faint smile lifts the corners of her mouth.

"Unless I prick my finger with a needle or drown in a wash basin, not much harm will come to me."

A flash of sadness washes over me, one of those waves that make you want to cry for no reason. Or maybe there is a reason. I don't know. I choke it back and shove it down, but I can feel my eyes moisten.

"Don't let what our people think stop you from being who you are. Not all tears are weak."

I sigh and straighten as Ani's hand slips back to her side.

"Come," she says, "we'd better go inside."

46

Ten Days

After our scant dinner of barley with a drizzle of yogurt, all of us, including Mihran and Shushi, sit around the stove with cups of tea. With oil for the lamps running low, only a few streets remain lit, making the night outside darker and more uncertain.

Baba sits close to the stove, cracking sticks we gathered from debris in the street and feeding them to the fire. The glow of the flames catches in his eyes. Taline sits at the table, but I think she has fallen asleep sitting up. Levon taps his foot like a rabbit, staring into the fire with those round, black pupils, his grip on the armrests turning his knuckles white.

I look over at Mihran beside me as we sit cross-legged on the floor. I wonder if he has ever known the comfort of a family. On the other side of me, I see Mama with Shushi on her lap, stroking her black hair with her fingers. I've never seen Shushi so calm and relaxed. In fact, it's nice not to have her speaking for once.

Everyone knows about Hovhannes—about the Tabriz Gate and the Turks moving into the city. Either from others or in the recent message. The rising fire of the old tower can be seen from most of the city. It keeps smoking even as darkness arrives. The article from the newspaper was unnecessary but confirmed what we already knew.

Only the crackle of burning wood, a sigh, or a cough comes from us. My heart aches, but I don't know why. I still hear Hovhannes singing, still see his hand raised and the pool of blood around him. The wounded *fedayi* in the hospital beds and the strong smell of their decaying bodies. The piercing eyes of the Turkish girl in the mosque—the one who pulled Hovhannes from the compound and into the Turks' sights.

Or does my heart break for my friend?

The conversation in the shop plays over in my head. Like a time traveler, I reenact what was said and what I should have said, how he would respond, how the outcome could have played out without me turning my back on him. How could my oldest friend become like all the other Turks? How could he talk of Allah and God as if they are the same? Allah stands for the murder of non-Muslims. My God is not a hateful God.

Baba clears his throat. "What day is it, Shushi?"

As if in a daze, she looks over at Baba. "The, uhhh, the fourth, I think."

Baba nods. "Ten days," he mutters to himself.

My stomach churns even after the small bit of food I just ate. It seems giving it food only made my belly hungrier. Father

Zakarian's words come back to me—his sermons of King David killing his enemies or all the different groups God ordered the Israelites to exterminate. Was God justified? He had them kill for the right reasons, right?

"How much longer can we fight?" Mihran asks, nibbling on his chewed-up fingernails.

Mama lets out a sigh and prayer at once. "Only God knows now."

Baba reaches over and grabs Mama's free hand that isn't brushing Shushi's hair. Ten days in, and Mama's voice sounds resigned to a fate the Turks wish on us. Hearing her sadness makes my heart sink. These have been the longest ten days I have ever known.

Levon slouches against the wall on the outskirts of the group. He pulls at a loose thread on his sleeve, the end slowly fraying and unraveling. I don't recall the last time I heard him speak.

"Listen," Baba says, breaking the awkward silence. "We must be prepared for whatever comes next. From what I've heard around military command, other key positions in the city are still held by us. Only the Tabriz Gate has been breached. The most important thing is to not give up hope."

"What is hope in these times?" Mama whispers to herself.

"How?" Mihran interjects.

Baba pauses. "What have they always taught you at the American school?"

Mihran thinks for a moment, rubbing his hands through his dirty black hair. "To always have faith in the unseen."

Baba smiles. "Exactly. The Scriptures say if we have God on our side, who can be against us?"

This eases Mihran's nerves. I can see it in his face. Mama agrees, mumbling something about God and protection as Shushi leans back into her chest, staring into the fire as her eyelids start to flutter.

I return to the mosque. How St. Boghos and Topchu could be temples for the same god in another world is beyond me. Maybe to an outsider, they are. Hamza could be right, but the shame I feel in entertaining such a thought proves to me my God is true. Allah is the murderous one. After all, the *pasha* all serve him.

"Let us pray," Baba announces softly and begins a prayer I've heard a hundred times at either a church or wedding feast. With each word and every mention of God, I feel the muscles in my neck and jaw tense until Baba's prayer finally ends.

May 9, 1915

The Square

47

New Recruits

When we enter military command, the room overflows with young boys. Some are old classmates, while others come from different schools. I recognize a few boys no older than ten.

"If they think they are joining the Big Guns, they have another thing coming," Nshan adds.

The youthful faces mix with the hardened features of the *fedayi*, who have witnessed more violence than they ever wanted. Each boy's eager eyes and nervous energy fuel the high-pitched chatter.

Two *fedayi* sit in chairs, one holding yesterday's report. Even through the noise, I can hear him reading:

"In the morning, enemy forces advanced toward our positions at Shoushants. Our sentries offered little resistance and were forced to retreat. To avoid encirclement, our comrades decided to abandon the village and take new positions on the heights above. The enemy set some buildings, including Garmro Monastery, ablaze. Around one hundred unarmed women and boys managed to escape the attacking horde and reach the city. This minor enemy success has not demoralized us."

Razmik pushes through and nearly knocks me to the floor. I can tell he hasn't washed in several days; he smells worse than yesterday.

A boy grabs my arm and yanks it. "Have you heard about the old bombs?"

He startles me, but I manage to respond, "Uhh, no."

"The Turks are using old bombs they found. They light the fuses and then launch them at us. We are going to cut them!"

Then he pushes past and disappears among the sea of youthful faces. I catch more being read by the *fedayi* nearby.

"At 6:11, a Turkish force of eighty men attacked our positions at Taza Kyahrez. Our comrades mounted a successful defense and killed a gendarme. Our sentries fired upon an enemy force approaching from Ourpat Arou and forced them to retreat. We killed a gendarme from our position there."

A screech of chairs scraping on the floor rises in the room. Charo's massive frame, draped in ammunition belts, stomps in and shouts, "My God! Why are all these kids in here?"

Jumping down the stairs, the thin figure of the professor lands and runs past us.

"Wait! Wait! Let me speak to them!" he shouts.

With his usual frowning mouth, Charo argues with his hands until the professor pats him on the shoulder. Then he turns and raises his hands.

"Quiet down! Quiet down, boys!" he shouts over the clamor. It takes a moment before the room falls silent enough for the professor to speak. He scans their faces with a hint of pride.

"Look at all these brave Armenian warriors who have answered the call—young and old. Each of you is needed in the ongoing battle against our enemy. As many of you know, the Turks are running low on ammunition and have found some old explosives from the armory. Though the battle in Ararout Square was a success and we destroyed the police station, the fighting continues. While the butcher, Jevdet Bey, tried to trick us into peace talks with some of our committee, he secretly attacked key positions and killed some comrades. Now we know we will never find peace unless these bloodthirsty wolves are pushed back."

A loud cheer erupts from everyone in the room, interrupting the professor. He raises his hands, trying to quiet them again. The young boys appear a bit confused.

"All of my young *fedayi*, your roles in this fight will be more important than carrying a weapon. Some will be messengers. Some will help bring rations of food to our sentries throughout the city. And some will be tasked with a dangerous and difficult mission."

His eyes land on us, the Big Guns, as he mentions this "dangerous task." Our current orders feel dangerous enough. Will we be given guns for the first time?

"My good friend Charo will be giving you your assignments."

Charo shoots a shocked look at the professor before the mass of boys surrounds him. Their hands grab at the bullets on his vest.

The professor gestures for us to follow him into the back room. We push through the boys as Charo tries to order them to be quiet. In the back room, the noise dies down.

Glossy wooden shelves line the walls, filled with countless books. Near one shelf is a round chair padded with red cushions. The only book in my house is the Bible. A portrait in a gold frame hangs above another wall, depicting an Armenian man dressed in a black suit with a cane, like the portraits I have seen of British and Americans.

The professor sees my face and says, "This house belonged to a wealthy Armenian family who fled when rumors of the village massacres started. Now, it is our command center."

Shushi runs her hands along the padding of another chair. "It's so soft."

"You wanted to talk to us, sir?" Nshan says, as if the professor needs reminding.

"Have a seat," he replies.

Shushi jumps into the chair before Mihran, nuzzling deep into the cushions with a sly smile. I remain standing as the others sit in chairs or on an ottoman.

"You five have been with the resistance since the beginning, so I can be frank with you."

His tone paralyzes me.

"Ammunition is low in the city. We've also noticed the Turks have been more selective with their munitions. As I mentioned, the enemy has somehow found antique weapons from the Balkan Wars that had been stored in the armory, to which we lost access after the Tabriz Gate fell. Now, they are using fused explosives as projectiles launched into buildings."

Razmik raises his hand.

"This isn't the classroom, Razmik," the professor says.

"Sorry. What does this have to do with us? We are just messengers."

The professor pauses for a moment, then sighs.

"Gunpowder was used inside these bombs to make them explode. As you know, ammunition, including gunpowder, is scarce. Our best strategy is to obtain it from these bombs before they explode."

"How do we do that?" Mihran asks.

The professor remains quiet, and his solemn, frowning lips can be seen just below his mustache. He removes his glasses and begins to clean them with a cloth from his pocket.

"I have a new mission for you."

48

A Dangerous Mission

I miss the lake.

In May, the cold air makes it a bad time to swim, but the sun feels warm on our shoulders, and the lake seems to come alive. The color returns to the water, and the dull, gray clouds begin to fade. Hamza and I would use bits of cheese as bait, sticking our rods on the shoreline and waiting for a bite, while I insisted he not tell Mama we used her good cheese. The once fond memory now stings.

Outside military command, we stand in a circle, looking at each other with expressions of confusion, fear, and disbelief. A loud explosion blasts from somewhere in the city. Not close, but loud enough to know.

Finally, Nshan speaks up. "Does anyone want to back out now?"

No one replies, but I can't help but look at Mihran. Nervous, trembling Mihran. Will he back out? When the time comes, will he be able to do what the professor has asked of us? The pause lingers.

"I never thought we would be this close to the fighting," Razmik remarks, rubbing his neck with his wide hand. A grin spreads across his face.

Mihran clears his throat. "You had no problem punching me in the face outside St. Boghos."

Raz smiles, and in a way, the irony makes all of us chuckle. "I mean a real fight."

Mihran shrugs. "Fair enough."

"What about you?" Raz says, turning the attention back to him.

Mihran's smile disappears, and a grave, pale look comes over him. His eyes dart away from our gaze as he shrugs.

"He can do it!" Shushi shouts, stepping forward toward her brother.

In a way, her confidence feels convincing, even if it isn't Mihran's. She glances at me, and she seems older now—not an impulsive, irrational girl but a young woman ready to fight.

"All right. I guess the Big—"

"Don't say it, Nshan," I interrupt.

He shoots me a surprised look and then sighs. "Let's go."

The professor told us to take a secret route through the backways and alleys toward the Tabriz Gate sector. The Turks have been launching old bombs from that position. As far as I know, none of us have been back to that area since Hovhannes was killed.

Some black cats lounge around the front doors of homes or crouch under debris. These cats used to roam as if the city belonged to them. In a way, I guess it did. Before the Turks, Kurds, or Armenians, there were cats. I wonder if they feel we have made a mess of their home.

"Are you going to tell your parents?" Mihran asks as we walk.

"Tell them what?"

"About the new mission."

I pause. "I don't know. I don't want Mama to worry."

He rubs his nose. "You should tell them just in case something, you know . . ." His voice trails off, and we walk in silence, trailing behind the others.

"Do you still hate the Turks?" I ask.

I expect him to answer right away. After all he has said about his dislike of them, his pause catches me off guard.

"I should."

"You have a right to," I reply.

"I do. But it is just different now. Especially after the tower."

"How is it different? The Turks are still trying to kill us."

"Hovhannes sacrificed his life for a little Turkish girl. Why would he do that if they were so evil?"

"Maybe he was just an idiot," I remark, feeling my jaw clench.

Mihran shakes his head. His long, uncut hair sways back and forth in front of him.

"No, I don't think so. Maybe he still sees others, even Turks, as God sees them."

"Who knows what God sees?" I blurt out. My cheeks flush hot as the words linger.

Mihran glances at me as we walk. The smell of smoke surrounds us—smoke, dust, and uncertainty.

"The minister at the orphanage talks about why bad things happen. Why God allows us to suffer instead of intervening."

"What does he say?"

Mihran scratches his thumbnails. "He always recites Scripture about God's divine plan for us."

My jaw relaxes, and I do my best not to sound annoyed. "What do you think about that?"

Mihran shrugs. "I want to believe it. Do you?"

His question catches me unprepared. Thoughts and doubts swirl in my mind, but voicing them feels like my family, living and dead, is watching. The old Bible stories return, where God strikes down His enemies.

"I don't know if I can follow a God who turns His back on His children."

A bitter taste lingers on my tongue. I can hear my mother's cries and see the disappointment in my father's and grandfather's eyes. Have I become a heretic?

Mihran nods without speaking—not in agreement, but not in disagreement either. I see it in his eyes.

"I have to believe what the minister says. I have no choice."

I kick at a small stone in the street. "I don't want to talk about God anymore."

The others walk ahead like worn soldiers heading back into battle. Shushi glances at us, her eyes filling with concern for her brother. The same concern I saw on her face at the Tabriz Gate tower, the same look that lingered in Hamza's eyes at the old spice shop, and a sense, a feeling, sinks into me.

A feeling I wish to avoid.

49

Breaking and Entering

A large blast rocks the city air. Ahead, the sky fills with a plume of dust, and debris rains down on the rooftops. The sound rattles in my ears, chest, and bones. Even Razmik slams his palms over his ears.

"I haven't heard a blast like that yet," Shushi shouts.

"Those must be them," Nshan responds, shouting as well.

"Are you sure?" Mihran asks, his voice cracking.

"He's right," I reply.

Nshan takes a deep breath and adjusts his glasses and hat. "Let's move forward."

Razmik stands next to me, arms crossed over his broad chest.

"I never thought when I went to war I'd take orders from Nshan."

I can't help but smile nervously. "Me too."

A wide grin spreads across his face as he slaps a hand against my back. I wait until he leaves before wincing and rubbing the spot. Shushi comes beside me and presses against my side.

"If something happens to me, look after Mihran. He's sensitive."

I nod. "Of course."

Some crows fly across the blue sky, only faint shadows of dust and smoke from the city. We walk past a pile of rubble and see the city wall—cracked and broken but still intact. Near the bottom, a patch of new stones covers a fallen section, perhaps rebuilt by workers overnight.

Men shout between gunshots, their voices sounding like they come from above. I scan the rooftops and see flashes of dark figures pop up, fire shots, and then duck down.

"Nshan!" I yell ahead. He turns around, and I point to either side.

"Come on!" he shouts, and we run left toward the nearest building. Without thinking, I grab Shushi's hand and pull her. I expect her to punch me, but she doesn't.

We huddle under the covered porch by the front door. Another strong blast sends dust and rubble into the air, shaking the building enough to sprinkle bits of stone from the roof.

Razmik rams his shoulder into the door, and it flies open. Our bodies spill into the room, and I fall on top of Mihran in a pile just inside the doorway.

Shushi slams the door shut.

"Boys," she chides, dusting her hands on her baggy trousers. Her bandanna hangs above one eye like a desert bandit as she shakes her head at us.

"Get off me," Razmik growls from the bottom of the pile, and without waiting, he stands, sending the rest of us to the ground again. We finally get to our feet. Above us, muffled voices of the *fedayi* come from the ceiling.

"Should we go up there?" Mihran asks. "Tell them our mission?"

Nshan looks around the room as he adjusts his glasses.

"They might shoot us by accident," he comments.

"Good point," Mihran agrees.

Shadows cover most of the room, but I can see the crude, worn kitchen table. Unlike at military command, there are no chairs—only piles of hay covered with blankets. No books or fancy chairs with soft cushions.

"Hey, where's my sister?" Mihran asks.

Our eyes meet, and as if sharing the same thought, we look toward the staircase, where a fleeting image disappears, heading up.

50

She's a Girl

I fly up the stone steps two at a time until I reach the landing. The possibility of getting shot flashes across my mind, and I wonder what it might feel like to have metal tear through my skin and muscle.

The upstairs mirrors the first floor. I search the area, and there she is, mouth hanging open, standing by the open doorway that leads to the roof.

"Shushi!" I whisper as loudly as I can, but she doesn't move.

Raz, Nshan, and Mihran gather on the landing behind me. Our warm bodies crowd together in the cramped space. I can feel Mihran's breath on my arm.

"Shushi! Get over here. Now!" Mihran shouts.

Slowly, she turns her head toward us and points at the landing. She mouths something, a strange smile spreading across her face.

"Shushi!" Mihran repeats, trying to sound like a father and stomping his foot.

"Hey! What are you doing here?" a voice shouts from the rooftop.

My blood freezes, and all of us except Shushi are paralyzed on the landing. Mihran stands so still his face retains an annoyed expression.

Shushi turns toward the balcony and takes a step toward the voice.

"*Parev*!" she calls.

"Shushi!" I shout-whisper again, but she is out of sight.

"Someone go after her!" Mihran cries out, coming to life.

I want to move and be brave, but the gunshots still echo outside, and my feet feel heavy. Even Razmik remains motionless, making a strange murmuring sound.

"Do something!" Nshan shouts.

Something propels me forward, and I run around the corner, half ducking as I scamper over to the doorway leading to the roof. The bright sun outside shines off the gray-washed stone. When my eyes adjust, I see Shushi crouching behind the wall next to two *fedayi* with their backs to me. The one closest to Shushi waves a hand, telling her to stay low. Shushi points at me, and the *fedayi* shoots a look over her shoulder.

Wait. Not his shoulder. Her shoulder.

The *fedayi* grabs Shushi by the arm and runs toward me, still standing in the shadow of the room.

"Get back! Over there!" she shouts, pushing us back inside.

I stumble toward the others as the *fedayi* swings Shushi by the arm and hurls her into us, nearly knocking me over as she crashes into my arms.

"*Oh Der Asdvadz im*!" she exclaims, clutching her rifle. "Who sent a bunch of kids here?" Her cheeks are smeared with dirt, and the front of her black uniform is powdered with white dust.

Nshan's courage returns. "Aram Manukian sent us."

"Aram sent you? To do what?"

Nshan pauses. We all know our mission, but none of us have actually said it out loud.

He clears his throat and adjusts his glasses. "We are here to disarm the bombs."

I feel those words deep in my chest. The others must too. Sending messages where fighting has occurred is one thing, but running into the fighting is another. Being face-to-face with a bomb is *very* different.

Her piercing eyes scan our faces, and she lowers her rifle to her side. She lifts her hand and pulls the end of her *khatch*. The fabric unravels and slides off her head, releasing her black hair around her shoulders.

"Stay over there until we tell you to come out, understand?"

We all nod like dolls during an earthquake.

She raises her rifle and returns to her position on the roof.

Shushi still clings to my arm, and once the *fedayi* leaves, she springs from my grip and faces me, her eyes wide and a huge smile on her face.

"She's a girl!"

"Yes, she is," Razmik remarks. His eyes stay locked on the woman outside, firing at the Turks.

Her finger points toward the roof as gunshots ring out again. Another heavy explosion booms somewhere outside. I look back at Nshan and Mihran. The same uncertain glaze spreads across their faces.

The same expression I can feel on my own face.

Araxie and Siroun

On the landing, we sit and wait as the *fedayi* on the roof continue to trade shots with the Turks. Gunfire. Bombs. Shouting. More gunfire. The fighting has a rhythm, like an old song. I saw it in the fights behind St. Boghos. All fighting feels like a dance that everyone is trying to lead.

Shushi leans away from us, trying to see around the corner. We sit against the wall and wait. Using an old mug, we pour drinks from a pitcher on a small table. I run my tongue over my lips and feel the dry craters. Razmik had brought rolls of fig *bastegh* he found downstairs. The sweet taste feels foreign on my tongue.

"How long will this go on?" Mihran asks.

"Too long," Nshan replies softly.

Outside, the sun glares, and my mind drifts to Hamza. I'm sure he returned to the Shamiram, to the safety of his home far from the guns and bloodshed. If he were here, would he fight against his own people? The Quran would not approve of Allah's people joining the infidels, let alone the Armenians. I think about how we used to skip stones on the lake when we were young, his rock always going farther or bouncing more, or those times playing seven stones, how our pyramid always withstood the other team's toss. We were the Big Guns before this all began.

The silence pulls me back from my memories. After such constant noise, the emptiness feels deafening. Shushi stands as footsteps approach from the entryway to the roof. The *fedayi* from before emerges. Her long, black hair hangs past her shoulders, strands sticking to her sweaty forehead. We jump to our feet when we see her. Shushi beams, looking up at the woman as if she were an angel.

"Are you all right?" she asks, propping her rifle against a wall.

"Yes. Is the fighting finished?" Nshan asks, standing straight.

She swipes her hair from her forehead, then searches her trouser pocket. "For now. So, you're here to diffuse bombs?"

We nod as she finds a loose cigarette, jamming it between her lips before fumbling for a match.

"Have you ever done this before?" she asks.

No one answers. She strikes the match, and it blazes to life.

"There's my answer. Most of us are in the same position."

She blows a plume of smoke into the air and watches it curl. The sharp smell of tobacco hits me. I watch the cloud dissipate, captivated by its swirls. Shushi watches the woman intently.

"My name is Araxie. Siroun! Come meet our new bomb squad," the woman calls to the doorway.

A moment later, a plump woman with thick eyebrows appears, rifle cocked on her shoulder. Her severe face scans us before turning to Shushi.

"You're joking," Siroun remarks, stepping over to her comrade with fingers pinched, begging for a smoke. Araxie rolls her eyes and hands it over.

"We've been messengers for a couple of weeks near the Tabriz Gate," Nshan informs them in his deepest voice. We wait and watch, but neither seems impressed.

Araxie notices Shushi's fixed gaze, which hasn't changed for several minutes. She turns to us and asks, "Is she all right?"

Mihran's voice cracks. "She is fine. She hasn't seen many girls—I mean, women—fighting."

Siroun exhales smoke, then offers the cigarette to Shushi. Without hesitation, she takes it and inhales deeply, making the tip glow.

"Slow down!" Araxie advises, reaching for the cigarette as Siroun bursts into laughter.

Shushi holds in the smoke with puffed cheeks before coughing and spitting. Araxie pats her back, trying not to laugh.

Mihran lays his head in his hands.

"Did you kill the Turks?" Razmik asks Araxie, standing with arms flexed, trying to make them look bigger like he does in front of every girl he meets.

"Maybe. We mostly shoot at a trench. Even the *fedayi* in the other buildings can't see the Turkish soldiers well enough to shoot accurately. We have to ration our bullets until we know we can get a good shot. Only those who try to run to the wall are easy targets. With those old bombs they keep launching, the dust makes it impossible to see. But now that you are here, that won't be a problem."

I can't tell if she is being sarcastic or truly believes that we know what we are doing.

"Well, maybe Tarzi can still shoot them," Siroun adds.

Araxie nods and smiles. "The arrow of God, yes."

My heart jumps.

"Tarzi? Tarzi Simonian?" I ask.

They both look at me. "Yes. You know him?"

"He's my uncle."

The two *fedayi* exchange a glance. Shushi finally stops coughing, her ashen face bent down to the rug.

"Looks like we are in good hands with a Simonian on our side," Siroun says.

"Can I see him?" I try to recall the last time I saw my uncle. Or my aunt.

"Not now. It's too dangerous. We can wait until dark when the fighting stops. Did military command send any food with you?"

"No," Nshan replies.

Araxie looks at Siroun. "Looks like coffee and cigarettes again." She turns back to us with a smirk. Something about her reminds me of Taline.

"Do you have knives or scissors?" Siroun asks.

"For what?" Mihran asks.

"*Astvats*! We're doomed," she exclaims, taking another drag before handing the cigarette back to Araxie. She points toward a wooden chest.

"To cut the fuse. Check in there. This house belonged to a seamstress, from what I can guess. There may be scissors. Others can check downstairs for a knife. Otherwise, you'll have to use your teeth."

Siroun chuckles at this bad joke.

Nshan and Raz walk over to the wooden chest and dig through its contents. They return with some pairs of metal scissors. Some are tinted blue or rusty, but they still open.

"There are only four," Nshan informs everyone.

An awkward pause lingers before Mihran breaks the silence. "You take them. I'll check downstairs for a knife or something sharp."

As Mama would have taught, I should protest and offer him my scissors. I feel their weight and the cool metal in my palm, and deep inside, I feel like I couldn't loosen my fingers from them if I tried.

As we examine our new tools, men's voices shout from outside. Siroun grips her rifle at the ready and heads back to the rooftop. Araxie stands and throws the remains of her cigarette on the floor, twisting her toe to snuff it out.

"What is it?" she calls out.

Siroun's solemn face appears in the doorway. She says nothing, and for Araxie, this seems to say everything. The two *fedayi* leave us in the room without any information. Razmik shoves his scissors into his pocket and scratches the back of his neck.

"Where did they go?" he asks.

"Come on," Shushi tells us and, without waiting, walks out of the room.

"Shushi!" Mihran calls out and chases after her, forcing us to follow. Soon, the blinding light strikes me in the face, and I lift my hand to shield my brow.

The two women stand with their rifles slung over their shoulders. A soft breeze blows Araxie's long hair back as she stares over the wall toward Mount Ararat. Razmik's mouth hangs open, and he may start drooling at any moment.

Slowly, we tiptoe to the stone wall around the edge of the roof. The Turks sit off in their trenches with their horses and artillery. However, what I see is far more terrifying than the Turks' guns.

52

Ghosts

They move like a herd of lost beasts.

Mothers.

Grandmothers.

Babies clinging to their mothers.

Young boys and girls.

Grandfathers stooping over, dragging their feet in the sand.

All are so covered in dirt, they look like they have climbed out of their own graves. Some have bloodied bandages on their heads, legs, or arms. A few hold stretchers covered in sheets from head to toe. No bags or oxcarts. Only themselves.

"Who are they?" Shushi asks, standing between Mihran and me.

"They could be Muslims from the city. I heard they are fleeing," Razmik replies.

"No," Araxie answers sharply. "They are Armenians."

"From the city?" Mihran asks.

"Villagers."

I return to St. Boghos and the story from the *fedayi* when we first snuck in. His news of the murders and attacks on the outskirts of the province.

"Which village?" I ask aloud.

"Bashkale. Saray. Arjesh. Alashgerd. Name one," Siroun interjects.

A mother holds her young daughter's hand, nearly pulling her forward. The scarf wrapped around her head covers her face. An old man near the rear collapses, but no one stops. Only a few men of fighting age walk with them.

"Where are all the men?" Shushi asks.

"Dead where they fought," Araxie replies, then mumbles something under her breath.

I've never seen spirits or ghosts, but I understand what those who have may feel. Most could think they are the dead, walking from this life to the next. Frail, thin, ragged bones. How many died just to get here?

"Shouldn't we help them?" Nshan asks.

"Unless we have orders to do so, the gates remain closed," Araxie says.

"That feels wrong," Nshan says. I have to agree.

"There's hardly any food for those in the city. Imagine letting in hundreds of starving refugees. What if a spy or an Armenian traitor loyal to the *pasha* sneaks in with them? It's not worth the risk," Siroun adds.

I look to the other buildings and see the shapes of other *fedayi* watching the parade of refugees outside the walls. I think I see

Uncle Tarzi and his ragged, gray beard in the silhouette, but I am not sure. With so little food and water, my mind may be playing tricks on me. Maybe there are no refugees, and I am back home in bed, asleep and dreaming a terrible nightmare. Soon I will wake up, grab a large breakfast around the table with Mama and Baba, Ani and Taline, Levon and Narek. We'll all be together before the Great War started and the Turks joined the Germans.

It's all just a bad dream.

Downstairs, I sift through drawers, shelves, and baskets for a knife for Mihran, but my mind wanders to the ghosts outside. Before we left the rooftop, a small girl saw us watching. She pointed at us and called for help. Others joined in, wailing and crying out like a wave until my ears and heart could no longer stand it.

"Do you think this will work?" Mihran asks, holding up a small, dull blade.

"Let's keep looking."

I find another knife with a wooden handle among some spoons. My finger runs down the edge, but it doesn't cut my skin.

"It's not sharp, but it's better," I say, handing the knife to Mihran. He takes it and rubs the blade on his thumb. His face sinks a little.

"You probably won't even need to use it," I try to reassure him, though I can't convince myself.

"Maybe there's a sharpening stone somewhere," he wonders and begins searching again.

I watch him dig around the kitchen.

"I've never seen anything like that," I remark.

"It's not great, but if I can find a sharpening stone, it should work."

"Not that." My tone sounds grave.

He stops, his tired eyes shining in the dim light. Tapping the knife blade in his hand, he leans against the nearby wall.

"I have."

"You have?" I exclaim.

"All orphans are refugees."

"That's different," I say.

He cocks his head and crosses his arms. "Different how?"

"Those outside have nothing. No home, no family, no possessions. They've lost everything."

A smirk crosses Mihran's face.

"What?" I snap.

"You're right. But orphans never had anything to lose."

I look at my feet. "I never thought of it that way."

"It's all right," Mihran says.

Guilt fills my stomach. Have I ever viewed Mihran and Shushi as refugees? Any orphan, for that matter? I've been so focused on myself and the battle against the Turks, Hamza, and Levon; I never saw the refugees in my own life. Levon. Is my brother a refugee now? Even with a family and a home, I can see him as just another face among the ghosts outside the walls.

Loud, stomping footsteps crash down the stairs. Raz, Nshan, and Shushi come around the corner holding their scissors.

"Araxie says we need to be ready for when the Turks start launching bombs into the city. It could happen any minute," Nshan informs us.

His words plunge into my gut and stick in my throat.

"I'm ready. I might not even cut the fuse; instead, I'll throw it back over the wall and blow those Turkish murderers to pieces," Raz says, pacing as if talking more to himself than to us.

"What about the refugees, Raz? Are you going to blow them up too?" Shushi counters in her typical biting voice.

He glares at her but continues pacing. "I'll throw it over them."

She shakes her head and dismisses him with a wave. Mihran seems unfazed and continues searching for anything to sharpen his dull knife.

I stand by Nshan and whisper, "Do you think the Russians will come soon?"

"I hope so. My father tells me they are defeating the Germans in the east and advancing." One of the lenses in Nshan's glasses is cracked.

An unsettling silence falls over us. I look around at the faces of my friends. They are more than that now—something more than family. Each of them comes into focus for me. Raz. Nshan. Mihran. Shushi. This strange moment feels sacred in an odd way. How could something holy occur outside of church? But the air feels thick with something beyond this world, something greater than the Turks, Armenians, Kurds, and their hatred for one another. All I know is that words are useless now.

Raz stops pacing, and we look into each other's face. Not quick glances but long, intense stares. Our eyes stay connected. No turning away or awkwardness. It's as if words don't need to be spoken to be heard.

Like glass shattering in the night, the sound of gunfire returns, and Araxie's frantic voice flies down the stairs.

"Get up! Get up! Follow me!"

The Dull Knife

With my mind swirling, we follow her out the front door. The shadows of the dim house fade into a bright, blinding flash outside. I try to cut back the glare but keep moving forward. My shoes wobble on the debris as I scamper across the street, following Araxie's figure.

"Three of you over there behind that building. You two follow me."

She points at Mihran and me. The other three run over and huddle in a gap between two tall buildings. Shushi pauses, looking at her brother, and he gestures for her to follow the others. The reckless courage in Shushi's eyes extinguishes like a blown-out candle, and I see the fear of a twelve-year-old girl being separated from her brother.

"Let's go!" Araxie barks, waving her arm for us to follow.

My pulse pounds in my temples. A few meters down the street, we cut into a small, abandoned shop. Just like the one from the last time I spoke with Hamza.

She pushes us into the shop, surveys the area, then snaps her fingers in front of our faces.

"Pay attention. Are you listening? See that square over there? This is where they have been launching the bombs with the fuses. If you see any bombs land over there, you are responsible for cutting the fuse before it goes off. Anything on that side, your friends will take care of. Understand?"

Her words sound muffled, as if she is talking with a hand over her mouth. Still, I nod. Mihran takes a few more finger snaps before acknowledging her. The way the corners of her mouth turn down reminds me of the same look Taline or Ani gives me when they don't believe me. For a brief moment, Araxie's face overwhelms me with comfort.

She sprints across the street and disappears between the buildings. Even with Mihran here, a loneliness I've never known settles on me. Gunfire sputters from the top of one building, and I see Uncle Tarzi's large beard and the old fez he always wears.

"Uncle!" I shout.

He continues firing over the wall without looking at me. I wait for a pause.

"Uncle!"

He lifts his head from the gun sight and looks around, searching for my voice.

"Down here!"

He raises his hand to shield his eyes.

"Suren? What the hell are you doing here?"

The question disarms me. Why am I here? Do I know why I am here, crouched in an abandoned shop with a pair of scissors?

"Get ready!" another voice near my uncle shouts, and diving back, a black object trailing smoke flies over the wall. It bounces off the building and lands in the square, rolling to a stop on the far side.

Araxie begins shouting, and I see Razmik's muscular body sprint toward it about fifteen meters away with his scissors in hand. The others shout for him to hurry. Every muscle in my body tenses, even those I didn't know I had.

The round object sits and sizzles like a firecracker, the flames burning down the wick with each passing second. Razmik slides to his knees and, with one quick flick, cuts the fuse below the sparks. The loose end burns out on the ground, and my body relaxes. I realize my nails are digging into Mihran's arm, but he doesn't seem to notice.

Razmik stands, raising a fist with a big smile.

"Grab it and bring it back, you idiot!" Araxie shouts at him.

Fumbling around, he finally picks up the bomb, holding it like a crying baby, and runs back to his position. Uncle Tarzi's voice comes down from above, praising Raz and yelling at me to get out of here.

From behind, I hear gunshots from the rooftops. With all the orders about saving bullets, I don't know what Siroun is shooting at. Mihran's shuddering breath is fast and erratic. His pale face and shaking hands scare me, but if we don't calm down, I may lose myself too.

I place my hand on his head and stroke his hair like I would a cat.

"Breathe, Mihran *jan*. Breathe," I say quietly.

He rocks back and forth with the dull knife fixed in his white knuckles. With each word, he seems to regain his breath. The rocking slows, and he sits on his trembling hands.

"Get ready!" Another shout comes from the rooftops.

Except the bomb doesn't land in the square but bounces off the side of a building and lands out of sight near the wall. Nshan begins to run out, but Araxie's arm smacks him across the chest, knocking him down.

A deafening blast blows rocks, wood, and dirt high into the air, sending a cloud above us. The debris sprinkles onto the roof. Across the street, Araxie pulls Nshan to his feet, slaps the back of his head, and drags him back to their post. I hear her high voice scolding him, but I can only catch every other word. Then she runs back to the house with Razmik's defused bomb in her arms and disappears.

"I can't do this, Suren. I c-c-can't. I want to go home," Mihran says.

"You have to. There's no choice now. We can't go back; otherwise, there will be no home to return to."

"Let's wait. Wait for the Russians to come," he says. Tears leak from the corners of his closed eyes.

Feeling myself losing him, I grip his shirt and pull him toward me. "Look at me, Mihran. Look at my face."

His eyes remain shut as he shakes his head.

"Look at me, please!"

He lifts his face and opens his eyes to slits. I grab the sides of his head with my hands and hold tight.

"We will make it out of here. I promise."

Whether I believe it or not, I have to say it. If not for him, then for me. His watery eyes look back at me, and he nods against my shaking hands.

"If a bomb comes our way, I will go first," I tell him, resenting the words as they leave my mouth.

"Ready!" a voice calls from above. My body tenses.

The object flies over the wall and lands on the far side of the square, closer to the others. But, as if responding to my words to Mihran, it ricochets, rolling toward us.

Everything suffocates me: the shop, the shouting, Mihran's tears, the smell of smoke, the taste of dust, and the sparks flying from the fuse just meters away. My body rebels. Go, you coward! Move! But I sit, the scissors stuck in my pocket, my hands still holding Mihran's face. I hear him call my name from somewhere, like an echo from another time, but my eyes are fixed on the bomb.

Something pushes me away. My hands are empty. Mihran. As the terror releases me, his skinny frame runs into the street toward the square, moving in slow motion, the dull knife in his hand. I open my mouth to stop him, but nothing comes out.

He sinks to his knees beside the bomb and begins to saw at the dense fuse. The flames devour the short rope, inch by inch, creeping closer to Mihran's knife until it touches the blade. All the voices rush back to me: Nshan, Razmik, Shushi, Uncle Tarzi. They scream for him to run, to get back.

Spark by spark, the wick shrinks closer and closer.

54

Blood on the Ground

Grit and dust sting my eyes. Rubbing them doesn't ease the pain, and I try to open them. Dirt coats my lips and tongue. Am I on the ground? A chunk of rock digs into my back as I roll over. Desperate to relieve the sting, I blink rapidly until tears wash it away.

Mihran. The explosion. The war. My inability to move when my time came to act.

I can't tell if the dirt in my eyes distorts what I see. Still, I climb to my feet and stumble forward toward the square. Is that Shushi crying? Or are the *fedayi* shouting at us from above?

As the haze in my eyes fades, I see Mihran lying in the square.

The pain disappears, and my heart pushes me forward. Is he moving? Is he dead? Several feet away, I kick something and look down to see Mihran's dull knife.

I collapse beside his body. The small stones dig into my knees and palms. Grabbing his shoulders, I shake him. His face is dark with streaks of blood and dirt.

"Mihran!" I call out. "Mihran! Can you hear me?"

He doesn't move. Doesn't respond. I can't see the scar over his eye that Razmik gave him so long ago. Shushi screams his name from somewhere in the buildings.

I shake my friend harder now.

"Mihran! Wake up," I shout in his face. "We need to get back to the shop!"

His eyes remain closed, and a warmth touches my knees in the dirt. I look down to see blood quickly darkening the mud around me. What if we both get shot out here? Or another bomb comes? I have to get him out of here.

"Come on," I yell and grab his hand. I pull back, expecting the weight of his body, but I crash backward onto the dirt and rocks. Mihran's body is still there, but I am holding only his hand.

Oh, God! I'm holding his hand. I fling it away from me.

My breath.

I can't breathe.

A sound escapes me that I've never heard before. Never felt before. Never knew was inside me.

"Grab the other boy. I'll get him."

A voice approaches from behind. I can't stop shaking. Then I feel two thick arms wrap around my waist. A wiry beard scratches my cheek and lifts me off the ground.

"Let's go, Suren *jan*. We need to leave."

Though I know it is my uncle, my body rebels, kicks, thrashes, and I'm screaming. Yelling. Cursing. Crying out meaningless words. I just need to scream. I grab at his sleeves and see my red handprints on his forearms, the dirty blood on my knees.

"He's still breathing," I hear a woman's voice.

"Get him to the hospital! Now!" Uncle Tarzi orders.

Araxie hoists Mihran onto her shoulders and runs out of sight. The tracks of my feet in the dust as my uncle pulls me away lead back to my cowardice. Struggling, I twist my body and see Araxie's silhouette down the street, followed by Shushi crying out her brother's name.

"Mihran! Mihran! Mihran!"

The others chase after her, calling her back, but she doesn't glance at them.

I feel his wet blood on my hands.

Uncle Tarzi keeps telling me it will be all right. I will be safe. Everything will be all right.

And I am still screaming.

55

Aftershock

I don't know how I ended up in this room. Uncle Tarzi has a wet rag and wipes my sticky hands. His sleeves are rolled up to his elbows. I can only watch him.

"Your friend will be OK," he tries to reassure me. But I know what I saw. I can feel his weightless hand.

Nshan sits and watches me as he cleans his glasses on his shirt. His shoulders slump forward, just like mine.

"Where's Mihran?" The words choke in my throat, but I manage to ask.

Nshan looks away.

"He's at the hospital. The little girl is with him," Uncle Tarzi informs me flatly. He dips the rag in a bowl of water and wrings it out. The pinkish water fills again.

"I have to see him. I have to." I begin to stand, but Uncle Tarzi pushes me back down into the chair.

"In time, but not now."

The room feels like a mouth trying to swallow me. Mouse droppings under the chair, cobwebs between the stove, a chipped hole in the wall where a bullet must have hit. Is Shushi all right? Can she forgive me?

An explosion roars outside. I flinch, cover my head, and see Mihran crouched beside the black bomb, sparks flying, the dull knife failing. I press into my eyes to push the image away.

The sound fades, and when I open my eyes, Nshan is next to me, wrapping his arms around my shoulders. Uncle Tarzi pauses, then puts the soiled rag into the bowl and walks away.

"Will he die?" I ask.

Nshan squeezes me. "I don't know."

The other voices in the room begin discussing bombs and counterattacks, military talk I only partially understand. Nshan hands me a glass of water, and I take a sip.

"He gave me his scissors."

"What?" Nshan asks.

"At the station. There were only four pairs."

Nshan rubs at his eyes.

"What if I had given him the scissors? What if I . . ."

"Don't!" Nshan barks.

I hang my head, my eyes fixed on the floor.

"I promised him," I murmur, my face flushing.

Nshan sighs, silent but still holding me. When he speaks, the world falls still. "There's a fine line between desperation and bravery."

Desperation. Is that what I am? Desperate for what? The bomb goes off over and over in my head, and with each blast, I try to find myself. To discover what I am really seeking. What am I fighting for? I wish God would fly down from heaven or Artavazd would break those chains and escape the Holy Mountain. Not for revenge. Or for victory. To tell me what I'm supposed to do. To tell me who to be.

"Where is Raz?" I ask.

"He is still down on the street, watching the square. He's diffused two bombs already."

How long have I been up here? Resentment starts in my jaw. Why wasn't he with Mihran? Raz didn't freeze like a deer. He would have run out, stood true to his word, defused the bomb, and saved his friend. I should have gone with Shushi and Nshan. It's his fault.

I turn and look through the window at the square. I realize we are upstairs in the building across from Araxie and Siroun. In the square, I see the small crater where the bomb exploded, the dark patch still beside it.

"Get ready!" Uncle Tarzi's voice comes from outside.

A black bomb flies over the wall, ricochets off one of the buildings, and lands in the middle of the square. From the buildings, I see Raz's shape run out, slide down, cut the burning fuse, and then return with the useless bomb in his arms. Like a trained dancer, his movements look effortless. No hesitation. No dropping the scissors. No wasted time.

I place my hands on the windowsill and see dirt and blood crusted under my nails. Mihran's blood. My eyes move to my trousers and the reddish-black stains on my knees.

Will I ever be able to wash his blood from my hands?

56

Never Hide from the Devil

The sun starts to fall. Though Ararat is far away, its silhouette feels like a shadow over the city. Still no God. Still no Artavazd. Is it morning or night? Has time changed somehow?

Raz and Nshan spent time diffusing more bombs while Uncle Tarzi opened them, dumping gunpowder into old, dry jugs from the abandoned home. All afternoon, I watched him fill three to four jugs on the table. How many bullets would that create? How many bombs? How many more days left to fight?

With the last light, Raz, Nshan, Uncle Tarzi, and I leave the house and walk the streets back into the city. The Turks never fight at night, but Araxie and the other *fedayi* stay to protect the position just in case.

With each step, I drag memories and sounds and smells behind me. Each step weighs me down. My fingers stopped trembling at some point. Nshan and Raz walk ahead, each carrying a jug of gunpowder. Uncle Tarzi is beside me, holding the last jug and scanning the area.

Raz and Nshan talk to each other just enough for me to know they are discussing me. I know it. They must be. About how I failed our group. Do they know I froze? To them, it may have looked like Mihran chose to go, not because I couldn't. But maybe they do know.

"What's on your mind?" Uncle Tarzi asks.

Snapped out of a daze, I turn to him and see his stern eyes, his mouth hidden beneath his bushy beard.

"Nothing," I lie.

He chuckles to himself.

"What's so funny?"

"Suren *jan*, you have always been a terrible liar. Just like your father."

"I might be better at it than you think," I reply flatly.

"I admire those who can't be dishonest. Me, your brother Levon, even Ani. We all have our secrets and work hard to keep them that way."

Farther away from the front, glowing eyes of cats begin to emerge from under boards and windows, from anywhere they may be hiding. They watch us pass, and I wonder if they sense our emotions. Can they feel my shame? My sadness?

"How far is the hospital?" I ask, keeping my eyes on the cats.

"Not far. But you need to know, you may never see him again in this life."

The thought lingers with me, but hearing Uncle Tarzi say it makes it feel possible. The image of Mihran with a sheet over his head tortures me. The memory of his hand in mine.

"Does your father know about Taline?"

I open my eyes. "No, I don't think so."

"Good. Especially for your mother's sake. I always told him that woman would break easily."

"What do you mean?"

He groans and continues. "I care for your mother. Like a sister. But there was something about how she let her tears flow like a waterfall. I told him, 'Vartan, that woman breaks too easily.' But no matter how stern I was, he just laughed as if I had told the most hilarious joke. Then he would kiss your mother on the cheek."

I consider whether I should be offended that he speaks this way about my mother. Should I be if it is true?

"What about Aunt Yeva? Doesn't she show her feelings?"

He lets out a deep, gruff laugh. "Yeva? The only emotion she shows is anger, and that is always directed at me. That's why she orders everyone around at the munitions workshop, the hospital—wherever she is."

He pauses and adjusts the jug of gunpowder in his arms. "Your cousin Tovmas was just like her. She could stare me down without flinching."

Tovmas. I had never heard Uncle Tarzi talk about my cousin. Not after they found her floating in the lake. But I don't remember. As a three-year-old, how could I?

He grows quiet for a moment.

"This life God has given us is a strange thing. Very strange."

He speaks as if talking to himself. "We are all Ottomans, but one wants to destroy the other. Same hair. Two arms. Two legs. They have two eyes but see different things. One heart, but feel different emotions."

Uncle Tarzi stops and places his hand against my chest. He sets the jug of gunpowder on the ground. I lift my face.

"Listen to me, Suren. I do not know how this will end. But God willing, whether we win this battle or not, promise me two things you will never do."

I nod, my eyes locked onto his intense blue gaze, the only one in our family with that color.

"Never forget who you are," he says, holding up one finger. "And never, *never*, hide from the devil."

He leans forward, pointing his finger at me. A tear slips from his eye and disappears into his beard. The famous fighter Tarzi? Crying?

"Promise me!" he barks, making me flinch.

"Yes, sir," I reply.

He examines me for a moment, then his eyes soften. Without a word, his calloused hand yanks me forward and presses me into his wide chest. His beard tickles my forehead, and slowly, I wrap my arms around him. My mind searches for a time when I hugged my uncle, but memory fails me.

Whether it has or not, it happens now, and no matter how new and foreign it may feel, my fingers grip his shirt. Squeezing tighter and tighter, I am determined not to let go until he does.

Uncle Tarzi remains silent for the rest of the walk. When we arrive at the hospital, he simply pats my shoulder and walks on without looking back. Never hide from the devil. Never run from your family. The promise repeats in my mind as I watch him leave.

Outside, I stand next to Raz and Nshan, facing the door. No one makes a move to enter.

"Should we go in?" Nshan asks.

"Yes," Raz agrees. He says it confidently, but still, no one moves.

What will we find on the other side of the door? Mihran with a sheet over his face? Even if he is alive, will he see me as a coward? Someone as lowly as the Turks? I told him it would work out. We would be OK.

"I can't," I say aloud before I can stop myself.

The others turn and look at me.

"You can't?" Nshan asks.

"I, I can't see him. Or Shushi. Not now. I'm sorry."

The heat from their eyes burns me, and I have to leave. I need to. I turn and flee from the hospital, away from my friends. From everything. The shame of my tears slips down my cheeks as my feet pound the dirt.

May 16, 1915

The Final Battle

57

Truth or Lies

A loud bang jolts me from my mat. Looking out the window, the bright sun shines across the rooftops. What time is it? I must have slept in. I check the bed but don't see Levon. I sit up and pull on a shirt before heading downstairs. Voices clamor in the main room—Baba, Mama, and even Levon, from what I can hear.

Downstairs, Baba and Mama stand near the open door, talking to Uncle Tarzi and Aunt Yeva. His squinty eyes are now wide and vibrant, hands flailing as he gestures wildly.

"It's true, Vartan! It's almost over!"

Baba rests his chin on his hands like a Greek philosopher contemplating something profound.

"Where did you hear this?" he asks. Mama wraps her arms around Baba's, leaning into him and murmuring with Aunt Yeva.

"Military command. Aram! Charo! Everyone. The Russians are coming, and those Turkish demons are fleeing when a real fight comes. Imagine if we had the Russian weapons," he chuckles to himself.

Levon sits at the table, oblivious to my presence.

"I will come with you," Baba says. He pauses, holds Mama's face close, smiles, and kisses her gently. A tear marks her cheek.

Seeing me for the first time, Baba strides toward his bedroom.

"Is the battle over?" I ask.

Baba, without stopping, replies, "Maybe. By the grace of God."

I glance at Uncle Tarzi, who whisks Aunt Yeva by the arms and begins to dance with her. I've never seen such joy from my uncle. Now he hums a melody, and Aunt Yeva smiles between her playful protests.

Mama holds her hands together and wraps her arms around my head.

"It's over! God has seen us!" Her words are choked by sobs.

She releases me and walks over to Levon, hugging him from behind.

"Suren!" Uncle Tarzi calls out.

"Yes?"

"Get dressed. You're coming with us," he orders.

"Where?"

"Stop pretending to be a hose! Go upstairs. Quickly!"

I roll my eyes and sprint upstairs. As I slip into my trousers, I wonder if the war is really over or if this is just another false hope we have to endure. Baba's watch and Hamza's *tasbih* sit beside my clothes.

"Suren!" Baba calls.

I grab both and stick them into my pockets before heading downstairs.

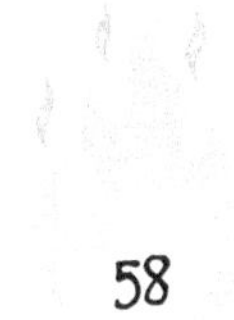

58

The Return

Between my uncle and father, we walk along the streets. From the shouts echoing across the city—women, children, and old men—the news must be spreading.

"How far away are the Russians?" Baba asks.

"A few days. Sooner, perhaps?"

"Do the Turks know this?"

My uncle cackles. "How could they not? They have better intel than we do. Reports of ships carrying Turkish citizens from the city across the lake have surfaced. From what I've heard in correspondence between Jevdet and our leaders, he has been bluffing and deceiving us before the

Russians come. I'm sure he'll try one last attempt to destroy us before he flees."

We weave between buildings and other citizens rushing about. Some shout and sing praises to God and the *fedayi*. Even with my young legs, the two always stay ahead of me.

"What has Aram said? And Charo?" Baba asks.

"They tell us to brace for the worst before it gets better."

"I wouldn't expect anything less."

Baba looks back at me. "Keep up, Suren. We are almost to the end."

The end. Those words terrify me. What end will it be? The war or the Armenians?

"What happens next?" I ask.

St. Boghos comes into view. I see the wall where we hid when we tried to join the battle, spying on those we ended up fighting alongside.

"What?" Uncle Tarzi asks.

"If the Russians come, what then?"

Baba dismisses my question with a wave. "We drink up and enjoy our victory."

"I mean, after that. Will the Russians stay forever? Will Van no longer be Ottoman? Do I have to learn Russian?"

Uncle Tarzi glances at his brother and juts his thumb at me over his shoulder. "Where does he get all these questions?"

Baba smiles. "One step at a time, my son."

Gunshots pop throughout the city. Whether Turkish or Armenian, all shots sound the same. I look up and see *fedayi* pointing their rifles to the sky, firing rounds into the air. Their joyful shouts echo across the city. Shouldn't they save their ammunition? The Russians aren't here yet.

The warm summer heat has arrived early, and I feel my clothes cling to my back. The blue sky above is clear and vast.

I look around but see no cats. If the war is over, they should be coming out and establishing themselves as they always do. Even as military command comes into view, not a cat crosses my vision. For some strange reason, this rattles my nerves.

Fedayi with raised guns dance and shout around the front entrance, smiles on their faces, some tilting bottles of *oghi* into their mouths. The terrible oud player sits outside, plucking away, but his song sounds much sweeter now. Young boys and girls, some I recognize as messengers from a week ago, jump around and dance with the *fedayi* as they sing:

Armenian heroes,
Armenian heroes,
It is our fatal time.
With a group of Armenian volunteers,
we must march on Armenia.

Uncle Tarzi, Baba, and I push through the rejoicing crowd. Sweat, alcohol, and cigarettes assault my senses as bodies collide into me, nearly knocking me to the ground.

Inside military command, a few *fedayi* continue to celebrate, and Professor Manukian and Charo sit at the map table, pointing and discussing something. Their brows and mouths are stern and tense. The professor lifts his face as we approach.

"The Simonians!" he exclaims, hugging each of us and kissing our cheeks. Charo just nods.

"I'm sure you heard the news," Professor Manukian remarks, gesturing toward the noise from outside.

"A well-deserved celebration," Uncle Tarzi says. The professor nods.

"A bit early, if you ask me," Charo comments, his hairy, broad arms folded across his chest.

"Sadly, Charo is right," the professor replies, pointing toward the map spread out on the table.

"What's the issue?" Baba asks. They all step forward and lean over the maps. I try to peek through the gap between Baba and Uncle Tarzi. Professor Manukian places a finger near the square where Araxie and Siroun were stationed. My gut sinks at the sight, and the sting of dust returns to my eyes, accompanied by a constant shame.

"Along the front wall of the city, the Turks have consistently shelled this area. But our scouts have reported that the Turkish troops are changing their position."

Uncle Tarzi and Baba exchange a glance.

"Changing how?" Baba asks.

"For a final assault," Charo says grimly, shoving a fat cigar into his mouth and searching for matches.

"We don't know for sure. But I wouldn't expect anything less from Jevdet," Professor Manukian counters.

"Let's return the favor," Uncle Tarzi replies, striking his fist on the table.

"With what weapons? Forks and spoons?" Baba retorts.

Uncle Tarzi glares at him like I used to at Narek or Levon, at least until we lost him to his mind.

The professor sighs, stretching his back and rubbing his neck. "Vartan is right. The time for fighting fire with fire is over. There are just no more bullets. And, as our waistbands show, the blockade of the Aykesdan passage has cut off our food supply. With the influx of refugees from the outer villages we've let in, there's not much left but faith."

I hear these words, and the cold hand of fear grips me. Faith? If I lack strong faith, what do I have to trust anymore? I scan the room and, stepping in from the front door, see Nshan and Raz. I freeze as their eyes meet mine and they start toward me. Is this what a rabbit feels like when it sees danger? Or a sinner before God?

I manage to move away from the table, my knees shaking with each step.

Nshan reaches me first. "*Parev.*"

"*Parev*," I repeat like a stranger.

I glance over at Razmik lingering behind Nshan like a bodyguard. Even with all the noise, the silence between us nags at me.

"So," Nshan begins, "you hear the news?"

"About the Russians?" I ask.

He nods. "It may be over soon."

His eyes drift away, looking around the room. He avoids my gaze as if it were poisonous. Razmik, on the other hand, stares deep into my soul.

"So you're a messenger now? With the children?" Razmik remarks, his tone dripping with sarcasm.

"Yes."

"Hmm," he grunts.

"Raz," Nshan says.

"What? I can't ask him why he left us?" Raz shrugs and throws his massive hands up.

Nshan doesn't reply. He just looks at me, lips pouting as if watching something pathetic.

The need to defend my decision rises in me, but the shame stifles it. What could I possibly say to make them understand without revealing how I contributed to Mihran being in the hospital?

"Have you been to see him?" Nshan asks, adjusting his glasses.

I move my eyes elsewhere. Anywhere else.

"You should. And Shushi, too," he adds.

"I know," I reply, my eyes drilling holes into the tops of my shoes. A loud chant starts up outside, and a swell of courage lifts my head.

"How is he?" I ask.

Nshan shrugs. "Alive, but he hasn't opened his eyes since that day."

"And Shushi?" Speaking her name pushes the guilt deeper into my heart.

Raz speaks up. "She hasn't left his side. Believe me, I tried."

Baba and Uncle Tarzi are deep in discussion with Charo and Professor Manukian at the table. The joy on Uncle Tarzi's face has faded, replaced by the same old expression I've known since childhood. Something must be coming. I don't know what, but I can feel it—something significant with no way back.

The door opens, letting in a loud roar from the *fedayi* outside. Two messengers enter, their bright eyes and smooth faces darting past Nshan and Raz to stop in front of me.

"Suren, do we have our messages?"

"Yes! Are we telling everyone about our victory?"

My cheeks flush, and as my eyes dart between my friends and these young, clueless faces, I manage to ask the professor.

They rush to the table, and I feel Nshan and Raz's eyes on me.

"What is your mission today?" I ask.

"Bomb squad!" Raz says, jutting his chin and revealing a long scar beneath.

I nod, rubbing the back of my neck, hoping to ease the heat in my face. The clamor of the two messengers fills the space between us, their shrill voices stabbing at my ears.

"Do you want to come? One last mission for the Big Guns?" Nshan asks.

Raz groans agonizingly.

"I . . . I don't know. I . . ." My words falter. Baba turns, sees me, and gives a subtle smile. I can't decipher its meaning right now.

Nshan and Raz exchange a look. Raz rolls his eyes and heads toward the door.

"We'll be near the square if you change your mind," Nshan says.

He turns his back and joins Raz by the door. Some *fedayi* in the corner share a cigar and clink glasses before downing their drinks. More chanting and singing come from outside.

"Suren!" one of the messengers calls. I look at him. "Are you coming?"

My head spins as I glance from the table to the messengers and then to the door. Back and forth, until I feel something rise inside, like boiling water in a kettle. Finally, the steam erupts. I tell Baba my plans and find myself outside military command, shouting for what's left of the Big Guns to wait for me.

Shushi's Fists

We stand outside the hospital, our eyes fixed on the wooden door with crude white letters. This is meant to be a place of healing, but not for the wound I carry. No medicine can ease my pain.

"Go in," Nshan tells me, a mix of command and suggestion.

I glance back, and he gestures toward the door. Taking a deep breath, I step forward, climb up the three steps, and push it open.

Inside, makeshift cots, beds, and blankets hold the wounded. Some have heads wrapped in bloody bandages, missing arms or legs. A symphony of groans fills the air. A few nurses tend to them, washing used bandages or cleaning saws, knives, and scissors. Taline, her head covered, walks in and sees me at the entrance. She approaches, drying her hands with a rag; the skin around her fingers is dry and cracked.

"I heard a rumor about the Russians?" she asks.

"The battle may be over soon," I reply, my tone flat and shaky. She studies my face, then hangs the wet rag over her shoulder.

"He's this way," she says, as if reading my mind.

She takes my cold hand and leads me through a room toward the back. As we pass through the doorway, I see him spread out on a stack of blankets. The cuts on his face have scabbed over but crisscross like a map on his forehead, cheeks, and chin. A red bandage covers the stump of his left arm—the very arm I dragged away from the explosion.

Sitting with her back to me, Shushi holds Mihran's other hand and hums a melody, unaware that I am right behind her.

I look at my sister, her eyes heavy, accented by dark circles. She comes to me and wraps her arms around me, giving me a tight squeeze I never thought she could give. Then she lets go and leaves me with my friends.

I listen to Shushi for a moment, hearing the sincerity in her voice as she sings to her brother. Almost as if the song will not put him to sleep but wake him up. Bring him back from the dream he is in now.

She pauses, slowly looks over her shoulder, and sees me standing behind her. She doesn't run to hug me. In fact, she says nothing. She stands, tears forming in her eyes, sliding down one by one to drop to the floor.

"Shushi, I'm sorry," I squeak. Before I can finish, she is in front of me, landing a stinging slap across my cheek.

"Where have you been? Why didn't you come and see him? Or me? I've been here for an entire week, waiting for you. Waiting for Mihran to wake up. Waiting for this war to end. Waiting and waiting for—"

"I know. I didn't know what to do," I begin.

Then she unleashes her hands and feet on me. Kicking my shins, punching my chest and stomach. The hits hurt as if she is hitting not just my body but my soul. I deserve them. She flails at me like a cornered animal until I pull her toward me and pin her head against my chest. I hold her and rest my chin on her hair.

As I tighten my grip, I feel her body relax, and she begins to sob—loud, uncontrollable sobs that dampen my shirt.

"I'm sorry," I repeat softly over and over. Soon, her arms wrap around me, holding me tight.

"I needed you, Suren," she repeats, each word piercing my skin.

I want to say something to fix it. Find the right words to make all this pain vanish. To fix Mihran and have him walk out of here. But no matter how hard I search, words don't seem enough.

"Has he woken up?" I ask Shushi.

She pushes away from me and wipes her palms across her eyes. "No. The nurses don't know if he will ever wake up."

The painful reality settles in. He could stay asleep for days, weeks, months, or just die quietly. The chance to make it right may never come, and that thought etches into my bones.

"Can I sit by him?" I ask. She nods, rubbing her puffy eyes.

The spicy smell of incense floods my senses as I sit on the floor. His brown skin looks ashen. I watch his chest rise and fall in slow, long breaths. I see no pain in his face—just deep sleep, far from where men hate each other.

I don't know what I feel or if he can hear me. But I know this may be my only chance to purge myself. Though Mama and Baba would tell me to see Father Zakarian and confess, I know the only person who can ease my guilt lies before me. Right now, I don't care if God forgives me.

"Can I talk to him?" I ask her.

"Go ahead."

She stands with her hip popped to the right and her hands resting on each side.

"Alone," I tell her, half asking, half ordering.

Her cheeks tense, becoming more defined—a sign I've noticed when she is about to explode.

"Please."

Her cheeks don't relax, but her eyes do. She straightens, brushes at the front of her shirt, her chin lifted like an aristocrat's.

"Two minutes."

Then she turns and disappears into another room, her chin still tilted up.

Watching her leave, I realize how much I missed her fire. The way she commands everyone's attention, even if she is impulsive and reckless.

I return to Mihran. My eyes rest on his chest, expecting it to stop rising at any moment, and my opportunity to confess vanishing forever. I must speak before the moment ends and my words drown me. His body remains still. The faintest twitch makes me think he is listening.

"I am so sorry. My word means nothing. My promise means nothing. I failed you. Shushi. Nshan. Raz. Professor. My family. Everyone."

His hand lies beside his body atop the blanket. I reach out and take it, placing my other hand over both.

"The truth is I am scared. Not just of the bombs or the Turks. But I'm afraid I may lose God also. I don't feel Him or hear Him. I'm afraid hate will replace faith in my heart, and nothing will be like it was. Artavazd will not escape the mountain."

What am I saying? I turn back but see no one listening and then worry about how much time I have left.

"I don't know what I am talking about. I just hope you can forgive me. If not in this life, then maybe the next if we meet there. I know you never had a family, but you are my brother, Mihran *jan*. Forgive me. I'll take care of Shushi. That is a promise I will keep."

My forehead drops onto our hands. Unlike before, I will not let go this time. I will hold it as long as it exists in this world.

"Time's up," Shushi says.

I lift my face, wiping to see if there are any tears on my cheeks before looking over my shoulder. I release Mihran's hand and gently place it back atop the blanket. Nshan, Raz, and Shushi stand near the doorway, watching me.

I glance back at Mihran, eyes like a hawk. Slowly, I meet my friends and follow them toward the exit. In my pocket, I feel Hamza's prayer beads, rolling them around my fingertips as we walk toward the city wall. Turk or not, I miss him now more than ever.

60

Back at the Tabriz Gate

I never thought I would return here.

Chunks of buildings have been bombed. Rubble spreads across the roads and the square, covering the spot where Mihran's blood spilled. The old shop where we hid has been reduced to debris.

I wait in the alley with Nshan and Raz. Shushi stayed with her brother, and I wish I were there too. Fear simmers inside me, but I grip the scissors in my fist, waiting in silence. No shouting or gunfire. Even with all the refugees flooding the city, the place is still.

"It's so quiet," Raz remarks, leaning against the wall and playing with his newly grown mustache. We sit facing each other.

"Did your father say anything?" I ask Nshan.

"No."

I lean out to look at the tops of the buildings. Some *fedayi* are on the rooftops on both sides.

"What about the two women who were here before?" I ask.

"They were reassigned elsewhere a few days ago," Raz replies, disappointment creeping into his voice.

A soft breeze whistles through the alley. A small cyclone spins down the street.

Raz throws his hands up and grunts. "Why haven't they launched anything at us?"

"Maybe they're saving their ammunition," Nshan answers.

"They're the government's army. Why would they be out of ammunition?" I comment, wiping sweat from my temple.

Nshan gazes up at the small patch of sky above us. The noonday sun is just beginning its descent to close another day that feels like a year.

"Something feels different," he mutters, opening and closing his scissors repeatedly.

My nerves get the best of me, and I jump to my feet. "I'm going to get some water. Do you want any?"

They both shake their heads, and I walk around the corner, entering the building where Uncle Tarzi stood watch a week ago. The room is mostly the same, except for a large hole in one of the walls facing the Turkish army, allowing me to see into another building nearby.

A pitcher with clay cups sits on a table. I fill one halfway and take a few sips, savoring the warm water on my tongue. Maybe we missed something. Was there a message we didn't receive? Have the Turks already packed up and left, and we're just waiting around, unaware? Maybe this final attack will never come.

Hamza's face flashes before me, bringing a flood of sadness. If the reports of ships carrying Turkish citizens fleeing the city are true, Hamza may be on one of them, taken away from me. Just like Mihran, I want to tell him I'm sorry. No, not just *want* to. I *need* to. I swallow the rest of the water and set the cup on the table.

When I step outside, I see a figure running toward us, waving something in his hand. I recognize him as one of the young messengers from military command. In his outstretched hand, he holds a sheet of paper. His voice reaches me, but he is too far away to make out what he is saying. I jog toward the alley.

"Someone is coming!" I shout. Nshan and Raz jump up and join me on the road leading to the square.

"What is he saying?" Raz asks.

Then I hear his words, fragmented at first, but they come together like a puzzle from a nightmare.

". . . bombing. The Turks are going to bomb . . ."

But the last phrases are drowned out by the blast behind us.

First one blast. Then another. A mix of debris and fire fills the air. A cloud of dust engulfs the square, followed by another blast thirty meters to the left.

Then another.

Fine pebbles sting my skin as I shield my face. Nshan and Raz duck down as we try to take shelter beside the building.

"They are bombing us!" Raz shouts.

"We know that!" Nshan snaps.

Another blast shakes the earth with such force that the ground trembles. Closer this time. The sound shocks my eardrums, making Nshan's words sound muffled.

"What?" I ask.

"Should we stay?" he says louder.

The door to the building opens, and two young *fedayi* sprint into the street, terror in their eyes as they run off with their rifles.

"There's your answer!" Raz yells.

With the door still ajar, a blast hits the roof and sends rubble into the air. A chunk of roof collapses and slides down the side of the building. We cover our heads as splinters and stones rain down on us, pelting us like hail. Dust stings our sinuses. I lower my hands from my head and rest them on my thigh. Something hard hits my hand—it's the beads. Hamza's *tasbih*.

"We have to leave!" I shout at the others.

Without waiting for a response, I run into the street, feeling the heat of the bombs and the sun on my back. Nshan and Raz's footsteps follow behind me. Explosions shake the ground, no longer landing in the square but chasing us down the street. The buildings explode beside us. My temple pounds as each hard step shakes the ground beneath me, traveling through the soles of my shoes and into my bones.

We pass the Topchu Mosque. The hospital. The bombs continue far away now, destroying areas near the front, maybe as far as Aykesdan. My lungs scream for rest, and my heart races to catch up, but I run because it's all I can do.

When I reach St. Boghos, I stop by the wall and lean on my knees to catch my breath. Nshan and Raz are no longer with me. They may have shouted for me to stop, but I didn't hear them. Didn't want to. I reach into my pocket and pull out the prayer beads, looking toward Ararat in the distance.

"God, please let me see Hamza again."

Sucking in a deep breath, I run toward the Shamiram.

61

The Gendarme Returns

The bombs roll like thunder across the city. From east to west, the deep roar surrounds me. I keep running through the streets past the abandoned market. Past mothers screaming and holding their children crouched in doorways. The cries of my people from the windows—no longer singing but praying.

As I pass the last buildings of the Armenian quarter, I see the cemetery ahead. Across it rises the skyline of the Shamiram. Behind me, smoke floats above the rooftops—a vision of the end days, as Father Zakarian spoke of from the book of Revelation.

I stand at the gate to the cemetery I have never entered. The headstones and tombs stand between me and my friend. If he is still there, I have to find him, and even Turkish ghosts won't stop me.

With my breath still heaving, I push off and run among the gravestones. I have no thought of jail or a beating by a gendarme. I dart between the headstones across the brown grass, unsure whether I'm stepping on the graves of Turks. They're dead, so why would that matter to them?

As I reach the end of the graveyard, the buildings lining the streets are much nicer than anything in my neighborhood. Even though I have no idea where in the quarter Hamza lives, I have to try. I make my way through the streets—no Turks, no gendarmes, no Armenians. No one. I expect to be stopped despite the absence of souls around. Even the towering mosque has no call to prayer.

I move in farther. Where am I? A row of shops sits dark and silent, and I turn down another empty street, down an alley that leads to a path deeper into the quarter.

As I step onto the path, someone grabs my arms, digging their fingertips into my muscles.

"Hey! What are you doing here? You should be on the boats!"

The familiar black uniform sends a chill through my blood. He must see the fear in my eyes when I look up at him. His eyes narrow on me. Wait! I recognize this man—the same young face and sinister mustache etched in my mind from that night with Baba.

"Hold on," he says, studying me closely. "I know you. You're that boy from the Armenian quarter. A dirty *gavur* just like your father!"

"Let go of me!" I growl through my teeth. I yank and struggle against his grip. My arm slips away, but he tightens his fingers around my shirt, spins me around, and wraps his arms around my chest.

"Stop fighting!" he snarls, shaking me.

"Never! I'll never stop fighting!" I scream, pulling and squirming, moving my body in any way to escape this monster.

I hear the sickening slide of a blade from its sheath.

This is it. I'm going to die. I will never see Hamza or my family again. I'll never have the chance to kiss a girl or raise my own family.

I close my eyes. My heart races against my ribs. Then something knocks into the gendarme and me. We tumble into the dirt and roll onto our backs.

"Get off me!" I hear the gendarme order, his voice strained.

I turn my head and see someone else grabbing the gendarme's wrists. The floppy hair and tall frame wrestle the knife away.

"Run, Suren!"

"Hamza!" I call out and jump to my feet, his face more swollen than the last time I saw him.

"You have to get out of here!"

"Let me help you."

My head swirls. Blood pumps through my veins as I prepare to attack. But when I move toward him, he speaks to me with an authority I've never heard from him in all the years we've known each other.

"Run now!"

I pause, my body struggling to move in either direction.

The gendarme curses and frees himself from Hamza's grip. He steps toward me, spies the blade in the street, and snatches it up. His eyes blaze with intense hatred. My body freezes, but Hamza runs over and wraps his arms around the gendarme's waist. Grimacing, the officer reaches down, grabs Hamza by the neck, and flips him around to face me. His arms lock my friend in place.

Pushing against the strong arms around his neck, Hamza screams, "Get home!" The vein in his temple pops out.

The distant bombs fade away, and I know I have to leave my friend behind.

"I'm sorry, brother," I shout, and, against all my instincts, I turn away and run toward home, wherever it may be.

From behind me, I hear Hamza's voice rise above the bombs, the violence, and the fear, screaming my name. It chases after me, urging me on, fueling my legs, and his words cling to me as I run through these foreign streets.

"Suren! Suren! Suren!"

62

Shelter

Somehow I weave through the streets of the Shamiram and dart among the headstones of the cemetery, running and tripping toward the bombs and the screams into the place I call home.

My legs burn. My lungs burn. Everything burns.

Memories swirl in my mind and collide with the future. I pass the market and the buildings I once found familiar. No cats. No shoppers. No children. Not even the faint call of a crow. The air cools as the sunset behind me meets the horizon.

I run until my hand slaps my front door. I push it open and stumble into my home. The faces of my family wait for me—

Baba, Mama, Taline, Levon covering his ears. Even Ani has returned. They sit around the table in their usual seats.

They look up at my disheveled face. The dirty skin on my cheeks is sticky with sweat, clinging my clothes to my body. The bombs continue their horrible crescendo outside, and Hamza's final cry echoes among the violent blasts.

Mama stands, pushing her chair back. Her eyes see through me the way only a mother's can. Something Baba has never really understood.

And I break.

Any attempt I make to stop the tears, the sobs, from coming becomes a casualty. I feel my face contort into that ugly expression I make. An ugly face to confront the ugliness of the world. The ugliness in me. Though tired, I make one last lunge into her open arms and collide with her soft body. All the tears I've held inside flood out of me, and for once, I won't stop them.

Her hands smell like flour and lavender as they caress my damp hair. Soon, I feel another body holding me and know it is Levon by the sharp edges of his elbows. Then the firm squeeze of Taline. Ani's soothing voice and comforting melody close to my ear. The last is Baba, wrapping his long arms around all he loves as the bombs continue to fall around us.

May 17, 1915

A New Morning

63

Retreat

Something stirs next to me, and I open my eyes to see Levon sitting up by the wood stove. He twists and cracks his back and then turns, smiling for once.

"We're alive."

I rub the crust from the corners of my eyes. A dull pain rests in my forehead, and sitting up makes it worse.

"That was a terrible night's sleep," I say, rubbing my head.

Mama and Baba are at the table, sitting across from each other, holding hands and sharing a look only long-married people can. Baba looks at us as we rise from the floor.

"My boys!" he sings, pushing himself from the table with his arms spread wide.

"Get dressed, and I will get the *jazva*. God knows we need it after last night," Mama says.

We head upstairs and change our clothes. My shirt and trousers smell so awful I consider tossing them into the fire. After washing and dressing, we return downstairs to the smell of coffee filling the room. For once, I actually want to have a cup.

"Here! Here!" Baba eagerly turns with two small, steaming cups in each hand. "I saved the last few beans for this very day."

We sit at the table and sip the hot coffee. I hate the taste, but I keep sipping. Something about the bitterness comforts me. Mama hums a melody and holds Baba from behind as he cleans the black sludge from the bottom of the cup. Normally, my parents' affection is disgusting, but today, it makes me smile.

"Where are Ani and Taline?" I ask.

Mama squeezes Baba one last time and turns around. "Taline left early to go to the hospital, and Ani—well, you know where she went."

"Wait," I say, "you knew about Taline? And Ani?"

Mama walks over and squeezes my shoulders. "A mother always knows. Besides, I have many eyes in this city."

I don't know if that is reassuring or terrifying.

"I can attest to that," Levon chimes in. For the first time, I see him alive and present, not lost in whatever horrible memories haunt him. I feel like I understand him in a way I never did before.

"Finish up! Hurry!" Baba orders. His excitement reminds me of a child getting a gift or how I felt as a boy every time he agreed to take me to the lake.

Levon and I chug down the rest of the coffee, and I scald the roof of my mouth. We kiss Mama and then head outside into the new morning.

The faint smell of gunpowder and smoke still lingers in the crisp air. But, unlike before, no gunshots or explosions can be heard. A flock of ducks flies in their V shape above us toward the lake. A few cats creep out from their hiding places with their ears perked.

"Is it really over?" Levon asks.

"Let's find out," Baba replies, and we head through the streets toward military command.

We don't have to go far before our question is answered.

Outside, women and children, both refugees and Van citizens, roam the streets singing and shouting. Old men and *fedayi* wrap their arms around each other and dance in the street, their legs kicking out together. Songs travel from windows and doorways. With each turn, more and more Armenians, some I know and some from the outlying villages, gather together. Many smile. Some sing. Others weep. For joy or for the ones they lost? Maybe both.

As I watch my people celebrate this victory, I think of Mihran, Hovhannes and his dying song, the *fedayi* in the hospital with sheets over their faces. The city streets grow more crowded, and soon, we have to work our way through mobs of people. I feel the prayer beads around my wrist and Hamza's voice calling to me from yesterday.

When we reach the military command, the *fedayi*, along with their wives and girlfriends, dance and drink, singing songs about the greatness of the Armenian people. Some musicians who used to perform near the taverns before the Turks came play outside. The banging of the *dhol* and the birdlike melody of the *duduk* spread through the crowd as the singer plucks at the oud.

Come, let's chant.
Let's shout with one voice.

Let's shout from our hearts: Long live Armenia!
Long live Armenia and freedom,
defender of the nation and the brave faith.

Ragged refugees mix in with the *fedayi* and dance with tears in their eyes. Some men, already tipsy from *oghi*, grab and shake us, pressing their faces close as they sing.

We push our way through and enter military command. More *fedayi* celebrate inside. Cigarette smoke and alcohol hit my senses. Charo stands by the map table with his arm around the professor's shoulders, each with a cigar hanging from his lips and a cup in one hand. A *fedayi* dances on the maps on the large table.

"The devil has fled! The enemy has retreated!"

The statement repeats and chants among the people. A swell of cheers rises after each phrase, and those with cups lift them up simultaneously. Emerging from the back room, Uncle Tarzi and Aunt Yeva hold each other.

I point toward them, and eagerly Baba pushes his way over as we follow. The brothers make eye contact, spread their arms, and collide into one another. Aunt Yeva sees us and grabs my face first.

"We won, Suren *jan*!" she says, then grabs Levon's face and repeats her words.

A whirlwind of songs, tears, and dancing swirls around us. Before Aunt Yeva can say anything else, I feel a hand on my shoulder and see the professor. His glasses are crooked on his nose.

"The Simonians! This victory would not have been possible without your help."

"The same goes for you, Aram," Baba says.

"The Turkish forces have fled. The Russians will be here any day, and our comrades in Aykesdan are flooding into the city with food. And more *oghi*!"

"If we're lucky, the Russians will bring vodka!" Charo shouts.

All the men laugh and hug each other, pushing me outside of the huddle. I watch from the fringes, and seeing them so full of joy makes my heart glad. But I can't shake Hamza from my thoughts.

"Suren!"

I turn around and see Nshan and Raz, smiles so wide across their faces that I hardly recognize them at first.

"We did it! The Big Guns helped defeat the enemy!" Nshan cries, grabbing and shaking me. Raz comes beside me and squeezes my arms so hard I fear he may have cracked my bones.

"To be honest, Nshan, I always hated that name," I confess.

"I know, but I don't care!" he cries out, then hugs me.

"Where is Shushi?" I ask.

Raz and Nshan's expressions change, and the smiles fade.

"You haven't heard?" Raz asks.

"Heard what?" I reply, but the sinking feeling in my gut already gives me the answer.

Nshan steps back. His expression tells me all I need to know.

Like a possessed person, I run past my friends toward the door.

Shushi's Song

In the hospital, the number of patients has doubled. *Fedayi* lie wounded, along with women and children. A young girl, no more than four years old, sobs in her mother's lap, a long, bloody gash poorly bandaged on her upper arm. Taline walks in from the side carrying scissors, string, and some wrappings. She doesn't even notice me standing there.

Near the back, I find Shushi lying next to her brother. A white sheet covers his face.

Her back faces me as I walk into the room, but she doesn't notice. I hear her soft voice humming a familiar song. The moaning and crying from other wounded *fedayi* and civilians fade away, and Shushi's song is the only sound I hear.

She sings an old song my aunt on Mama's side used to hum to me. When I asked her what it was about, she looked into my eyes, held my cheeks in her wrinkled hands, and said, "Words would only destroy its power." When I asked Mama what it was called, she said it was "Tikranakerti Ororotsayin."

As Shushi hums the melody, I think of Narek and wonder where he is. Is he alive, or is he under a sheet or buried in a mass grave somewhere? I may never know.

Walking cautiously, I move toward her. She still doesn't look at me, even though I am beside her. I sit next to her and place my hand on her shoulder. She doesn't move and continues to hum her song for her brother. Reaching up, her hand touches mine, and we sit together. As Tati said, words would only destroy this moment. The truth is we have saved our home, but at a cost.

Though I have no words for her, I have my tears and my time, and I give them to her as distant celebrations rise across the city.

After I stand and leave her beside Mihran, I notice Taline watching me from the doorway.

"I'll look after her for now. When I'm finished, I'll bring her home so she's not alone," Taline assures me.

Outside the hospital, I join Nshan and Raz, who must have followed me here. A group of men, women, and children walks through the street, clapping and singing.

"How is she?" Raz asks.

I shrug. "Her brother is dead."

The celebration fills the space between us. Then Nshan clears his throat and says, "Let God shine a light on his soul."

Raz and I bow our heads, make the sign, and respond together, "Amen."

I watch the procession pass by.

"It seems wrong," I comment.

"What does?" Raz asks.

"Celebrating when others have lost so much."

To the west, I notice black smoke against the blue sky.

"Where is that smoke coming from?" I ask.

The others follow my finger pointing at the sky.

"It looks far away," Raz says.

"Yes. From Aykesdan."

"I thought the war was over?" I ask.

We decide to follow the crowd toward the Tabriz Gate to see what is happening. Like fish in a school, we mix with the refugees and Van Armenians singing songs of Armenia's heroism. The evidence of the battle is visible in the sides of buildings and the rubble lining the paths. Curious cats perch atop the stones and watch the procession. Somehow, the Topchu Mosque remains untouched by the war.

After some time, we reach the Tabriz Gate, and the smoke has grown thicker. I can taste the ash and embers in the air. A large group of *fedayi* from Aykesdan stand where the Turks had been just a few weeks ago. They embrace the refugees and *fedayi* from the Old City, and a crowd gathers around the entrance to Aykesdan.

Black clouds billow overhead.

"Ask someone," I urge Nshan. He finds a bearded *fedayi* who turns toward him, his right eye covered by a patch.

They finish, and Nshan walks over to us.

"What did he say?" Raz asks.

"The smoke is from the Turkish quarter." Nshan's expression is grave.

"Why from the Turkish quarter? All the Turks have fled."

He looks at Raz and me before answering. "Revenge."

I hear cheering, and down the street, the smoke begins to build at the Topchu Mosque. A crowd of *fedayi* holding torches stands outside the ornate wooden doors.

Revenge.

I look up at the smoke as the sky turns ashy gray, and I realize what he means.

"I have to go," I tell them, darting and weaving through the celebration as I run west toward the Shamiram.

65

The Past in Flames

For weeks, no one walked these streets or gathered in the squares, and today I can hardly make my way against the crowds.

Fear fuels my legs and lungs. My heart races as I maneuver better than I thought I could. It's as if my senses are heightened, and I dance on light feet across, around, and through the celebrating crowds. The buildings block my view of the distance, and the smoke of Aykesdan hangs like a shawl over the city. But I keep moving forward until I pass my home, the abandoned market, and make my way toward the cemetery.

Some *fedayi* carry what look like wooden sticks wrapped in

damp rags. Another group walks with long-handled hammers or shovels propped on their shoulders, all moving toward the Shamiram. As I pass, I hear one say, "Those monsters deserve it. They tried to destroy us; now they will have nothing to return to."

The men cry out with a cheer. When I reach the cemetery gate, I stop.

Across the rooftops and from windows, orange flames rage from the Turkish homes. At the center, taller than everything else, the dome of the Shamiram mosque blazes—like a giant torch warning the world not to underestimate Armenians.

My feet feel like stones. The blood drains from my face, and I hear Hamza's words from yesterday—his cries to send me home, to be safe. The blade in the gendarme's hand. I see us swinging from a rope and splashing into the lake. I hear his broken Armenian, see his wounded eyes in the old Kurd's shop, smell the incense on his clothes after attending mosque. I feel his *tasbih* around my wrist as if he is here with me. What I cannot feel is whether he is alive or dead.

The *fedayi* and some old men from the villages, with their unlit torches and hammers, walk past me, trampling over the graves of generations of Turks. They smash headstones and cheer as they point toward the tall flames licking the sky and casting black smoke across the city. Walking toward me, men, women, and children carry chests of jewels, fine plates, chairs, woven rugs, and anything else they looted.

I watch the flames grow and the smoke overshadow the city from all sides.

Unable to stand, I collapse onto my knees, watching the consuming flames, whispering, "From the Aegean to the Euphrates."

66

Three Candles

I don't know how far I've walked, but my feet stand on the doorstep of St. Boghos. The wooden door with the iron handle stares back at me as I pull it open. The scent of rosary and incense washes over me.

Votive candles light the altar. From one end to the other, small flames flicker as the door closes behind me. I walk down the center aisle, past mothers, wives, and sisters bowing their heads in the pews, probably praying for those lost in the battle. Maybe for all Armenians.

Walking toward the altar feels like dragging a ball and chain behind me. I don't know why I am here, but somehow my feet move across the rugs. I trudge forward until I reach the front. Picking up three candles, I light each one and place it beside the others. I wonder if those praying in the church care that I lit a candle for the soul of a Turk to be placed next to their loved ones.

After lighting the candles, I don't pray. I just watch the flames burn. Burn like the Shamiram. After a moment, I turn and sit in the first pew, actually falling into it, leaning my elbows on the end closest to the aisle.

I close my eyes and see Mihran, Hamza, Narek. Their faces move across the darkness behind my eyelids in an endless cycle. Even in the church, I can sense the faintest stench of smoke from outside.

I hear a rustling sound near me, and I open my eyes to see the ends of the priest's *shabig* hanging just above his feet. I look up, and Father Zakarian, solemn and quiet, looks down on me. He doesn't smile, but there is compassion in the wrinkles around his eyes.

"May I join you, young man?" he asks, gesturing toward the seat next to me.

I scoot over to make room for him, and he eases himself down with a grunt.

Father Zakarian exhales, resting his hands on his lap and looking toward the candles illuminating the front of the church.

"I'm afraid there may not be enough candles," he says quietly. "We will need God's guidance more than ever."

I pause.

"I don't think God is here anymore, Father."

The words escape me like a burdened sigh. In an odd way, relief washes over my muscles.

Father Zakarian strokes his beard and stares at the altar. "You may have a point."

I turn my face from the altar toward him.

He looks at me. "Doubt is part of faith."

"I'm not sure that makes sense to me."

"All the heroes of the Bible had doubts: Moses, David, Job, St. Peter. That doesn't mean God abandoned them."

I nod. "It feels like He has."

"It can feel that way."

My eyes fix on the three candles. Are the flames brighter than the others? I don't really know. Father Zakarian looks over my head out the window at the darkening skies.

"Father," I begin, "Is it wrong to hate?"

He sighs. "I'm glad you asked that question."

"You are?"

"That is because God is still with you."

"How? I should be joining the others in the Shamiram. The Turks deserve it."

Father Zakarian lifts his arm and places it around the back of the pew. "There are many things we deserve in this life. Not all of them are good, whether we are Turks, Armenians, Kurds, Germans, or even the French. But God took pity on all of us and didn't give us what we deserve. When you feel that, you know He is still with you. When you feel nothing, then it is time to worry."

The wooden cross hangs at the altar, and I stare at the tortured figure of Jesus.

"He didn't die for hate," Father Zakarian remarks, pointing at the cross. "He died for what we deserve, even for the things we've done to punish ourselves."

I absorb his words in my soul. They stew inside me, and the faces of Hamza, Mihran, and Narek return. But the despair in their expressions is gone. Instead, they smile back, and I'm unsure if I deserve it.

"I don't know what the future holds for you, me, or any of us," Father Zakarian continues, "but I know that if we can forgive, light will overcome the darkness."

He pats my shoulder and rises from the pew, straightening his tunic. He crosses himself and turns down the center aisle, blessing those with bowed heads.

I watch the three candles burn, flickering even in the darkness. On the sides, I notice how the wax drips down like tears.

Then I lower myself, resting on the kneeler, and bow my head.

Epilogue

July 31, 1915
City of Memory

Baba and Levon place the last of our belongings on the ox-cart. Bags of clothes, heirlooms, food, and everything we own pile above the sides of the cart. For seven people, it seems like a meager amount. Some from Aykesdan have several carts filled. The nonessentials still sit where they've always been.

"That's it," Baba says, dusting off his hands and shirt. Levon walks toward the cart's long handles and tests the load's weight.

Mama, Ani, Taline, and Shushi stand in front of our home. Well, what was our home. Their head coverings are tucked snugly into their collars. Mama's eyes are puffy, and I fear they may always be that way. Shushi brushes her hand at the edge of her head covering with a scowl.

It is a hot summer day. Normally, we walk and sing in the streets, throwing buckets of water at each other to celebrate Vardavar—our one day to prank others without getting into trouble.

But not this year.

A warm breeze sweeps through the streets, cooling the sweat on our skin. The city buzzes with movement as others, like us, pack what they can carry. Baba sees some neighbors down the street with sacks slung over their shoulders.

He turns back to us, forcing a smile. "At least we have this cart."

Nobody smiles back.

"We should get going," Levon suggests.

We exchange uncertain glances before looking back at our home. The wooden door is shut tight, and the windows are boarded.

Mama places one hand on the door and the other over her mouth, leaning forward until her forehead rests on it.

"Generations upon generations have walked through this door," she says between sobs that choke her words. "No more."

Ani and Taline come beside her. I join my sisters and place my hand on the door as well. Mama looks at me with her puffy eyes and takes her hand from her mouth, caressing my cheek.

Then Ani places her palm on the door.

Then Taline.

Until all of our hands feel the grain of our door for the last time. Shushi stands back, hesitant at first, but then she joins me and places her hand next to mine.

Once our tears have dried, we grab our small bags, and Levon lifts the oxcart handles. With a loud creak, it begins rolling, and we follow, holding all we have left.

Others join the march through the streets. To me, it feels more like a funeral. The festive celebration when the Russians rode through the streets is a distant memory. Now, tears and solemn faces carry crying babies and inquisitive children. No songs. No smiles.

An old man with a face like dried dates grumbles, seated on a donkey.

"The Russians betrayed us."

An older woman, maybe his daughter, replies, "They couldn't stay here forever, Baba."

We pass parts of the city that had been rebuilt during the few months Van was ours again, as it was before it became Ottoman. The time when Professor Manukian ran the government. New homes, a police station, government buildings—all built and ready. Now, it will all be Turkish again.

"Are we heading east?" I ask.

He doesn't look at me but keeps his eyes straight ahead. "There's nowhere else to go."

"So much loss for nothing," I remark.

Baba places a hand on my shoulder. "They call Van the 'City of Memory.' That is exactly what we've left here. One I hope echoes forever."

I raise my eyes to my father. He doesn't look at me but gazes instead toward the horizon. A single tear slips from an eye and falls into his beard. Of all the things I admire about him, his tears make me the proudest to be his son, and I slip my hand into my pocket, feeling the time he gave me at my fingertips.

Up ahead, I see Nshan with his family. Raz is with him. I guess his father finally drank himself to his grave, though no one knows for sure how he died. I guess Mihran and Raz have more in common now. I watch Nshan between his parents, and as if he knows I'm watching, our eyes meet. I nod, and he nods back.

We funnel through the gate at the city wall, pulling our cart among a sea of people. At some point, Uncle Tarzi and Aunt

Yeva join us without a word. As we push through the gate, we emerge facing a trail of Armenians snaking across the desert to the east. The flag we raised at Cannon Rock after we won the battle still waves above the city. Not much can be seen ahead except for the tall peak of Mount Ararat. Like a watchful eye, it follows me—my family, my friends, my people—as the river of refugees travels into the unknown.

I stare up at the snowy peak, feeling the beads of Hamza's *tasbih* on my wrist. A presence walks with me. Not physically, but in a way I can't describe. Whether it is Hamza, Mihran, or Narek, I can't say. Perhaps it could be God.

Next to me, I see Taline. Her cheeks glisten slightly under her eyes. Seeing her cry, I can't help but voice the thoughts that have plagued me since we closed the door for the last time at the place where we were all born.

"They won, Taline."

I feel her arm slip around my bicep and squeeze. Her weight hangs on me like it used to when we wrestled.

"I don't think so," she replies.

"Really?"

She looks off and smiles. "We survived."

I nudge her, and she nudges back harder. I hate to admit it, but she is right.

I look ahead at Baba, trailing behind Levon and the cart as he holds Mama around the waist. Ani and Shushi follow. All of us walking toward the mountains into a strange and uncertain future.

They will call us rebels, but we are survivors.

Together.

Author's Note

Did any of this really happen?

The answer is yes—and no.

Suren and his family, the Big Guns, Hamza, and most of the characters in the novel are not historical figures, but their inclusion served to add depth, conflict, and empathy to the narrative. Aram Manoukian was a very real person who not only became the military leader in the resistance to the Turks but ran the Armenian government in Van. Sadly, he is a forgotten hero in a muddled, suppressed era of history for various political reasons. On the other side, Jevdet Bey, the "Horseshoer of Bashkale," was a real Turkish leader known for devious and horrific acts against minorities in the Ottoman Empire during World War I, including nailing horseshoes to people's feet during interrogations.

Children often were chosen to dismantle bombs—some as young as nine years old. Girls and women like Taline and Ani worked as nurses and provided care and sustenance to those fighting. Araxie and Siroun are fictional, but many women grabbed weapons and fought in the *fedayi* during the resistance. And, unfortunately, the novel's ending events are also factual, leading to uncertainty and resulting in the Armenian Diaspora. However, many Turks did defy the *pasha* and are responsible for saving countless Armenians, ensuring future generations at the cost of their own lives.

Some aspects of the story required a bit of creative license. Some of the *fedayi* patriotic songs were not written until after the Armenian Genocide occurred, and some of the events did not occur in the order narrativized here. For the reader interested in the hard facts, I have included a further reading section.

Regardless, the Defense of Van, during which the forty thousand or so Armenian citizens of the city fought and defended themselves against oppression, truly occurred—an event lost to the wider world that needs to be retold. Stories of survival, perseverance, and courage never grow old, and what Aram Manoukian and real-life figures similar to Suren and Hamza did should not be footnotes in some history book but a testament to the resilience of the human spirit to strengthen the future by looking at the past.

After reading *Never Hide from the Devil*, I hope you feel inspired and curious, eager to learn more about this suppressed event and also to fight against the odds for what is good, just, and worthy. I learned much from Suren's story, and I hope you did too.

Acknowledgments

To be honest, I was a little terrified to write this book. Focusing on such a sensitive time in a cultural group's history, when millions were murdered, I wanted to do it right. Doing poor research and just making up characters and events without any context or advice would not be acceptable. That's why there are so many important people to thank for their input into Suren's story.

A huge thank-you goes to Dr. Khatchig Mouradian, who sacrificed his time, resources, and limitless knowledge to answer all of my questions and provide feedback on early drafts. Honestly, I don't know how I could have written this story without his help.

Much gratitude goes to Dr. Ronald Suny, Aram Mjorian, Astrid Kamalyan, Laura Michael-Gaboudian, and Lara Vanian-Green for their Zoom conversations, phone calls, recommendations, and invaluable input and support.

Without Nadine Takvorian's artistic eye, insight, and help with Western Armenian, this novel would have had a fatal flaw, so I am very grateful for her help in providing authenticity and feedback.

To Holly Thesieres Monteith and Cynren Press, thank you for taking a chance and pioneering this novel, bringing Suren's journey and the history of the Armenian people into the world. It is my hope that the Armenian Genocide will finally be unveiled and shown for what it truly was.

Where would a writer be without beta readers to give honest feedback? A huge shoutout goes to Celia Cunningham, Khatchig Mouradian, and Sarah McQueen.

Two very important beta readers who deserve some honor are Hailey and Cailyn McQueen. They helped shape this novel into what it is, even if it meant telling Dad when something sucked or should be changed. I forgive you. *Te amo mucho*!

I would have never known about the Armenian Genocide if it weren't for the Simonyan family (Abel, Sara, Gabby, Isaac, and Elizabeth). Aside from being amazing people and close friends, they have accepted an *odar* like me and been a blessing to my family with their generosity, faithfulness, and Armenian coffee. It's not a coincidence that the main character shares their name.

To my family and friends who always support me in my writing, thank you for having my back and being constant and faithful.

For all the other authors, scholars, and anyone else who provided endorsements for my novel, I am eternally grateful.

Thanks to God, who gives me grace even when I don't deserve it, comforts me when I am brokenhearted, and guides me even when I think I know what I am doing.

Most importantly, I give thanks for my incomparable, stunningly gorgeous wife, Christina, who makes life worth living, gives me honest feedback on my writing, and infuses beauty into this world with every word, movement, and action. I love her more than words could ever express.

Guide to Pronunciation

Characters

Ani (AH-nee)
Aram Manukian (A-ram MAH-nook-yahn)
Hamza (HOM-za)
Levon (LEH-von)
Mihran (MEE-rahn)
Narek (NAR-eck)
Nshan (NEE-shahn)
Razmik (ROZ-mick)
Shushi (SHOO-shee)
Simonian (si-MONE-yahn)
Suren (SOO-ren)
Taline (TA-leen)
Tarzi (TAR-zee)
Vartan (VAR-tahn)
Zakarian (za-KAR-yan)

Other Terms

Adana (AH -dah-nah)
Ayeksan (AYE-kes-dahn)
Fedayi (fe-DIE-yee)
Jazva (JAHZ-va)
Kufta (KOOF-tah)
Shamiram (SAHM-eer-ahm)
Topchu (TOPE-choo)
Van (VAHN)

Further Reading

Akam, Taner. *A Shameful Act: The Armenian Genocide and the Question of Turkish Responsibility*. Metropolitan Books, 2007.

Bagdasarian, Adam. *Forgotten Fire*. Dell Laurel-Leaf, 2000.

Balakian, Peter. *The Burning Tigris: The Armenian Genocide and America's Response*. HarperCollins, 2003.

Bogosian, Eric. *Operation Nemesis: The Assassination Plot That Avenged the Armenian Genocide*. Little, Brown, 2015.

Bohjalian, Chris. *The Sandcastle Girls*. Vintage, 2017.

Do, Λ. *Van 1915: The Great Events of Vasbouragan*. Gomidas Institute, 1917.

Ghiragossian, Alicia. *Screaming Labyrinth: The True Story of the Armenian Genocide Through the Eyes of My Father*. American University of Armenia, 2015.

Houshamadyan Association. "Houshamadyan Project." https://www.houshamadyan.org/.

Hovannisian, Richard. *Armenians Van/Vaspurakan*. Mazda, 2000.

Mouradian, Khatchig. *The Resistance Network: The Armenian Genocide and Humanitarianism in Ottoman Syria, 1915–1918*. Michigan State University Press, 2021.

Suny, Ronald Gregor. *"They Can Live in the Desert but Nowhere Else": A History of the Armenian Genocide*. Princeton University Press, 2015.

Suny, Ronald Gregor. "Tsarist Russian and the Armenians of Van, 1914–1915." YouTube video, November 21, 2016. http://www.youtube.com/watch?v=CFIgfy2nioU.

Walrath, Dana. *Like Water on Stone*. Ember, 2015.

Waterman, Victoria Atamian. *Who She Left Behind*. Historium Press, 2023.

Questions for Discussion

1. What do you think is the meaning behind the title *Never Hide from the Devil*? What were your expectations?
2. Suren, an Armenian Christian, and Hamza, a Turkish Muslim, are best friends. How do you think their relationship was affected by the events taking place in the Ottoman Empire? Can you find connections to your own experience where certain beliefs and ideologies of the time strained your relationship with someone close?
3. Why do you think Turkish government officials and citizens dislike Armenians?
4. Vartan, Tarzi, and many of the citizens reference the events of Adana. Why does this have so much significance for the Armenians in Van?
5. Suren's family is divided if they should stay and fight or flee like others have. Why is this such a difficult and divisive decision for them? What would you do if you faced the same decision?
6. Why doesn't Vartan want Suren, in his time considered a man at his age, to join the *fedayi* and fight the Turks?
7. Do you feel Suren's choice to disobey his parents is right?

8. As Suren and his friends take missions, in what ways does Suren change? Name specific moments when his character shifts in positive and negative ways.
9. How does Suren and Hamza's relationship change throughout the novel?
10. Consider the members of the Big Guns—Razmik, Nshan, Mihran, and Shushi. Which character is your favorite or least favorite? Why?
11. The scene at Ararout Square is a powerful and tragic moment for Suren and the Big Guns. Why do you think Suren makes the choice to leave?
12. What happens to Hamza after the incident in the Shamiram quarter?
13. Suren struggles with his faith throughout the novel. What significance is there in this journey when he has the conversation with Father Zakarian?
14. After reading the novel's ending, what do you think will happen? How do you feel?
15. Before reading this novel, what did you know about the Armenian Genocide?
16. The novel is written in first person, present tense. Why do you think the author made this choice? How does it affect the novel as a whole?
17. How does this novel differ from other books about genocide and the Holocaust that you've previously read?
18. Why do you think the Armenian Genocide is not as prominently taught in schools, as are World War II and other conflicts? Why isn't a figure like Aram Manukian more well known as a hero?
19. The Republic of Turkey denies the Armenian Genocide ever happened, unlike other countries responsible for crimes against humanity. Why does Turkey remain firm on this stance?

20. Why is it important for writers, artists, filmmakers, and other creatives to continue to write stories about genocide, discrimination, and other atrocities?

Photo by Hailey McQueen

N.T. McQueen is an avid writer and dedicated college lecturer. With a master's degree in fiction from California State University, Sacramento, McQueen has brought unique perspectives on human nature to readers in his captivating novels *Never Hide from the Devil* (Cennan, 2026), *The Cry of Dry Bones* (2021), and *Between Lions and Lambs* (2011). His writing has been featured in *North American Review*, *Stonecoast Review*, *Entropy*, *Sunlight Press*, *Atticus Review*, *Dappled Things*, *Grief Digest Magazine*, and *Foreword Magazine*. He lives in California with his wife and daughters and enjoys fishing, traveling, and a tasty cup of coffee.

Stay in the conversation.

We invite you to join Cynren Press's

Margin Notes

—where we share thoughtful essays,
early looks at forthcoming books,
and conversations that extend
beyond the page.

cynren.com/margin-notes

www.ingramcontent.com/pod-product-compliance
Lightning Source LLC
LaVergne TN
LVHW020040110826
845155LV00029B/574

* 9 7 8 1 9 4 7 9 7 6 7 1 9 *